RAISING
WILD
GINGER

RAISING WILD GINGER

A LACLAND STORY

BY
TARA WOOLPY

BATS IN THE
BOATHOUSE
PRESS

MINOCQUA, WISCONSIN

For Dana

Thanks!

Tara Woolpy

The characters and events described are fictitious. The town of Lacland and all its inhabitants exist only in our imagination, although Edward, Sam, Maggie and Gillian regularly blog with Tara at http://www.batsintheboathouse.com/lacland-news-blog.html

Bats in the Boathouse Press
PO Box 685
Minocqua, WI 54548
Batsintheboathouse.com

ISBN 978-0-9832033-2-2

Cover photo: iStockphoto.com/Mustafa Arican
Design by Pat Bickner, anewleafcreative.com
Author photo: Jerry Woolpy

For my girls
Sarah and Anna

ONE

✽

For our anniversary, Sam and I trekked in to the site of our first kiss. With our Boston terrier, Daphnia, scouting the path ahead, we hauled a picnic lunch through a quarter mile of wetland to the grove by the stream where we'd waited for the emergence.

I spread out a blanket. Sam opened a cooler and grabbed the bottle of sparkling cider and two plastic champagne glasses. He popped the cork and poured. Little bubbles fizzed up from the bottom of the glasses. Handing one to me, he smiled and toasted, "To us."

Four years ago, we'd met in the late afternoon every day for two weeks, hoping to catch mayflies in their annual ephemeral swarm, an event where, if I understand correctly, in one afternoon the whole population mates. On that last day, I'd arrived late to find Sam and the mayflies already there. I swung up my camera and, looking through the viewfinder, I'd seen everything I'd been waiting for, too.

That's the picture I keep on my desk. Sam, arms outstretched, head flung back, laughing as hundreds of beautiful white-winged insects fly around him. I'd wanted that for the book cover, but the art director decided it wasn't properly academic. She went for a close-up of a male mayfly perching on a blade of marsh grass, wings held high, tail filaments catching the light, his huge eyes scanning the sky for a mate.

As the light began to fade that afternoon, we'd stood in the middle of the grove, our shoulders almost touching, peering at the camera preview screen. I remember trying to feel heat from his body and watching his face, memorizing the curve of his eyelashes, as I clicked through the images. Eventually he looked up, and that's when we kissed.

Four years later and I still couldn't believe my luck.

"To us," I agreed. Our glasses touched. I sipped the syrupy juice and leaned back on my elbows. We had an amazingly good life.

Then Sam said, "You know, I really would like children," and I groaned.

"What?" he continued. "Look, Edward, I know we've been over this but—"

"Sam, darlin', I'm too old for kids."

"Don't be silly. Men older than you have children all the time. And it isn't like you'd be making one from scratch. I think you'd make a great father."

"No, you'd make a great father. I'm a better uncle. Let's not talk about this now. Come." I patted the blanket next to me. "Lie down and let me distract you."

He laughed and handed me my sandwich. "Food first, you old lecher."

After lunch, I pulled him down beside me on the blanket. The wet earth beneath us smelled of spring, and the nylon of our bulky jackets rustled. "The thing about an early spring picnic," I whispered into his neck, "is that, while we don't have mosquitoes, it's also too cold for people."

"We might have seen another mayfly emergence."

"But we didn't, and there's something sharp poking my hip. Let's find Daphnia and go home."

Later, covers pulled up to our necks, Sam lay spooned against me. I stared into the curly mat of his hair. He's younger, smarter and much better looking than I am. He's also usually right. "I'll think about it," I whispered.

"Thanks."

❧ ❧ ❧

We packed the usual dozen or so into St. Sebastian's for the Tuesday noon meeting. I took a seat next to my sponsor, Henry. Last week's Sunday School projects hung above our heads, butterflies made from tissue paper and clothespins. A woman in gray, whose name I never remember, agreed to chair and we began. I looked around the group— no first timers, but a few still early in recovery.

After the readings, our chair said, "This is a discussion meeting. Does anyone have a suggestion for a topic?"

I cleared my throat. "Hi, I'm Edward. I'm an alcoholic and an addict."

"Hi, Edward," the group chimed.

"I guess I want to talk about resentment." I fiddled with my coffee cup. "My partner really wants to look into adopting . . . making a family. The thought scares the crap out of me. He grew up in this white-bread family where punishments fit the crimes and everyone was hyper- normal—at least until he came out, but that's another story. I don't have any idea how to do that, what that kind of family looks like from the inside. I feel scared of the responsibility, the time, and I think, deep down, terrified I'd turn into my mother and really mess someone up. It's not something I want him to want, and I can't seem to shake feeling angry and resentful, even though I know that's poison for me, my sobriety and for our relationship. I'm hoping this meeting will help me get over myself. With that, I'll pass."

Someone else took up the topic of releasing resentment, an alcoholic favorite, and the meeting continued. By the time we stood to hold hands and repeat the serenity prayer, I felt better than I had in weeks.

Henry asked, "Got time for coffee?"

"Sure. How about we meet at the Rise and Shine? The coffee's awful, but the pie's good."

At the Rise and Shine Café, cracked green vinyl booths line the wall opposite the lunch counter. Old-time diner food. I've been a regular all my life. It's gotten a little better since Irene and her sister Claire took over, but not much. The smell of grease still envelops you as you pass through the front door. Sam'll come here if he's really hungry. For me, the place remains delicious with memories of the grandfathers taking us for chocolate chip pancakes on summer Sunday mornings.

Henry and I took the back booth. As Irene poured our predictably bitter coffee, I wondered if I looked as unchanged to Henry as he did to me. Over a decade ago, he'd taken on the job of steering this messed-up, rich, white, gay guy toward something like sanity. He didn't look different to me from that first time I'd stumbled into a meeting, fresh from two hundred and seventy-four days in jail, followed by twenty-eight in treatment, and looking for something to convince me that life without drugs and alcohol was better than suicide. Big and black, ten years older than me, already sober twenty-some years and married for longer, he breathed out a cloud of patience developed through years of sobriety and social work, and looked like hope to me. He still does.

"So Sam wants babies." He chuckled.

"Not babies, he's thinking kids, maybe refugees." I took a swig of coffee and dumped in more creamer. "He's got some great arguments. No question about it, we have plenty to share." I shook my head. "But I'm not sure I'm the Mother Theresa type."

Henry stirred sugar into his coffee. Irene brought two slices of rhubarb-apple pie, warmed so that golden flakes of crust glistened against the ooze of pink filling. I forked a bite into my mouth and rolled the tart sweetness along my tongue.

Henry spoke. "Have you thought about a compromise? Maybe foster care? It's cheaper and faster than adoption, and it could be temporary if that's what you wanted."

"So you think I should give in?"

"Man, this is good, isn't it?" He held up a forkful of glistening pink filling. "I think you should keep an open mind, that's all. How badly does Sam want kids?"

"Badly. Ever since he visited his sister and her family last summer, he's talked about it off and on. It triggered this family thing in him, and it's like an itch he can't quit scratching." I stuck my fork into a ridge of crust, watching it crumble, catching the crumbs and popping them into my mouth. Food is my only remaining addiction. I'm not giving it up.

"I thought he wasn't in contact with his family." Henry wiped the edges of his mouth with a napkin.

I shrugged. "It's complicated. His father won't acknowledge his existence, but Naomi, his sister, keeps in regular contact. They talk on the phone, email. Over the past few years the three of us have seen each other a few times in neutral territory, and last year he met her family. She's scheduled to spend some time here early this summer. His mom pretends to his dad that she doesn't communicate with him, but sends little messages through Naomi. It gets confusing."

"Sounds like it." He sipped his coffee. "Sam's good for you. Those early years I knew you when you were involved with what's-his-name—"

"Rob," I supplied.

"Right, Rob. Where is he these days?"

"New York, last I heard. He got a job as a personal assistant for some magazine editor." I shrugged. "But that was a couple of years ago, so who knows."

"Well, he wasn't healthy for you. You really struggled in that relationship."

"It didn't help that he was constitutionally incapable of fidelity."

"Uh-huh. I don't see you having that trouble with Sam."

I shook my head and smiled. "Sam was born faithful."

Henry nodded. "People like that don't come along every day." He pressed his fork into the few remaining crumbs on his plate. His eyes met mine. "I have this girl. She's from downstate and has been through a rough time. Before next school year, we'd like to get her out of the town she's living in and find her somewhere around here, at least for a while, until we can get her something more permanent. When you were talking in the meeting, I thought maybe you're the right people to take her on."

"Why?"

He shrugged. "She's already been bounced from a couple of homes. She tends to make wives uncomfortable. I think she could use a safer kind of father figure than she's had so far."

"Oh." I leaned back in the booth, letting the coffee cup warm my hands.

"You could think of her as a different sort of refugee." He smiled.

I nodded slowly. "Interesting."

"Talk it over. Do whatever's best for the two of you. If you're interested, give me a call and I'll come over to the house, talk with the both of you, fill out some paperwork, and get the process started." He smiled again. "You think you can prove you're healthy, financially stable and have enough room for a foster child in that mansion of yours?"

"Okay, I'll talk to Sam. You really think I could do this?"

"I really think you could be good at it, but you've gotta do what works for you. What Sam wants is important, but you need to know your own limits too." He tented his arms, folded his hands together and rested his chin on his thumbs. "You've grown up more than you know, my friend. Give yourself time and I think you can figure out that next right step."

As we stood to go, Henry said, "I'm having an open house on Saturday afternoon to celebrate my birthday. Can you both come?"

I smiled. "I'll check with Sam, but I bet we're free."

"No presents," he said. "We've got more than enough crap around the house. And bring big appetites. Fran's already cooking."

I grinned. "Appetites we've got."

From my car on the way home, I phoned Sam at work.

"Hi," he said, "can you stop at the store and pick up some pasta? I talked Maggie into coming over for dinner with a jar of homemade tomato sauce."

"Excellent. I'll see if I can pick up some appropriate bread and a bag of salad."

He sighed. "We really should learn to cook."

"So you keep saying."

"I've got to get to class. Thanks for shopping."

"I love you."

"Me, too."

❧ ❧ ❧

As I pulled into the garage, I glanced at Gillian's house next door, where Qian practiced skateboard moves in the driveway. Gillian lent the house to the university for use by visiting faculty, and for the past few years it had felt like we were living next to an international guest house. Qian's mother, Bo Lin, was almost done with her sabbatical and soon they'd pack up to head back to China. I knew that feeling. Sam and I spent our first year together in Amsterdam during his sabbatical. As the end neared, I felt torn. I'd made friends and I loved the city, but I also missed my home.

And when I came home, I left Gillian in Amsterdam. Who'd have thought I'd be the one to hold down the home front while she spent our golden years abroad? It's like the Dalai Lama said in that movie, "Kundu": things can change just like that.

Gillian's my oldest friend, my next-door neighbor, my sister, my co-conspirator in life, not to mention the best cook I've ever known. We've been linked since childhood by our grandfathers, two men who lived, made a fortune, and died together, leaving all their money to the foundation that Gillian and I control. I always contend they were gay and Gillian, while she allows it's a good possibility, points out that our very existence could be cause for doubt. Now she's living in Amsterdam while I keep the old homestead in repair and watch the foreign professors come and go.

I let Daphnia out the front door and spotted the afternoon paper slumped against the step. Above the fold, the headline called out in big letters that after years of delay, our congressman was finally headed to jail. There was a bad picture of Jack, the guy I'd spent twenty years loathing as he made Gillian miserable. I was glad she'd been out of the country throughout the scandal of the divorce, his bribery trial and the endless appeals. Maybe now that it was over and he was headed to prison, she'd come visit.

I stared at the picture, hearing the clang of prison gates closing. The memory never fades. It's been years. I can go weeks without thinking about it and then something will trigger my memory—a story in the paper, a guy showing up at a meeting sporting an ankle bracelet, the phrases "drunk driving" or "vehicular assault," and I'm back there amid the bright lights and constant noise.

Most of what you hear about prison is bull. I wasn't raped in the shower or shanked in the yard. I did spend nine months stuck in cacophonous, soul-sucking boredom. Like anywhere else, money helps. My mother could talk the judge into the harshest sentence possible, but she couldn't keep Gillian from stocking my prison account with money and my care packages with cigarettes and chocolate.

I threw the paper on the dining room table and went to work. I spent the afternoon editing two images I'd agreed to donate for a Nature Conservancy brochure. I fiddled with the magenta in a sunset until my eyes crossed. Still, it was easier than the old days when I would have been stuck for hours in an acrid darkroom. Around four, I took a break and headed for our basement where, years ago, I'd converted the old rec room into a gym. Back then, I was struggling to keep Rob's attention and had spent hours pumping iron, trying to force myself into the hard-body he'd wanted.

These days I trot along on the treadmill. Sam's thirteen years younger, so I'll probably die first, but I'd like to stick around long enough to enjoy a life together.

By the time Maggie and Sam pulled up, I was considering a few images from Madrid for the book and playing tug-of-war with Daphnia. I watched out the window as Maggie parked at the curb and Sam waited in the driveway. As they greeted each other, I was struck by how related they looked—about the same height and lean. Actually Maggie borders on skinny, with that wonderful dark, curly hair. Maggie looked like Sam's slightly older sister, but their DNA couldn't be more different; Sam DaCosta's a Sephardic Jew only two generations off the boat, and Maggie Mazzoni is the daughter of an Italian butcher and an Irish nurse, who I'm sure never counted Abraham, Isaac and Jacob among her next of kin.

I like Maggie. It seems to me that we've been to some of the same dark places, but we never discuss it. There's something tangential about our friendship. She's Gillian's best girlfriend and Sam's closest colleague at work. Sam and Gillian are sweet people. They grew up loved and it shows. Maggie and I—well, that shows, too.

I opened the door as they started up the steps. Daphnia bounded down, wagging his whole body in greeting before jumping to plant his little paws on Sam's thigh. Sam picked up the dog and held him as he squirmed and licked his face and tried to lunge toward Maggie.

She reached a hand over and obligingly scratched his ears. "Hi Daph, how's the poop-eating business?"

Sam averted his eyes. "Oh, he's been over that for, um, weeks."

"Uh huh," Maggie said. "I'm still not letting that tongue anywhere near my face."

"Great to see you." I hugged her and stood aside to let them through. Sam and Daphnia kissed me in passing.

"God I love this view." She stood by the kitchen window, looking out at the lake. "So what have you been up to lately, Edward? It seems like I haven't seen you in ages."

"Polishing his book." Sam took the tomato sauce Maggie handed him and went looking for a pan.

"A book? I didn't know you were working on a book."

I felt myself blush. "It's not a book yet. But I collected some nice images of urban wildlife in cities like Paris, London, Rome, Amsterdam and I think—shit, I don't know what I think."

"They're great," Sam exclaimed. "He caught all the great landmarks: Buckingham Palace, the Coliseum, the Eiffel Tower—only the focus of each picture is a pigeon, a squirrel, a rat, raccoons, even a pet ocelot. They're funny and sad and beautiful."

"I'd love to see them sometime." Maggie leaned against the counter, watching us puttering in domestic bliss in what passed for cooking in the Rosenberg–DaCosta household.

I grinned at her. "Sure. If you twist my arm, I'll show you everything after dinner."

She sighed, one hand on her forehead like a swooning B-movie heroine. "I can't tell you how long it's been since a man made that kind of offer."

"What about Paul Johnstone? I thought he made that kind of offer all the time." Sam winked at Maggie.

"Who's Paul Johnstone?" I shook pasta into boiling water.

"Chair of the history department," Sam said. "He's hot, for an old guy. And he seems to find his way into the science building and past Maggie's office more often than you'd expect."

"What I'd expect and what really happens in academia seem to be completely different things." I stirred the pasta, which was forming alarmingly large clumps. "It always sounds more like you're high school students than college professors."

"Feels like that, too." Maggie gave Sam a look. "Paul's a great guy. And he's not much older than Edward."

"Ouch," I said.

"And I'm about as interested in him as I am in Edward."

"Any time you youngsters are ready, you can feel free to change the subject," I grumbled into the pot.

Eventually, we got dinner on the table. I turned to Maggie. "So, you have any plans for after the term ends?"

She shrugged. "Mostly work. I've got a big grant that starts in June."

"The drug company collaboration?" Sam asked.

"Yes. And that's all I get to say about it." Maggie speared a lettuce leaf. "I signed all sorts of confidentiality papers. I can tell you that they're sending over a doctoral student as part of the deal."

Sam's eyebrows shot up. "They're sending you a student? What about funding any of the students you've already got?"

"Part of the deal. And it works out well for me. They've already trained this guy so he'll be ready to do the technical work from the get-go. Anyway, no summer plans." She tore off a hunk of bread. "I was going to visit my sister in San Diego so I can remember all the reasons I didn't marry some redneck guy and have a bunch of snotty-nosed kids, but it looks now like I'm stuck in the lab all summer. You guys doing anything exciting?"

I looked at Sam, who shook his head. "No, not yet."

"You're coming to the end-of-term picnic, aren't you, Edward?" Maggie asked after a pause.

"Am I?" I asked Sam.

He smiled. "It'll be better than the holiday party, I promise. It'll be outdoors. We can play volleyball."

"I guess I'm coming," I told Maggie. "But if he abandons me to that geologist again, I'm out of there."

"You left him with Carter, didn't you?" Maggie accused Sam.

"I went to get punch, and by the time I returned they were already up to the Cambrian."

I shuddered dramatically. "It was hideous."

Maggie patted my arm. "I'm so sorry I wasn't there to rescue you."

She turned to Sam. "You're a cad."

He shrugged apologetically. "I wasn't thinking. I'll be better next time."

After Maggie left, Sam and I walked down to the dock. I pulled him close as we stood looking out over the water, listening to the waves lap against the shore. I recounted my conversation with Henry.

"Huh," he said. "Troubled teenage girl—hadn't thought of that possibility."

"I don't know what I think yet," I told him. "We're really good, right now, like this."

"I know," he whispered, leaning into me.

"But we can keep talking." I watched the play of moonlight and wind across the waves.

❧ ❧ ❧

I woke in the dark, hot and sweaty, my heart pounding. The clock said three a.m. Taking a deep breath, I tried to relax. My favorite nightmare, the one where I watch through my windshield as three kids tumble in slow motion around the back seat of the station wagon. My car keeps pushing and pushing into theirs. I can see Zoe Barnes's terrified face in her rearview mirror. I watch as first little Ben, then Amber, and finally Zach crumple onto the seat. Can't tell you how much of the dream is memory, how much reconstruction, but I bet Zoe has dreams like mine. This was the part I avoid remembering. I went to prison and eventually walked out, picked up my life and went on. Zach tried to get home from dinner at his grandma's and won't ever walk again.

I slid out of bed and pulled on my robe. Might as well start the coffee. Fourteen years and I hadn't yet fallen back to sleep after the dream. Before heading down to the kitchen I stopped in my office, turned on the computer and transferred $10,000 into the trust account I'd set up for Zach after the accident and another $10,000 into a checking account I share with Zoe. It doesn't stop the images, but it's what I always do after the dream. I deposit, she withdraws. Maybe after her own dreams, maybe when she watches Zach wheel himself to school.

We don't talk much. He's going to Stanford in the fall. I know because I'm paying the tuition. Seemed only fair since over the years I've made him too rich for financial aid. Least I could do.

Two

※

"You want to help me kick up a stream?" Sam stood at the end of the bed, pulling on an ancient pair of jeans.

I blinked at the clock. "It's not even six."

"Come on. It'll be fun." He jostled my foot. "You can bring your camera."

I squinted at him. "Did a grad student stand you up or something?"

Sam held up his cell phone. "Down with the flu. But it's okay. I like you better."

"That'll be a comfort to me when my boots flood." I swung my feet over the edge of the bed. He handed me a pair of sweats, a long-sleeved tee and a sweatshirt. He's hard to resist when he has his boyish charm thing going.

As I stumbled into the garage, clutching my giant coffee mug, a camera bag slung over one shoulder, Sam was stuffing equipment into the back of his ancient blue hatchback. Daphnia bolted past me and leaped through the open door onto the passenger seat. Sam crammed one more box into the back and slammed the hatch shut. I slid onto my seat, wrestling Daphnia onto my lap.

He pulled out of the garage and headed north into the early morning light.

I turned Daphnia so he'd quit licking my chin. "What are we studying this morning?"

Sam glanced at me. "Bugs. What else?"

"Will it take a long time?"

"I have class at eleven." He dropped a hand to my thigh. "Thanks for coming—you're a lifesaver."

We left the town behind and drove into the woods. Sam turned onto a secondary road. Red pines loomed above us, interrupted by the occasional stark white birch. Daphnia curled into a compact bundle and I leaned back in the seat to sip my coffee and watch the scenery slip by.

Gravel crunched beneath the wheels as Sam pulled onto the shoulder. I stepped out, inhaling the sharp cold forest smell. Daphnia trotted to the nearest clump of grass, sniffed delicately and peed.

Sam opened the back and tossed me a pair of slick green chest waders. "Hard to flood your boots in these."

I kicked off my shoe and slid my foot into the cool rubber sleeve of the boot. "Never underestimate my ability to fall."

He leaned against the bumper as he slid into thigh-high boots. "You're more graceful than you think you are."

"Right." My fingers curled around the camera, my reminder to look around.

Sam passed me a long-handled net and shouldered his field pack. He pushed through the tall grass and into the woods, with Daphnia bounding ahead and me trailing behind. As we slogged through mucky ground on our way to the stream, I got a good shot of a bumpy brown bullfrog nestled in the canary grass.

I heard it first, the clatter of water bouncing over rocks. The air felt cooler near the stream. I could smell wild mint. We stepped around a willow and there it was, a sparkly rush of blue past moss-covered rocks, lit perfectly in the morning sun. I took a quick dozen calendar shots.

Sam stopped at the water's edge and grinned. "Now aren't you glad you came?"

I got that grin, too.

"Okay." I hung my camera on a tree branch. "Where do you want me?"

Daphnia watched from the riverbank while Sam shuffled toward me, dislodging whatever lived under those rocks and I waited downstream like a spider in its web. I really hope that kiss at the end isn't part of Sam's standard sampling protocol. It could get him in real trouble.

Larvae of all sorts cascaded from the net into Sam's enamel pan. He threw back a few minnows, handed me tweezers and we picked through, tossing feather-tailed mayflies, husky stoneflies, hard-bodied beetles and curly, wormy things of all kinds into his sampling bag.

"Kids really like doing this." He dropped a mean looking dobsonfly into the bag.

Sam bent back over the pan and I stared into his curls. "Uh huh."

He sealed the bag and retrieved the net. "That was fun. Let's do it all over again."

❧ ❧ ❧

Sam dropped me off at home on his way to work. I had a meeting downtown with the Neskame Wetland Association. They wanted someone to shoot the images for a brochure and a dog-and-pony fundraiser slideshow. More pro bono work, but I don't mind. I'm not in it for the money, and the Neskame's a beautiful place. So I agreed to spend some time out there and see what I could get.

On the way back, I passed Harding Elementary. Must have been recess, because kids came pouring out, ricocheting off fences, playground equipment and building walls. I stopped, parking across the street to watch. I was reminiscing about the time I broke my arm because Jim Connors hopped off his side of the teeter-totter when a large, middle-aged woman crossed the street toward me. I rolled down the window.

"Have you considered a less conspicuous surveillance vehicle?" she smiled. "Shiny red BMW convertibles tend to get noticed."

"Hi, Tess. I'm just watching and remembering. Are you patrolling for bad guys?"

She grimaced. "Ever since that kid was abducted over in Collinville they've got one teacher on playground duty and another watching the street. I guess it's a scary world out there, although, to tell the truth, we worry more about divorced dads than pedophiles."

"Do the dads really sit and watch the kids like that? I thought that only happened in movies."

"It happens. Breaks your heart." She patted my car roof. "I'd better get going. Try not to look like you're stalking the children, okay?"

I nodded and started the car. "Sure thing. I'll see you next Thursday at the Nature Conservancy board meeting." As I drove off, I could see her strolling back toward the school fence, starting another trip around the perimeter.

❧ ❧ ❧

I got an email from my agent, Kathy Caldwell, saying *Sport Fisherman* was looking for an image of an eagle catching, holding or eating a fish, and did I have one? I wrote her back that the whole idea was trite, overdone, and derivative, but yes, I had some. I attached my three best. Had she spoken to anyone about the book idea? I asked, and hit send.

"Hey, Daphnia, wanna go for a walk?" He appeared almost instantly and quivered with excitement as I pulled his leash from a hook on the wall. If only we were all that easy to please.

"April is the cruelest month." Who said that? As Daphnia and I emerged from the house into a beautiful spring afternoon, the only potential cruelty was that eventually we'd have to go back inside. Our road runs from downtown up a steep incline and along a ridge around the southern shore of the lake. Daphnia and I headed uphill. For the first part of the climb, houses shelter walkers from wind off the lake, but by the summit, the lakeside houses literally recede, as the roofs peek from below and steep driveways fall down into garages that cling to the cliff.

Years ago this all belonged to Gillian and my grandfathers, wealthy businessmen from the city. They built, and sold for millions, Rosenberg and Wolf Tool and Die. In the twenties, they started spending weekends up here. Eventually they bought most of the south shore as property after property was auctioned for taxes during the Depression. They sold most of it before they died, leaving us the two large adjacent lots where our houses sit. And money, lots of it.

The wind kicked up whitecaps along the lake. I zipped my coat. A squirrel crossed the road and bolted up a tree. Daphnia strained at his leash. "Pass obedience school and I'll think about it."

He looked at me, looked at the squirrel, looked back at me.

"No dice." I walked on, pulling him reluctantly behind me. After a while, he gave up and trotted ahead, once again at the end of his lead. "You have some experience of me as a parent," I said to him. "What do you think?" He must not have heard me over the wind because he didn't answer.

About a mile's walk from the house, there's an old path down to the lake. The current owners tried for a while to keep people away, eventually settling for erecting a sign disavowing responsibility for broken bones. Daphnia arrived there first and sat, patiently waiting for me to unclip his leash before he disappeared over the cliff edge. I followed more cautiously.

The summer we were ten, Gillian took her first life-drawing class at the Y. I was in my pirate phase. My mother forbade it, but when I came down for two weeks in August, the grandfathers let me wear my eye patch all day. On the last Saturday of my visit, Gillian talked me into modeling for her. She grabbed her sketchpad. I donned my plumed hat and we scrambled down this hill, gravel bouncing ahead of us. She posed me on a near shore boulder peering through an old paper kaleidoscope out over the lake. She didn't get the proportions quite right, but for a ten-year-old? The drawing's in the upstairs hallway where the grandfathers hung it. The framer tried, but couldn't clean off the dirt smudges or iron out all the creases, so it stands as a testament both to Gillian's skill and my clumsiness. Climbing the hill one-eyed, I tripped over a branch, fell backwards into her, and we both tumbled down to the shore.

In the hospital, my mother turned her icy tongue on Grandpa Rosenberg, castigating him for indulging my childish dress-up games. She flung me into the Volvo's back seat. For the entire two-hour drive home, she lectured my father about the impropriety of his father's life and for letting me play with "that girl." She turned around once, saw me crying, and told me to be a man, that pain was character-building. I wiped my tears. But in fifty-plus years I've never managed to build the character she had in mind. I'm not a six-figure lawyer with a slim wife and several brilliant children. Instead, I've spent my days slogging through mud in search of the perfect picture or trapped in the sexy intimacy of a darkroom or lately, sitting in front of a monitor, cropping and tinting the less-than-perfect results. And I've spent my nights – well, my mother has never did approve of my nights. But it's been years since I approved of her at all, so I guess we're even.

I reached the tiny strip of rocky shore in time to see Daphnia plunge chest deep, chasing a pair of Mallard ducks. "You'll be sorry," I told him as he waded through the chilly water, but what I really meant was that I'd be sorry when I had to carry the shivering dog the last half-mile home. He clambered out of the water and shook, which, since he doesn't have much fur, managed to neither wet me nor dry him. I sat on a boulder to watch the lake while Daphnia explored the beach.

The lake felt as familiar as breathing. When I was a kid, it was the safest place I knew. My parents brought me down most weekends and left me with Gillian and the grandfathers for weeks at a time during the summer. Although she clearly relished the time away from me, my mother always referred to the visits to "your grandpapa" or, if she was talking to my father, "your father's house," as if Grandpa Wolf and Gillian didn't live there as well. When she did acknowledge Grandpa Wolf or Gillian, it was to note what a bad influence they were on me. I loved those visits.

When my mother wasn't around, the grandfathers let me get dirty and wet, taught me to canoe and sail, bought me my first camera, and later, set up a darkroom in a spare bedroom upstairs. They didn't make me sit still, play tennis, practice the piano or be nice, although they were insistent on kind.

"Come on, Daph," I called, "time to go home."

They'd have taken in Henry's broken girl, no doubt about it.

❧ ❧ ❧

Friday nights, Sam liked us to make a big culinary production for the Sabbath. That meant no pizza, TV dinners, or deli food, although the kind of frozen meal that served a family was all right. I selected a package of beef teriyaki to defrost, checked to make sure we still had some bagged lettuce, found candles for the Shabbos candlesticks, set the dining room table for two, and bounded upstairs toward the shower.

I loved Friday nights. The rabbi didn't need Sam for the evening service, which tends to be more family-oriented. We went a few times. But mostly we skipped synagogue and stayed home together. Another thing likely to change with a kid.

As I rinsed off, the shower door opened and Sam stepped in. I moved sideways so he could fit under the stream. He closed his eyes and leaned back, letting the water hit his forehead and cascade down his body.

"Rough day?" I turned him so I could wash his back.

"Not terrible. But I'm glad to be done with it." Grabbing the shampoo, he pulled me back under the warm spray. I helped him massage the soap into his hair.

Eventually we made dinner. The microwave is a wondrous thing. The sun was setting over the lake when Sam lit the candles, singing the blessing in that amazing rich tenor that always gets me. As we ate, we watched the light leach from the sky, leaving a darkened landscape illuminated only by houselights across the way.

"So tell me about your day." I forked tangy meat strips into my mouth.

"It's that time of year." He swirled the ice in his water glass and sipped. "We're close enough to the end of term that we're all ready for it to be over, but there's still so much to do. So everybody's grumpy, students and faculty alike." He put down his glass and picked up his fork. "How about yours?"

I told him about the meeting with the Neskame Association and about my potential eagle sale. "Daphnia and I climbed down the cliff." I nodded toward the dog curled in a corner chair. "While we were down there I was thinking about my mother."

"That's unusual," Sam said dryly.

"Do I talk about her too much?"

He looked at me for a long moment while stirring his food. "Talk, no. But for a fifty-three-year-old guy whose mother lives a thousand miles away, so he sees her maybe once a year and after four years, hasn't even introduced her to his lover, I think maybe she's in your thoughts too much."

"Wait, have I met your mother and forgotten about it?" I asked, stung.

"No, you haven't met my mother, but if she ever returned a letter or phone call I'd be delighted to introduce you." Sam attacked his salad.

I took a deep breath. "I'm sorry. That was out of line." He looked up and softened, so I continued, "And you're right. I should get over Mom. I'll get right on that. Tomorrow."

He laughed. "Here's what I've been thinking lately, Honey. Everyone needs family. For whatever reason, you and I don't get to keep our birth families, so we have to make our own."

"We have each other." I tried not to sound too defensive.

He nodded. "And Maggie feels like family. So does Gillian, although more like a distant cousin now that she lives so far away. We even have Henry and Fran as parental figures, more for you than for me, but still. What we don't have is the next generation down."

"How about Daphnia?" At the sound of his name, the dog lifted his head and looked expectantly at me. "He's the son I've always wanted."

Sam shook his head, looked at his plate and toyed with a piece of meat.

I broke the silence. "I know this is important. I'll try not to be flip. But I worry. We have only so much time together as it is. My work is flexible, but yours, not so much." I paused, scooping up one last bite of teriyaki as I tried to find the right words. "When we do have time, we're really together. Having someone else around would change that. This afternoon when you came home, would that have been the same with some teenager watching TV down the hall?"

Sam smiled. "Maybe it would have been better. Illicit is sexy."

I closed my eyes, trying to picture the place with children. But of course, there had been children running all over the house and I'd been one of them. I remembered the grandfathers' faces as they watched us. Maybe Sam was right. Scooping up our plates, I escaped into the kitchen to find dessert.

❧ ❧ ❧

"Good morning." Sam sat on the edge of the bed. "I need to leave for the synagogue in about half an hour. Are you coming?" His hair glistened, still wet from the shower.

"Sure." I reached for the coffee cup he held out to me. "Did you run this morning?"

He smiled. "Only ten miles. I've got a long way to go until I'm in shape for the Lakeshore Marathon."

I gulped coffee. "I'm grateful when I can do two." I swung my legs over the side of the bed. "I know, I know, you think if I ran outside I wouldn't get bored and could go longer. But I get enough of the weather with work. Are you in charge this morning?"

He nodded. "I said I'd open up and lead the morning prayers every Saturday until Rabbi Talia's father gets released from the nursing home. That way she can spend time with him before the Torah service." He shrugged. "I told her I'd take the whole thing, but she feels an obligation."

Before Sam, my main connection to my ancestral religion was a fondness for bagels and guilt. I'm still not as comfortable in a synagogue as he is, but who could be? He studied to be a cantor before going into biology. He can chant Hebrew all day long. Now he coaches the bar and bat mitzvah kids. On Sundays during the school year, there's a small parade of adolescents passing through his study and the house fills with sounds more like the mating calls of tree frogs than anything approaching sacred text. The fact that no one in the congregation has objected to their offspring being taught Hebrew by an openly gay man is either a tribute to their tolerance or to Sam's skill. Probably a mixture of both.

"I'm glad they weren't ordaining gay rabbis back when you were in school or I'd be doing good works in some progressive congregation," I told him.

"You'd make a lovely rebbitsen." He smiled.

"A what?" I stood and stumbled toward the bathroom.

"The type of rabbi's wife who runs the Sisterhood and keeps the women in line."

I could hear him laughing as he rummaged in the closet, probably looking for a clean shirt for me.

"Give a whole new meaning to Sisterhood, wouldn't it?" He appeared in the bathroom doorway.

"Ha ha," I mumbled, my mouth full of toothbrush.

Sam managed to get us there on time, even though I arrived with bagel crumbs down my shirt and a small wet coffee stain on my pants. A cluster of people stood waiting for Sam to open up. Once inside, he climbed onto the bimah and I slumped into my usual seat near the back, nodding to old man Gordon and the Guttmans as I passed.

As I slid in beside Liv Bloomberg, she smiled, patted my arm and pointed one crooked finger at the page number in her prayer book. Soon we were chanting, "How lovely are your tents, oh, Jacob."

When I reappeared in this community of people who knew me as a child, most kept their distance. Liv told me to be patient, that it might take them time to get comfortable around a gay jailbird junkie. She'd winked and told me to stick with Sam and everything would work out. Everyone loves Sam. As I looked around the sanctuary, I realized she had been right. Despite my bad Hebrew and worse past, the congregation had embraced us as a couple and pulled me back into the tribe. With some exceptions, of course.

The Saturday morning Torah service tends to be a haven for adults. It's long, mostly in Hebrew and not very kid-friendly, so children don't show up except for the seventh-graders, who the rabbi forces into coming at least half the time in preparation for their bar and bat mitzvahs. We're a small congregation. There are usually only a handful of thirteen-year-olds each year and the rite of passage ceremonies get clustered in the spring. So after New Year's, they become regular attendees. The first sulky adolescent arrived about half an hour into the service. Brittany Goldstein sullenly followed her mother to a seat near the front. When Sam started coaching her last fall, Bob and Vera Goldstein made it clear they expected great things from her. I watched her now, wondering what it would feel like to shepherd a teenager through that particular hurdle. Her hair, hanging over the pew back in carefully arranged curls, seemed to whisper secrets I couldn't quite hear about adolescence, obedience and betrayal. Okay, maybe I drifted off a bit. Like I said, it's a long service.

As usual, Sam stayed up there to help through most of the service, even after Rabbi Talia arrived, but he came back to sit with Liv and me through the closing prayers. We stood and sang and wandered into the community room for bagels, Manischewitz, or in my case, grape juice, and conversation.

As everyone stood eating and talking, Rabbi Talia strode up to us. "Shabbat Shalom. Thanks so much, Sam."

"How's your father?" I shook her proffered hand.

She shrugged. "No better, no worse. Thanks for asking. How are you guys?"

Sam smiled. "Good, thanks. Only a month left in the semester and I can almost see the end of the tunnel."

"Any plans for after school ends?" She moved us toward the food table.

"Actually," I said, surprising myself, "we're thinking about becoming foster parents." Sam looked at me open-mouthed. I smiled sheepishly at him and faced the Rabbi. "We're still considering. Maybe we could come talk with you about it sometime?"

"Of course." She smiled, looking from one of us to the other. "Catch me before you leave today and we'll set up a time next week." She nodded to us both and moved on.

Sam turned to me, his hand on my arm. "Really?"

I shrugged. "I honestly didn't know I was going to say that, Sam, otherwise I would have talked with you first, but, well, we are thinking about it and it wouldn't hurt to talk with Talia."

He grinned widely. "I love you." He squeezed my arm. "Stay here, I'll get us some cookies." I watched him walk off, a graceful runner's stride. I prayed, please don't let me fuck this up.

❧ ❧ ❧

Henry and Fran live in a rambling old Victorian north of downtown. Henry greeted us each with a warm hug and ushered us into a living room overflowing with family, only to abandon us as the doorbell rang again. Ignoring the grandchildren running by, I introduced Sam to Henry's eldest, James, a thirty-year-old lawyer now living in the city, and William, the baby who'd driven home from college for the

event. Fran led us to a table laden with a large aromatic roast, sliced
ham, mashed potatoes, potato salad, egg salad, beet salad, green beans,
baby peas, grilled onions, creamed corn, homemade rolls and biscuits.
Desserts covered a side table.

"My God, Fran," I asked, "who all are you expecting?"

She laughed, a single deep musical tone, developed over years
of singing in the choir and smoking in the anteroom. "I'm a feeder,
always have been. Eat up, boys. There's plenty." She whirled back into
the kitchen.

Her daughter, Ruth, smiled at Sam and handed him a plate. "Hi,
Sam, nice to see you. And how've you been, Edward?" she asked me
tightly.

"Good, thanks." I reached for a plate and forked a slab of roast beef
onto it. "You?"

"Fine." She turned toward the kitchen, hauling two of her children
with her. "See you at school," she called to Sam over her shoulder.

"Chilly," he whispered, spooning potatoes.

"Can you blame her? She's Zoe Barnes's best friend," I murmured.
"All things considered, after what I did to Zach, I'm grateful she's polite.
And it looks like she isn't taking it out on you. That's good. I suspect
your life could get difficult if the departmental secretary disliked you as
much as she dislikes me."

"It's 'Program Assistant,'" Sam mumbled.

A couple of guys from the Thursday St. Andrew's meeting arrived,
teasing us as they filled large plates with food.

The party spilled into the backyard. A group of us sat in lawn chairs,
enjoying the unexpected warm afternoon sun. I watched Sam laugh as
he played touch football with some of the older kids. Henry pulled up
a chair beside me.

"Happy birthday."

He nodded. "Thanks." We watched as younger kids wandered
onto the field and the football game disintegrated into tag. "He's good
with them."

"I know. And he's happy." We watched a while longer in silence.
"I know you don't want any birthday presents, but I thought that as
long as your whole family was here you might not mind a portrait. In

about an hour, the light should be perfect. What do you think?"

He beamed. "That would be great. Really nice of you."

"Good. I'll get the equipment out of my car."

When everyone was assembled into a tableau with Henry and Fran at the center and their kids and grandkids arrayed around them, I looked through the viewfinder and snapped, feeling like I'd captured a transient moment of the American dream.

༄ ༄ ༄

Naomi flew in on a Tuesday. I stayed with the car while Sam ran in to meet her. You're not supposed to park in the loading zone, but it's a small airport. The only time a security guard ever confronted me, all he wanted to talk about was my car. So I sat in the driver's seat, lolling in the late afternoon sun. I must have slept, since the next thing I knew, Sam was leaping into the back seat, Batman and Robin style, leaving his sister to open the car door and slide in beside me.

She smiled. "Hello, Edward."

Last visit, we'd moved to the cheek-kissing stage, so we did. It was getting less awkward. Naomi's what we used to call a storefront lawyer. Her husband, David, teaches at an urban high school. I think their problems with my influence on Sam's lifestyle have a lot more to do with my money than my gender. Donations to her legal aid center help, but old prejudices die hard. Also, since she's the only member of Sam's family I'm allowed to meet, getting to know each other requires navigating a lot of potholes.

"So," Sam was saying, leaning forward from the back seat. "How's the family?"

She smiled. "Hectic. They say it gets easier as they get older, but I haven't seen it yet. It's the after-school stuff that gets you. Hanna's caught up in soccer, and Alma joined a gymnastics team, which has me waking up in the middle of the night wondering if I'm anything like the other pushy moms."

"Isn't she young for a sports team?" he asked.

Naomi shrugged. "She's nine. There are a couple of first-graders on the team, so she's not the youngest. I worry, too. She seems to love it, though. Of course, her best friend is on the team, so what can you do?"

"How's David?" Since I hadn't met him, I threw in the question to be sociable.

"Good. He's got a great group of students this year, which is a big relief after last year when that group of punks tried to blow up his chemistry lab. Gives me hope that by the time Hanna gets to high school there might be a few decent kids she can date."

Sam laughed. "As I remember, you didn't date any decent guys in high school and you survived."

"Yeah, but that was then. The bad boys now are doing crack and meth. But enough of that, how are you guys?"

ॐ ॐ ॐ

Naomi likes ethnic food. She also lives in Boston where she can do a culinary world tour from the subway on the way home. I drove to our closest equivalent, El Serape, a dive sort of like the Rise and Shine but with beans and guacamole.

Over food, Sam gave her the short version of our possible foster fatherhood. She listened in a quiet, lawyerly way and asked the occasional question. I emptied the chip bowl twice.

Finally, she pushed her almost empty plate away and leaned back in the booth. "I really don't know about that type of law." She smiled. "We don't get much call for foster care or adoption in employment law. But I do see plenty of children getting treated badly. Seems to me if you want to and can afford it, taking in this kid could be a good thing."

Sam's shoulders relaxed. "I'm glad you think so."

"Of course, your lives are likely to change in ways you can't even imagine." She took a long swallow of iced tea. "Gymnastics and soccer are nothing compared to what you're signing on for, especially if she's been abused. Those kids can be hard to rescue."

The check came and we walked out into a warming day. Almost May and the world was greening up again.

ॐ ॐ ॐ

Wednesday morning after breakfast, I packed one waterproof bag with camera gear and Sam packed another with snacks. We keep a few plastic kayaks hanging along one wall of the boathouse. There are a couple of nice paddling routes around the lake. Nothing longer than an hour or two, but that's enough to exhaust my shoulders.

We slid three brightly colored boats into the water and paddled toward the far end of the lake. Sam and Naomi surged ahead. With my camera in hand, I lagged behind. The light wasn't perfect, but they paced each other beautifully, paddles arcing in exact synchronous angles.

The best paddle route involves hugging the lake edge for about a mile, and ducking under a little bridge, into the wetland channel that eventually dumps you into Bear Lake. Really, it's more a culvert than a bridge. I always have to hunch down to pass under.

I'd fallen far enough behind that I felt completely alone with the slap and swish of water around my paddle. At some points, the channel narrows so you have to angle the paddle steeply if you don't want to knock vegetation into the boat. Taking my time, I got a nice shot of a row of turtles sunning themselves, a frog peeking out of the muck and a heron feeding in the shallows as I entered Bear Lake, which really should be called Bear Pond, but what does it matter? Sam and Naomi drifted nearby. She was talking, he was laughing. I watched until they spotted me, and paddled over to join them.

❧ ❧ ❧

We didn't talk about the "third rail" until the night before Naomi was to leave. After dinner, we sat before a fire in the living room, huge bowls of chocolate ice cream cooling our laps.

"So how's Mom?" Sam kept his eyes on his spoon as he brought ice cream to his mouth, his voice almost flat.

Naomi inhaled. "Not great. She's forgetting little things. It's not Alzheimer's. The doctors think she might be having small strokes." She looked down, swirling ice cream with her spoon. Finally, she smiled sadly at him. "She sent her love."

Sam nodded. After a moment, he asked, "And Dad?"

She shrugged. "The same."
She watched her brother steadily.
He nodded again and changed the subject.

⁂ ⁂ ⁂

Something woke me. I stared at the dark ceiling for a moment before I realized the muffled sobs were coming from the pillow beside me. I curled myself around him and he buried his face in my chest.

Nothing is as cruel as families.

The next morning, after we dropped Naomi at the airport, I called Henry and told him to bring over the papers.

THREE

"So what changed your mind?" Henry asked, settled into our couch with a cup of tea, his satchel open beside him. Daphnia jumped onto his lap. Henry held up his cup, managing to keep it from spilling. He set down the cup, and held onto Daphnia, who strained to lick Henry's chin. He eventually persuaded the dog to lie still and be petted.

"A lot of things," I said, "but I think Naomi's visit and something Rabbi Talia said about Tikkun Olam, our responsibility to heal the world, really tipped me over. That, and how happy Sam looks whenever we talk about it."

Henry scanned the room. "Where is he now?"

I glanced at my watch. "His last class today didn't end until about fifteen minutes ago so he should be home soon. Maybe we can start filling out papers?" I paused and smiled at him. "It's funny, but I'm really nervous about this interview. I know it's crazy. Years ago we sat in this same room and I told you about every hideous thing I'd done in my using days, and I swear I wasn't as scared of what you'd think as I am now."

Henry chuckled. "It's the nature of the process. You can relax. We already ran the background check. Nothing I didn't already know came back, so you're clear. After that, it's all up to my discretion, and if you'll remember, I'm the one who suggested this. Here." He passed me a sheaf of papers. "Start filling these out. Nothing like paperwork to calm a man."

I began filling in my name and address. "You want me to put Sam's name on the same line with mine?"

"We should talk about that." Daphnia jumped down and Henry crossed his ankle over his knee. "The state doesn't say one way or another about licensing gay couples to foster parent. I brought two sets of paperwork if you want to fill them out separately. Otherwise we'll put one of you in as the spouse."

Daphnia started barking and ran to the front door. Sam walked in, peeling off his jacket.

"Hi, Henry." He strode forward to shake hands, ignoring Daphnia nipping at his shoelaces.

Henry pulled him into a quick embrace. "Hey, Sam."

I patted the seat beside me, and Sam flopped down, letting the dog lick his face in greeting. When Sam had been thoroughly washed and Daphnia lay contentedly across his lap, I said, "Henry was asking whether we want to fill these out separately or as a couple."

"Does it matter?" Sam absentmindedly stroked the dog.

Henry shrugged. "In this case, probably not. There's a slim chance that you could get denied on the first go-around if you fill it out as a couple, but as I was telling Edward, the law isn't clear."

Sam stared into space. "I think we should apply as a couple. None of this makes any sense to me otherwise."

I smiled. "Okay then. Since I already started filling in the boxes, you're the spouse."

"Cool. I always wanted to be a spouse."

The paperwork didn't take long at all. We answered "no" to most questions (previous marriages, other children, history of mental illness or child abuse complaints), provided our address, directions to the house, and two non-related references (Maggie and Rabbi Talia), described the living arrangements, and I wrote a short essay explaining my incarceration. The last page consisted of essay questions about our parenting attitudes. Henry suggested we email him the answers to those after we'd had some time to think.

"Have you decided where she'll sleep?" He picked up his clipboard and pen.

"The green room at the far end of the hall upstairs." I looked at Sam, who nodded. "It'll give her some privacy and her own bathroom, but she'll need to pass our room to get downstairs and out."

Henry nodded. "Sounds like a good choice. In a bit you can walk me around the place and show me exits and fire extinguishers." He smiled from under his bushy eyebrows. "Or more probably, I can show you where the fire extinguishers will be."

After skimming the papers, he looked up. "There's a set of classes you're supposed to go through. I'm going to waive most of them for now. The material is more pertinent to people taking in babies and little kids. If you decide you want to keep doing this, we can talk again. But I think you should get some training in dealing with traumatized and abused children. There's a workshop down state next weekend." He looked at us questioningly.

Sam wrinkled his brow. "I think we're free?"

I nodded slowly. "Um, sure, sounds fun."

Henry chuckled and made a note. He put down his clipboard. "This might be a good time to talk about Ginger.

"Her name is Ginger?" Sam asked.

Henry nodded. "Ginger McIntyre. She'll be twelve next month." He pulled a snapshot from the folder and handed it to us. A very thin blond girl wearing heavy eyeliner pouted into the camera.

"Twelve going on thirty it looks like," I said.

Sam studied her. His eyebrows lifted and he glanced at me.

"Like I said, she's had a rough time. It's all in here." Henry handed me the file. "But the short version goes something like this. Her mom died of an overdose when Ginger was about six. After that, Mom's boyfriend took over. We don't think he's Ginger's father, but it doesn't matter, he's not getting her back under any circumstances."

"What did he do?" Sam asked softly.

Henry looked thoughtful. "We're not exactly sure. She doesn't want to talk about it, or doesn't remember, it's hard to tell which. What we do know is that by the time she ended up in the system, she had gonorrhea and crabs, as well as vaginal and anal bruising." He gestured to the folder. "Read it on an empty stomach."

"Holy shit." I stared at her picture.

Sam swallowed hard. "Poor thing." He looked up at Henry. "How about him?"

Henry looked down at his hands and shook his head. "We don't know that either. He's still at large. We didn't rescue her. She made her way into the system by not showing up at school for a week. Lucky for her, she had a first-year crusading teacher who got worried and dropped by to see how she was doing. She found the kid all alone in a filthy apartment, no food, no money, no dad. Guess Ginger came home from school one day and he was gone."

Sam swallowed. "Wow, where is she now?"

"Right now she's in a group home. It's a temporary solution, but we don't have anywhere else to put her. She's . . ." Henry paused, searching for the word, "seductive. It's not uncommon among girls who were sexualized early. You can think of it as conditioning. She's been taught that sex will make her safe. She's a smart kid, scores incredibly high on standardized tests even though she almost didn't pass fifth grade, and she's on the edge of failing sixth. She's been kicked out of five foster homes so far. She steals and lies, but mostly she's too damn sexy. And it isn't only young boys who fall for it."

"Sounds like a handful," I said. "How about her grandparents?"

Henry shook his head. "We haven't found any. There probably should have been more of an effort or at least an investigation when her mom died, but," he shrugged, "we're so overbooked that it must have slipped through the cracks. Now . . ." he trailed off. Clearing his throat, he continued, "I'm gonna leave the file with you for a while. Think it over. I don't mean this to pressure you, but frankly, you're her last chance. Still, don't do it if you think you can't handle her. She doesn't need another rejection."

I nodded and watched Sam, who'd been staring intently at her picture. He looked up at Henry. "So when would we get her?"

"Our treatment plan has her moving up here right after school ends, first week in June. The idea is to try to get her into a different emotional space by September so she has a fighting chance of making it through junior high."

Into the silence that followed, I tossed, "And in September?"

Henry shrugged. "If you're happy and she's happy, we're happy. Otherwise we go to plan B."

"What's plan B?" Sam set the photo face down on the coffee table.

Henry smiled. "We don't have one yet. Right now, you're plans A, B and C."

"But no pressure." I eyed the folder.

"Welcome to fatherhood. There's always pressure."

"So if her mother's dead and her father's either unknown or abusive, no grandparents, then she's theoretically available for adoption, provided everything worked out, that is." Sam stopped and looked at me apologetically.

I smiled and told Henry, "You might as well sign us up for that class. It looks like we've made up our minds."

❧ ❧ ❧

After dinner, Sam and I bundled up and hung a flashlight on the bow of my old aluminum canoe. Almost full, the moon lit up the familiar landscape. We paddled in silence broken only by the slap of water and the call of an owl.

"You ready to go back?" I asked when Sam stopped paddling.

"Not yet." He stowed his paddle and turned to face me. "Do you really think we can do this?"

"Having second thoughts?" I rested my paddle across my knees.

"It's all so real, so raw. How will I know what to do?"

I smiled. "It's funny, but for the first time since we started talking about this, I'm feeling like maybe it could work. It won't be 'The Brady Bunch,' that's for sure. But on the other hand, we've got to be better than where she's been."

"I suppose you're right." He trailed a finger in the water.

"I'll call Henry and tell him not to process our paperwork until after the workshop next weekend. That'll give us another chance to talk with Talia and gain some idea of what we're getting into."

Sam nodded, turned back around, and we paddled home.

FOUR

⚘

T he file sat unopened on the kitchen table until Wednesday
when the cleaning service came and I slipped it into my
briefcase and stowed it in the closet of my office. It wasn't that
I thought my overworked cleaning women would read the damned
thing. Even if they wanted to, they wouldn't have time. But it was the
only thing I could do right then to protect Ginger.

Thursday morning I tried to work, but eventually gave up and
picked up Henry's list of essay questions. How the hell was I supposed
to know my strengths and weaknesses as a parent? Closest I'd come to
parenthood had been as the funny, drunken uncle to Gillian's children.
"I have a good sense of humor," I wrote. Maybe Sam could answer
that one. He has great strengths, although I have to admit I'm the one
to come to for weaknesses. "Many people have experienced trauma in
their own lives. Have you? Have you discussed these events with your
spouse?" I was emailing this to Henry, for God's sake. I wrote, "Sam
knows everything about me and so do you." I decided I'd have to get
approved or disapproved without the frigging essay answers.

I gave in and pulled the briefcase from the closet, retrieved the
file and stretched out in my old leather easy chair. Outside, the sun
broke through the clouds. Sunlight fell through my office window,
cascading across my calves and warming my feet. I opened the file,

looking again at the photo of Ginger, trying to envision the personality behind the sullen, over-painted face. I turned to the other papers: a police report, medical records, placement and discharge forms for each of her temporary homes with the names inked out, a couple of crappy report cards, and a psychological evaluation that didn't add much (withdrawn, acting out, symptoms of PTSD—no shit, Sherlock). The story of Ginger's life laid out in dry professional prose seemed even more horrific. How the hell was she supposed to survive that?

I closed the file and walked it across the hall to the spare bedroom we'd converted into Sam's home office. I laid it carefully on his desk, picked up my field camera bag and called Daphnia. I didn't much care if anything good came out of the expedition. I needed to do something to change the images running through my head. Within minutes, Daphnia and I were speeding down the interstate on our way to Neskame to see what we could see.

❧ ❧ ❧

I caught the four o'clock meeting at United Lutheran, stopped for pizza on the way home, and managed to arrive seconds before Sam. He smiled and nodded toward the box. "Health food?"

"Sure, I got extra olives and mushrooms—aren't those vegetables?"

"Olives are technically a fruit, but I'm not in the mood to argue."

"Hard day in the salt mines?" I kicked the door closed behind us.

Sam set down his satchel, sloughed off his coat, and bent to pet Daphnia. "My own fault. Test day." He inclined his head toward the bag. "There are eighty-two intro bio midterms in there awaiting my magic pen."

"Midterm?" I carried the pizza into the kitchen with Daphnia and Sam following close behind. "You're only a couple of weeks from finals. How can this be midterm?"

"Good point." He slung himself into a chair and peeled a slice out of the box. "If it's not a quiz or a final, it's a midterm. Not always appropriate, particularly in this case, since I'm not giving a final and the next couple of weeks are for project presentations. So you could call this an early final, but I didn't, so it's a midterm."

"What's your schedule like tomorrow?" I held a pizza slice above my mouth so I could catch the long string of melted cheese.

"I've a lab meeting at eight, class from nine to ten and after that I guess I'm grading all day. Why?"

"We have to be at the retreat center by Saturday afternoon for our abuse workshop. I was thinking we could drive down tomorrow and stay overnight in town, have dinner at that great steakhouse by the river and spend a relaxed morning before the fun begins. Let Izzy Guttman open up on Saturday. You know he wants to."

He took a huge bite of pizza and chewed thoughtfully. "It sounds like a great plan, but did I mention eighty-two tests to grade?"

Daphnia was sniffing around my shoes, so I dropped a piece of crust for him. I took a deep breath. "I'll help."

His eyebrows shot up. "Really?"

I nodded. "But just this once. I hate tests. Didn't like taking them, and I'm sure I won't like grading them. But if it's the only way to get a romantic weekend of abuse together," I shrugged, "well, a man's gotta do what a man's gotta do."

"That's a very sexy offer, you know." Sam smiled at me.

"Oh, I hope so."

Saying that I ought to be able to handle the first two pages of the test since they consisted of fill-in-the-blanks and short answers, Sam carefully wrote me a key. I did the dishes by wrapping up the leftover pizza, throwing away the box and our napkins and wiping down the table. Since I couldn't fortify myself with scotch, I made extra-dark hot chocolate. We built a fire and sprawled across the couches, each with a stack of forty-one tests.

After a mind-numbing hour, I looked up at him. "If you have to do this very often, they don't pay you enough."

"I know," he said, his eyes not leaving the page.

After another hour, we traded stacks, and by ten, we were adding up numbers and assigning grades. "It will take me awhile in the morning to get the grades entered." Sam yawned. "Can you pick me up at noon, and we'll leave from school?"

I nodded, rubbing my neck. "Qian Lin next door said he'd dog-sit. I made him promise to come over right after school tomorrow to hang out with Daphnia for at least an hour and again three times a day through the weekend, but I bet he's here more. I don't think he's made many friends."

"Can you imagine spending your freshman year in a foreign country?" Sam shuddered. "High school was bad enough in Rhode Island, and I spoke the language."

"I'm sure he'll be glad to get home," I said. "Maybe he's even got a girlfriend waiting for him. Or a boyfriend, I suppose, but I don't think so."

Sam laughed, stood and stretched. "Let's get some sleep. Thanks for helping with the grading. It was really sweet of you."

"What happened to sexy?" I said, following him upstairs.

He just smiled.

❧ ❧ ❧

I arrived at the university early and decided to stop by Maggie's lab to say hi. I poked my head through the doorway. Except for the clicking and rustling of hundreds of caged rats, the place looked empty, so I stepped in to write her a quick note, shuddering slightly at the faint musky smell.

A deep voice asked, "Can I help you?"

I turned to see a tall, blond, muscular man of about twenty-five emerging from behind a bank of rodent cages. "Hi. I'm looking for Professor Mazzoni. It's not important. I can leave her a note."

"Maggie should be back any minute." He turned back to his contraption.

Just then, she walked in. "Edward, how great to see you. You're here to pick up Sam?"

I nodded, aware of a sudden alertness from the man in the corner. Maggie saw my glance. "Did you guys meet yet? This is my new grad student, Bill O'Brian. Bill, this is my friend, Edward, Sam DaCosta's . . ." She paused.

"Friend," I supplied, holding out my hand as I crossed the lab space.

Bill's face transformed from an indifferent scowl to a radiant smile, his handshake firm and perfectly timed. "Nice to meet you. Dr. DaCosta's a great guy." He dropped my hand and faced Maggie. "I should have some preliminary data by late this afternoon."

"Great. I'm out of class at four. Shall we meet in my office after that?"

He nodded and disappeared again behind the rats.

"I'll walk with you down to Sam's office." She led me out of the lab.

"Nice to have met you," I called to Bill, who gave me a short wave and another dazzling smile. Once out of earshot, I said, "Nice arms."

She blushed. "Nice everything."

"You aren't . . ."

"No." She shook her head. "He's my student, for Pete's sake. But you've got to admit he's fun to look at."

"Very. But watch yourself. He strikes me as the dangerous type."

She waved dismissively. "Relax. He's a kid. Now tell me, are you guys really going to some sort of sex workshop?"

I laughed. "Either you weren't paying attention or Sam mumbled. We're going to a foster parenting workshop."

"That doesn't sound nearly as fun." She turned down Sam's hallway. "I had this great picture of the two of you learning all sorts of acrobatic—"

"Stop," I said. "I find that sentence too disturbing for words, starting with 'I had this great picture.'"

Sam appeared in his doorway. Laughing, Maggie abandoned me. "Have a great weekend." She waved to Sam as she walked away.

He handed me his satchel, grabbed his coat, and closed the door. "Let's get out of here now. I called in sick to a committee meeting. If anyone asks, you're taking me home to bed."

"That's a reasonable alternative plan." I scrambled to keep up with him.

He grinned. "Love your flexibility, but let's get out of town while we can."

❧ ❧ ❧

St. Alban's Retreat Center, an hour drive west of Auburn Falls, is bordered on one side by state forest and the other by an organic farm run by nuns. On Saturday morning, we checked in at the registration desk and a nice middle-aged woman who might have been a nun handed us a thick packet of material, nametags and our room assignment.

"Well, at least we're roommates." I opened the door to a long room in which four sets of bunk beds were punctuated by eight identical desks and bureaus. Three of the bottom bunks already held suitcases or other markers.

"Top or bottom?" I asked, strolling toward the remaining bunk. Sam looked at me, one eyebrow cocked. "Right, how about we flip for it?" I pulled a quarter from my pocket.

"Leave the top bunks to the young, Edward," a voice boomed from the doorway.

"Henry! I didn't know you were going to be here."

He shrugged, patted my back and shook Sam's hand. "Continuing education credits. I thought you might like the support and I can always use a refresher." He pointed to a bottom bunk across the room. "That's me, so I'm hoping you don't snore. Afraid Fran says I do. Hope you brought earplugs." He laughed. "Toss your stuff on the beds and let's go find some food."

After lunch, about twenty of us gathered in the conference room, a large open room with pine paneling. Some of the windows that spanned two walls stood open so we could hear birds. The room smelled of pine. Classrooms have never been within my comfort zone, so I steered us to a set of seats from which I could see both the forest and the farm. Five hours later, we broke for dinner.

"An afternoon like that must cut down on the food costs," I said, as we walked toward the cafeteria. Sam nodded, still pale.

Henry said, "The point is to desensitize you so that you can handle it when these kids tell their stories. And to bring out any of your own if need be." He took trays and passed them to us before collecting his own.

I picked up silverware and napkins. "Isn't there a danger that we'll become callous?"

He nodded. "That's always a danger. More for those of us who work with hundreds of kids than for foster parents. But if you're ever going to convince some child that what happened to them doesn't make them a freak, well, you'd better not freak out. You can, and should, show that you're angry about it. But revulsion doesn't help anyone." He accepted a giant serving of potatoes and a slab of meatloaf from a smiling middle-aged woman.

I nodded to her to dump food on my plate as well.

"Just soup, thanks," I heard Sam say behind me.

"You can relax now." Henry poured coffee from a giant dispenser. "After dinner we'll move on to more mundane problems like getting kids to do homework and dealing with friends." He guided us to a table. "Turns out they're still kids with normal kid issues."

"That's a relief." Sam sat beside Henry.

"Are you all right?" I asked.

"I'll be fine." He swirled his spoon in the soup. "The slide show got me." He smiled weakly. "You're right, photography is a powerful tool. That image of the boy with the burn scars—" He shuddered. "Doesn't matter about the earplugs, Henry. I don't expect to sleep tonight."

❧ ❧ ❧

By the drive home, we were negotiating parenting strategies and debating the choices made by various participants in the role-playing exercises. Monday morning I called Henry and told him to go ahead with the paperwork.

"Already did." His chuckle rumbled across the phone lines. "You're approved as long-term foster parents. Better get her room ready. You've got about three weeks, give or take a weekend."

I called Sam. "Congratulations, Dad."

"No shit," he breathed. "Wow."

❧ ❧ ❧

"No geologists," I said, glad I'd talked Sam into letting us take the convertible. The last Friday afternoon in May, sunny, almost hot, the blue sky stretched above us like the inside of a balloon.

"The grad students have challenged faculty to volleyball. You can cheer us on." Sam smiled, leaning back. The wind plastered his hair flat against his forehead.

"And there'll be grilled meats?"

"All your favorite food groups." He ticked them off on his fingers. "Hamburgers, sausages, potato chips, coleslaw, baked beans and potluck desserts."

"Potluck? Did we bring anything?" I glanced at the back seat.

He shook his head. "I paid the higher no-thanks-I-won't-be-bringing–a-dessert price."

"Good man."

"It looks like we'll get a nice crowd this year," he said as we pulled into the half-full city parking lot.

"It's a great day for a picnic," I agreed, "even with academics. Now let's be clear before we start. Am I your friend or roommate?"

"Both." He smiled. "I don't think anyone really cares. Or if they do, they wouldn't admit it. After all, I have tenure. Still, a little discretion might make the old guard more comfortable."

"So Snookums is out? How about Pookey? Squeeze bunny?"

"Stop." He laughed. "This is an academic gathering. No levity."

"Right. Can't tell you how much I look forward to these events." I opened my door and stepped out, following Sam across the park toward the community shelter, where Ruth and a couple of young women were setting out food. "Is that really part of her job description?" I nodded in Ruth's direction.

He shrugged. "No one ever said we were progressive. If it weren't for Ruth I'm sure we'd all stay locked in our labs like the crazy, antisocial scientists we are." He steered me toward the volleyball court.

It took a ridiculously long time to negotiate the volleyball game rules. Each side had enough members for two teams, so they settled on a complicated rotation scheme that, as far as I could tell, left everyone sitting out most of play. It worked out for me, though, since Maggie and Sam ended up at opposite ends of the roster and I was never left without one of them to protect me against the ever-present threat of dogmatic conversation.

"So you're really going through with this foster fatherhood thing?" Maggie asked as we watched Sam score the first point.

"She arrives Friday. Her room's set and we're about as ready as we can be."

A graceful young black woman spiked the ball, evening the score.

"If it's anything like my sister's house in the summer, you can kiss your free time goodbye." Maggie clapped and shouted, "Good job, Paul!" as a balding man with extraordinarily skinny ankles made a saving dive for the ball.

I shrugged. "We've set up a schedule. Sam's taking off Fridays and Mondays all summer so I won't get stuck with all the work. We'll see. Hey, is that Paul Johnstone, the history guy you were talking about?"

"Uh huh, I'm up." Maggie sprinted into the rotation as Sam sauntered out.

"Nice point," I told him.

"They'll win. They always do. It's good to get in a point or two before the blood bath begins."

Maggie served, and the ball flew low and hard into the pack of students. Big Blond Bill knocked it back over the net. Paul dove but missed, losing the point.

"Maggie's got a nice serve," I said.

"Yes, she does."

"Do you think either she and Billy or she and Paul are sleeping together? Probably Billy and Paul aren't, am I right?"

Sam frowned at me. "Did you miss that earlier discussion about discretion?"

"What's that, Snooky?" I whispered. "Oh, yeah, now I remember. So that's Paul the history guy." I looked from him to Big Bill. "I like him better. Interesting ankles."

"Shut up and cheer or I'll feed you to the geologist."

FIVE

※

The bell rang. We looked at each other for a long moment. Sam picked up Daphnia. I took a deep breath and opened the door. Henry stood on the step, a tattered workout bag slung over one shoulder. The girl beside him stared at the ground. She was smaller than I expected, maybe five-two and ninety pounds, and wore a turquoise tee shirt that might have fit a toddler but barely covered her chest, leaving a long expanse of thin, white flesh that ended in low-rider jeans so tight I wondered how she could have sat through a four-hour drive. Long beaded earrings hung from her ears and silver bangles circled her skinny wrists.

Henry smiled. "Edward, Sam, I'd like you to meet Ginger McIntyre. Here they are, Ginger. The big one is Edward and the good-looking guy is Sam."

She looked up at me. Dark eyeliner and bright orange lipstick made a mask of her face and I had trouble reading her expression. Then she smiled a big, toothpaste billboard grin and I saw how scared she was.

" Hi, Ginger," I said. "Welcome. Please come in."

She turned her beam on Sam, who smiled and stood aside to let her pass.

"What a cute little dog," she gushed, her voice soft with a touch of kid-lisp. "What's her name?"

Sam stroked the dog's ears. "His name is Daphnia."

She looked up at him. "Like from Scooby-doo?"

Sam sighed. "You're thinking of Daphne. This is Daphnia. He's named after a kind of zooplankton, because of how he holds his front legs straight up sometimes, like a Daphnia." Sam held up one of the dog's legs and waved it. "Really, he can look a lot like a Daphnia."

"That's weird." Ginger leaned in to pet him, laughing as the dog licked her chin. Sam passed him to her. She cooed and nuzzled Daphnia, eventually setting him down.

Henry handed me the duffle bag. "I'll check in with you in a couple of days. Take care, Ginger. Be good."

Ginger walked into the living room followed closely by Daphnia. Henry waved and left. I closed the door and we watched Ginger peruse the room.

"Nice place," she said finally.

"Thanks. You hungry? We've got a cheese pizza in the oven. There's Coke in the refrigerator." Sam trailed off.

She frowned. "I don't really like Coke. Do you have root beer or cream soda or anything?"

"Come look for yourself." He led the way.

Ginger stopped when she entered the kitchen and stared out the plate glass window at the lake. Sunlight sparkled off the water. "Who lives there?" she asked, pointing to the boathouse.

"Um, nobody," I said. "There's a guest room upstairs and we store the boats below. We'll show you around later."

"Wow, that's really cool. Can I sleep there?"

"No. House rule is that no one under eighteen stays there alone." I snuck a glance at Sam, who nodded his agreement with my new house rule.

She shrugged. Sam opened the refrigerator door and gestured to her.

Ginger scrutinized the contents for a moment. "Can I have this?" She pointed to a sparkling fruit drink.

"Sure." Sam handed her the bottle. "You want a glass?"

"No, thanks." She twisted off the cap. Sparkly pink polish covered parts of her ragged nails. I pointed her toward the garbage bin and she tossed the cap.

"You like music?" I asked. "We probably don't have anything you'd like, but there's a radio."

"That's okay, I guess." She took a pull of her drink.

I showed her the controls on the stereo. Soon the house filled with a not unpleasant beat. Sam set out the pizza, three plates and napkins and we settled in to our first family meal.

"So, Henry said you guys are faggots," Ginger said conversationally, peeling the cheese from her pizza, feeding it to Daphnia and picking at the crust.

Sam choked on his soda.

I shook my head. "I bet he didn't put it that way."

She smiled uncertainly. "Not exactly. But it's what he meant."

I smiled back. "It's not exactly what he meant since that would be an insult and Henry likes us. But Sam and I are a couple, if that's what you're asking."

Sam cleared his throat. "We should probably talk about house rules."

She nodded, wiped her fingers and started ticking them off. "Let me guess, no drinking, no smoking, no drugs, no sex and in by ten."

I laughed. "That's a good start, except you're twelve so you'll be home by sunset. And until we know you better, you won't be out alone anytime. We don't keep alcohol or drugs in the house, so don't bother looking for them."

Sam continued, "Let's see, what else is against the rules? Stealing, skipping school." He looked at me.

I nodded. "And make-up on anyone under sixteen."

"What?" Ginger erupted. "No. That's crazy and unfair!"

Sam shrugged. "It's really not negotiable. Wash it all off tonight and starting tomorrow you'll show the world a fresh face."

"But I look ugly without makeup," she whined. "Everyone will think I'm a jerk."

"I tell you what, I'm a photographer. We'll take before and after head shots and look at them again in a year. If you still think this is the best look for you," I shrugged, "we'll reopen the discussion."

"I probably won't even be here in a year," she said, head in hands.

"Then I guess it won't be a problem," I told her, "but in the meantime, no makeup."

She considered me for a long time and cocked her head. "I can't believe you're going to make me walk around looking stupid. Can I at least use cover-up?"

"Only if you have an actual zit." I glanced at Sam for confirmation.

"Lip gloss?"

Sam stepped in. "We'll see how it goes, and after a month or so we'll consider lip gloss."

"Fuck," she said, "this sucks."

"Oh," Sam added, "no swearing."

She scowled at him.

I offered Ginger a second slice of pizza. She shook her head. Taking one myself, I sat back. "It's not all bad, Ginger. Chores here are minimal—help with the dishes, don't make too much of a mess and keep your room clean. We'll make sure you have everything you need, ask your opinion on major family decisions and do everything we can to keep you safe."

"Yeah, right," she muttered. "I've heard that before."

"Well, this time it's true." Sam popped the last bite of crust into his mouth.

We gave Ginger the grand tour of the house, ending with her room. It's a pleasant space, with dormer windows facing the lake. A soft breeze rustled through the forest green curtains. The only change we'd made in anticipation of Ginger's arrival was to empty the closet and upgrade the clock radio. "We can redecorate later if you like," I told her. "In the meantime, settle in, make yourself at home. Bathroom's across the hall and the towels are clean. We'll be downstairs if you need us."

She nodded. I left but Daphnia stayed. Last I looked, he was standing on the bed, his forelegs propped against her shoulders while she stroked his back with one hand and scratched behind his ears with the other. At least one of us was connecting.

Downstairs, Sam and I sat at the table and watched the sunset, Sabbath candles burning discreetly in the corner. Maybe next week we'd introduce religion.

❧ ❧ ❧

Sam sprawled on the couch, buried in a novel. I sat in my favorite chair, laptop on my knees, skimming the *New York Times*. We both looked up at the whisper of bare feet descending the stairs. Sam glanced at me, eyebrows raised. I returned my gaze to my screen, listening as the padding got louder. I looked up and thought, the guy who taught her this couldn't be human. And according to the police report, he was still out there somewhere. I tried to smile at her, standing at the edge of the living room dressed only in her tee shirt and panties, hands on her hips, smiling strangely, her face still thick with paint. Daphnia sat at her feet, his ears up and head cocked expectantly.

"Hi, Ginger," I said.

Goosebumps puckered her skin. Sam reached for a throw and handed it to her saying, "It's funny this time of year. Warm all day but chilly at night."

She wrapped the blanket around herself and turned to go.

"Wait, have a seat," I said. "You want some cocoa? There's ice cream if you like."

She shook her head but sat in the armchair. Daphnia leaped onto her lap. She stroked him gently.

"Where'd you get the bruise?" I nodded toward a yellow-green mark on her left shin.

"Um, soccer," she mumbled, tucking her calves beneath her.

I looked at Sam. He didn't believe her either. This kid came from a scary place.

"You like soccer?" Sam asked. She shrugged. "What position do you play?"

She shrugged again. "I'm not very good. I get scared when the ball comes at me."

He nodded. "We didn't have soccer when I was a kid, but I never liked those ball sports—football, softball, basketball. When it came to athletics, I was always more the track and cross-country type."

"What's that?"

He laughed. "I guess they don't have it in grade school. You might get to try next year in junior high. Easiest sport in the world. You run."

She looked at him skeptically. "That's it?"

He nodded. "Run like hell and the fastest person wins."

She scratched Daphnia's ears and nodded. "That's cool. How about you?" she asked, appraising me. "Were you a big football guy?"

I shook my head. "I hated football. My last sporting adventures were in Little League." No need to mention that I'd been too busy passing a joint to learn to pass a ball. "You sure you don't want some dessert? I think there's a box of cookies somewhere if ice cream doesn't appeal. Myself, I'm thinking caramel, chocolate swirl with hot fudge."

She considered. "Maybe a little bit, with extra hot fudge."

I grinned, snapped my laptop shut and stood. "A girl after my own heart. Sam?"

He shook his head. "I'm fine, thanks. Hey, you guys want to watch a movie?"

"Sure," I said. "You two pick it out, I'll get the ice cream."

I returned to find Sam showing Ginger his entire collection of superhero-themed films. She shrugged and said it didn't matter. Sam thought for a moment and selected Christopher Reeves in *Superman*.

As Superman spun the earth backwards, reversing time, I looked over to see Ginger sleeping, Daphnia curled against her. I signaled Sam, who smiled. We rose as quietly as possible. I could smell the artificial strawberry scent of her shampoo as I leaned down to scoop up Daphnia and carry him to the front door to go out. I watched Sam wrap the throw around Ginger and pick her up. She stiffened instantly. Sam dropped her back on the couch.

"Um, bedtime," he said into her wide-open eyes.

She nodded and stood.

I let Daphnia back in and the three of us followed her rigid shoulders up the stairs. At her doorway, she turned to face us. I watched her tight eyes for a moment before saying, "Good- night." I watched her slump onto the bed. Daphnia immediately jumped onto the bed, circled beside her and dropped down in a curl, his head resting across her thigh.

We slipped into our own room, shut and locked the door and flopped onto the bed.

"Oh, man." Sam shivered. "That was exhausting. Do you think she was trying to seduce us with that whole Lolita look? If she was, she sure didn't seem happy to get touched."

"I don't know. Probably she doesn't know. I was really shaken when I saw her standing there like that. Could you tell?"

"Only because I know you. I thought I might throw up. Ice cream? I was glad I could keep my dinner down."

I shrugged. "You know me—I eat when I'm nervous."

"You were right. I'm creeped out. This is not going to be good for our sex life."

"Right. But I thought we made a good team." I propped myself up on one elbow and looked at him. "You were so cool handing her that throw. I guess we can forget showing her physical affection for a while. So let's put on our thickest jammies and cuddle up. Sex is probably overrated anyway."

Sam pulled an empty beef jerky package from his pocket. "This was on the floor outside her room. It explains Daph's sudden loyalty shift."

I wrinkled my nose. "Ugh, that stuff will make him sick."

"Do you think we can convince her to do something about her hair?"

"What is it you don't like? The blue streak, the two inch roots, or the over-the-eye, Veronica Lake look?"

"Do I have to pick one?"

֍ ֍ ֍

We'd mapped out something like a treatment plan with Henry before Ginger came. The idea was to try to rework her outward persona before launching her into Lacland preteen society. So, until she scrubbed her face and changed clothes, we were confined to quarters.

Saturday morning, Sam left early for the synagogue. Around ten, Ginger appeared downstairs in the same clothes she'd worn when she arrived. Daphnia trotted behind her. I opened the door and let him out. He rushed to the nearest tree, peed and ran back to scratch at the door.

"Looks like you've made a friend." I opened the door and Daphnia bolted past me to jump on Ginger.

Ginger nodded and knelt to pet the dog.

"Frosted flakes, granola, or toast? Daphnia prefers these." I handed her a bag of dog treats. "Easier on his system than beef jerky. Try not to give him too many."

She gave an embarrassed smile and nodded. After a moment she said, "Frosted flakes. Can I watch cartoons?"

"Sure." I handed her a bowl and gestured toward the cereal and milk. "You want juice or anything?"

She shook her head, filled her bowl about halfway with cereal, sprinkled on some milk and headed into the living room. I poured myself another cup of coffee and a second bowl of cereal and followed.

I waited for the commercial break to say, "About last night . . ."

She nodded, looking into her cereal bowl. She wiggled her toes, scratching Daphnia's belly.

"It was nice watching a movie together." She looked up. I cleared my throat. "I want you to know that you don't need to . . . We're not looking for . . ."

"I get it," she said. "You don't like girls."

"No, I mean, yes, that's true, or not like that, but it's not what I wanted to say." I took a deep breath and tried to collect my thoughts. "You don't have to sell yourself to us to stay here." I stood. "I'll be on the back porch if you need me."

She turned her attention back to the television.

I wandered out to the screened porch. The lake looked dark green under the overcast sky. A light breeze rippled the water and rustled the leaves. Birds sang and I could hear the whine of a jet ski in the distance. I breathed in the rich piney spring air, savoring a moment alone. The door opened. Daphnia trotted over and leaped into my lap. The wicker creaked as Ginger sat in the chair beside me.

"Hi," I said.

"Hi." She was silent a long moment before adding, "So what do I call you?"

I looked at her. She looked much younger and less angry without the caked-on makeup. "Hmmm, that's a good question. Does it seem too soon for Dad?"

She winced and nodded. "My stepfather made me call him Daddy." The word curled out like a threat.

"So that's out," I said and she nodded. "Well, for now how about calling us Edward and Sam? Although Papa one and Papa two has a certain ring, don't you think?"

She smiled.

"And you. Shall we introduce you as our daughter, foster daughter, Ginger the kid who lives with us, our houseguest Princess Gingersnap?" I wiggled my eyebrows.

She laughed. "I guess you can call me your daughter if you want." She shrugged. "I mean, it doesn't matter. Whatever you like."

"Okay, daughter, let's do some breakfast cleanup." I briefly touched the back of my knuckles to the arm of her chair, thinking even that might be too much but not wanting the moment to pass without contact. "After that we can work on those head shots I promised."

By the time Sam got home, we were busy creating a makeshift portrait studio against the boathouse wall. I hoped the white lapboard would make an interesting but not overwhelming background.

"Good, you can hold the reflector." I handed him the shiny cloth disk. "Here, Ginger, let's test it out. Sit on the stool and look at Sam. Yeah, that's good, but I think we need another foil. I'll get it while you go up and 'put on your face,' as they say."

Ginger grinned and sprinted toward the house.

"How was the service?" I asked Sam as we followed more slowly.

"Good. I made an appointment for us all to talk with Rabbi Talia a week from Wednesday. Are you free?"

"I think so. I cleared the calendar for the next couple of weeks. Do you think it's too early?"

He shrugged. "I warned her we might cancel if it didn't feel right. But it would be nice to introduce Ginger and show her around so we can start taking her with us." He paused. "I missed having you there."

I nodded. "Let's hope we can find our way to cohesive by then."

I rummaged in my equipment closet until I found the big reflectors I'd used back in my misspent youth when I'd done head shots for young actors in exchange for, well, perhaps "gratitude" is the best word. I recruited Sam to carry one while I shouldered the other, my camera and tripod. Bo Lin and Qian watched us set up from their deck. Ginger appeared. She'd changed into a clean, tiny black tee shirt and a matching ruffled skirt that showed her belly button and threatened to do the same for her panties. She walked delicately across the dock, beamed a smile at Sam, Daphnia, me and the Lins, perched on the stool and looked seductively into my camera.

I played along, snapping away like a fashion photographer, calling, "Look over here, beautiful, now look down. Yes, that's it. Good," and thinking about how much I hoped she'd later hate the slutty, campy images.

"Okay, that's the before." I straightened. "Now go wash your face and come back down for our after shots. And remember, no makeup, not even the mascara and lip stuff you tried to sneak in with this morning."

She frowned for a moment and ran back up to the house. I looked up at the Lins still on the deck. I waved to them to come down. "I'm doing portraits," I shouted. "You want one?"

Bo blushed, looked at her son, back at me, grinned and started across the path that joined our two houses. Qian followed slowly. Sam sprinted to the end of the dock to greet them while I fussed with the stool and reflectors.

Bo smiled and shook my hand. "Good morning, Edward," she said in her beautiful, although heavily accented, English.

"Good morning." I shook her hand. "It's nice to see you. I was afraid you might be leaving soon."

She smiled from beneath the brim of her wide sun hat. "We have another month. After that we'll go back." She looked sadly at her son as he slouched across the dock toward us. "It is time to go home."

I settled her on the stool with Qian behind her, arranged his hand on her shoulder and positioned Sam with the hand-held reflector so that the light lit her eyes and amplified her slight smile. Then I set about trying to coax a smile from Qian. When it suddenly appeared, I clicked through several frames.

I stopped and heard Sam say, "I'd like to introduce Ginger. Ginger, this is Dr. Lin and her son, Qian. They live next door."

Everyone murmured hello. I turned to see Ginger standing beside Sam and almost laughed. She had not only scrubbed her face but changed her clothes as well, choosing a baggy, stained pink tee shirt over dirty yellow shorts. Clearly she wasn't leaving anything to chance in an attempt to derail the after shots. Without the camouflage, her dark brown eyes looked even bigger. She cracked a smile, a touch asymmetrical, and I thought I'd never had an easier assignment.

Bo gave up her seat to Ginger, pulling a reluctant Qian away with her. I again adjusted Sam's reflector and looked through my viewfinder at a scowling, pouty Ginger. Borrowing Bo's hat I covered Ginger's hideous hair and started my fashion photographer routine, trying to jolly her into a smile. Nothing worked until we all heard a great squawking and a splash, as Daphnia leaped into the water chasing ducks. I've had years of learning to wait for those moments. Ginger looked toward the sound and laughed. I held down the shutter button and caught twenty shots before she returned to her look of doom.

જ જ જ

We were sitting around the kitchen table playing Parcheesi. Ginger watched Sam pull the lasagna from the box and plop it into the preheated oven.

"So, you guys don't cook much, do you?" She rolled the dice and counted out her moves.

"Um, no," Sam said. "We keep meaning to learn but . . ."

"So is that why you got me?" She handed me the dice.

Sam turned around to stare at her. I looked at the dice in my hand. "No," we said, almost simultaneously.

She looked from one to the other of us. "So why did you? You don't want sex. I don't think you need the money?"

"No." I cleared my throat. "We're putting that in a college savings account for you."

She blinked. Sam gave me a look. We hadn't planned on telling her that yet.

I stuttered, "Or maybe that's what we're going to do. I guess we'll see."

She shrugged. "Daddy used to say that nothing's free. And I've been through enough of these placements to know he was right."

I rolled the dice and moved my piece. Sam sat back down in his chair. While he took his turn he said, "We're looking to feel like a family. It's as simple and as complicated as that."

She looked at him, then at me.

"Your turn." I nodded toward the dice.

❧ ❧ ❧

A steady Sunday afternoon crowd strolled through the mall. The occasional stranger's glance let me know what an odd group we were, two well-groomed middle-aged men and their pet Lolita. We found our way to the juniors section of a large department store.

"I don't really care what she wears," I'd told Sam earlier, "as long as it looks like she can breathe."

He'd been sitting cross-legged on the bed, skimming the table of contents of one of his scientific journals. "Not looking like a professional would be good."

And so here we were, flipping through racks of brightly colored little shirts and pants.

She picked out a pair of jeans with hearts etched in sequins on the pockets. I found the same pair in the next size up.

"Take them both to try," I suggested.

She rolled her eyes at me. "I'll look fat in these." She pointed to the pair I held.

"You couldn't look fat if you tried. Please, do it to prove me wrong."

She shrugged and, taking both pair, sauntered into the dressing room.

Sam, who'd been studying a dress display, looking thoughtful and out of place, gave a little start. "Wait here, I'll be right back."

I watched him stride across the aisle to where two blond amazons stood trying on hats. He spoke with them briefly, with gestures and nods in my direction, and ambled back to me, sporting a self-satisfied grin.

"What was that all about?"

He smiled.

Ginger appeared, modeling jeans so tight I found it remarkable she could walk. She struck a pose, one hip cocked provocatively.

"Um—" I was interrupted by a lyrical "Professor DaCosta."

One of the young women appeared next to Sam, followed by her companion. They stood gracefully before us, available for worship. I glanced at Ginger, who stared at them in thinly veiled awe.

"Taylor, how nice to see you." Sam sounded rehearsed.

"What are you doing here?" Taylor asked, flirtatiously. "Shouldn't you be in your lab playing with bugs?"

Sam laughed. "We're shopping. I'd like you to meet my daughter, Ginger. Ginger, this is Taylor. She was in my senior seminar last term."

Ginger smiled shyly.

"Oh, isn't she cute?" Taylor gushed. She turned to her friend. "I remember when I was that age. I used to dress like that. Imagine wearing anything that tight now. But when you're a little kid you think it's sexy or something. Guess you don't know how silly you look." She smiled a bright, condescending smile in Ginger's direction. "Nice to meet you." Looking up at Sam she waved. "Good to see you, Dr. D. Have a great summer." She spun on her heel and they disappeared, leaving a whisper of perfume and the sense that we'd been blessed.

I turned to Ginger in time to see her disappearing into the dressing room. I looked at Sam, who grinned.

"Biology major, theater minor," he explained.

"Beautifully staged, but a little harsh, don't you think?"

He shrugged. "Maybe. But I bet it works."

When Ginger reappeared, her clothes fit nicely. Over the next two hours, we'd purchased an entirely new wardrobe, including one outfit remarkably similar to what Taylor had been wearing.

Small towns mean small gay communities where everyone knows way too much about each other's business. So I knew Antonio's real name (Jimmy), that his last lover left him for his own ex, that he'd had a short affair with Rob back when we were together, and that he'd probably be willing to keep the shop open late on a Sunday to rescue Ginger's hair. I also thought it best for my own serenity to send Sam across town for Chinese takeout while he worked.

Ginger's protests faded in the face of the hushed fountain, hardwood floors and golden lighting of Antonio's Day Spa and Salon. Antonio/ Jimmy greeted me warmly, looked hopefully around for Sam, before turning his odd mix of arrogance and fawning on Ginger, offering her mineral water or tea and gushing. "Such a pretty face, and those eyes!" He picked up thick strands of hair, cocking his head to one side and studying her in the mirror. She stared at him, her expression guarded but not unfriendly.

Finally he said, "I think you want to keep the length?" She nodded. He continued, "The color is interesting, very edgy, but I think not quite right for this season."

I sat two stools down watching, my face as neutral as possible, trying to imagine the appropriate season for Ginger's current look. Maybe spring in hell.

Antonio convinced Ginger to let him shape her hair and "try a new color, something fresh for summer." He winked at me as he whisked her away for a shampoo, but I'd already mentally doubled his tip. By the time Sam arrived to pick us up, we had ourselves the spitting image of a fresh-faced, innocent twelve year old. I couldn't shake the feeling that it had all happened way too easily. The inner makeover was likely to take a long, long time.

Six

*

onday morning, Ginger was still asleep when Henry arrived with an avalanche of paperwork. We sat at the kitchen table drinking coffee. Outside the sun lit the boathouse a blinding white and sparkled along the tops of waves. Henry brought out the file we'd returned the week before and handed us a letter from the guardian ad litem, specifying our rights in the care and feeding of Ginger McIntyre. Henry'd already made appointments for her with the counselor, medical doctor and dentist, and he slid a list of addresses, dates and times across the table to me.

Ginger appeared, blinking sleepily. Daphnia trotted behind her. Henry smiled, barely acknowledging her change in appearance. "Hey, Ginger, how was your weekend?"

She looked at us with a half-smile. "Okay."

After letting Daphnia out and pouring herself a bowl of cereal, she disappeared into the living room.

Henry raised his eyebrows at us and smiled. I preened a little under his approval. Sam smiled vaguely into his cup. Henry took a deep breath. "I would expect her to be fairly cooperative. We had a long talk before I brought her over. She knows that her next stop is probably a permanent group home."

"And I thought it showed we're amazing dads." I poured more cream into my coffee.

He smiled. "I'm sure you are. Otherwise she wouldn't be here. But it may be a while before she really opens up. In the meantime I hope she's relatively pleasant."

I nodded, reaching behind me to open the door so Daphnia could breeze past on his way to the living room. "Seems like she's doing her best to please, sort of flailing around looking for the right note. So far she's tried sex and food, smart guesses really, even though . . ." I trailed off as Sam jumped up and walked to the counter, filling the kettle for a fresh pot of coffee. His back stayed rigid while I told Henry about the first night.

Henry smiled slightly. "That's typical of what she's done other places. I hadn't heard her offer to cook before."

Sam emptied the old grounds into the sink and rinsed the pot, his back toward us. "Maybe that's because sex clearly won't work with us."

"That's another reason she's here." Henry's eyes were on Sam's back. "So what's your plan for the week?"

I shrugged. "Maggie's coming over for dinner to meet Ginger. If they get along, she thinks she might be able to put her to work a few hours a day in the lab, washing test tubes and taking care of the animals, that sort of thing. Of course, since she's so young she'd technically be volunteering or interning or something. It'll give her something to do besides watch TV all day." I didn't tell him I'd promised Maggie I'd pay the kid under the table.

"Nice idea. Of course, as you know, it's illegal for her to have regular employment, but volunteering," Henry smiled, "that's another issue. It might be good for her to be around all those brainy types. And it could be a while before anyone gives her a babysitting job." He gazed thoughtfully at Sam, still busy grinding coffee and fussing with his French press. "So how are you guys doing?"

I started to speak, but Henry gave me that sponsor look, the one that says, take the plugs out of your ears and stuff them in your mouth. I took a deep breath and sat back in my chair.

"It's hard," Sam said after a long moment, his voice barely above a whisper. He turned to face Henry. "Aside from the weird sex stuff, she seems like a good kid, I guess. But she feels so disconnected, cold, maybe. I don't know, I'm having a harder time than I thought I would and every time I think about what probably happened to her—" He shuddered.

"Give her some time," Henry said quietly. "She's been through a lot. In the end, kids are amazingly resilient. But it can take a while. Eventually, if she's safe and loved, she'll warm up."

Sam nodded. "I'll be fine. It's just hard." The kettle whistled and he poured. Henry and I waited for more, but instead Sam announced, "If you guys don't need me anymore here, I'm going upstairs to see if I can find a recipe for dinner tonight."

"What?" I asked, jerking back, almost tipping over in my chair.

He pushed down the coffee plunger and refreshed all our coffee. "Look, if we're going to convince her we aren't looking for some sort of Dickensian kitchen slave, one of us has to learn to cook. We can't keep feeding her frozen lasagna and TV dinners."

"Right," I said, and Henry nodded with a smile.

After Sam left, I looked at Henry. He shrugged. "So give them both time. And you might be extra good to him for a while. It's that emotional vacuity that always got Fran, too."

"You fostered? I didn't know that."

He nodded. "For a while. But it got to be too much."

"For Fran?"

He shook his head. "No, she's a wonder. She always managed to melt them in the end. I couldn't take it anymore." He swirled his spoon around his cup. "It began to feel like I could never get away from wounded children."

I nodded, sipped my coffee and fingered Ginger's papers.

"How about you?" he asked. "How is it going for you?"

I laced my fingers together and tapped them against the table in a gesture that reminded me suddenly of my own warm, ineffectual father. "It's not easy. I know this is going to sound horribly callous, but I kind of like the game of it." I laughed. "It's like playing chess in the dark. I don't know if I'm winning or losing, but so far I haven't heard anything break, which I take as a good sign."

He laughed. "Be sure and let me know if you figure out where they keep the flashlights."

I walked Henry to the door. Ginger waved a distracted goodbye, her eyes glued to the screen. The cartoons appeared to have an Asian, *Speed Racer* influence, all big eyes and round faces, but what did I know? Ginger seemed to like it and Daphnia still appeared besotted with Ginger, so I figured the household as a whole was batting fifty percent. I hugged Henry, sent my love to Fran and took the stairs two at a time to see if I could improve the average.

I found Sam in his study scrolling through recipes that looked way too complicated. He nodded as I entered, so I closed the door and crossed the room, resting my hands on his shoulders. He kept his eyes on the screen but gradually softened into me until his head rested against my stomach.

"I know I'm being a shit," he said after a while. "I got us started on all this and now," he sighed, "I'm not sure I can handle it."

I kneaded his shoulders, pressing my thumbs along the top of his scapula. "It'll get easier," I said, not at all sure that was true. "Why don't you go in to work? I'm okay here today and maybe doing something productive will make you feel better."

He turned to look up at me, his face filled with a guilty sort of hope. "Are you sure?"

"We'll be fine."

"Okay, but I'm still cooking dinner."

"I live in gratitude and awe."

I let Ginger watch cartoons all morning while I fussed with the contrast and the scale in an image of rabbits in the park behind Notre Dame. I went back and forth between two slightly different versions until I couldn't judge the difference. Checked my email. Kathy said she had some ideas for pitching the book, but the tone of her email didn't encourage celebration.

Finally, I put work aside to process Ginger's shoot. It is all a game, I decided as I chose a "before" shot that caught her thick, caked mascara in a particularly unflattering light. Great smile, I thought as I clicked through possible "after" shots. For my next trick, I'd like to make it appear more often. I cropped both final choices to headshots, printed eight by tens and left them on the drying rack, destined to spend the next year in my file drawer.

For lunch I probed the edges of my culinary prowess with turkey and swiss on whole wheat (mayo, no mustard for Ginger, vice versa for me). In a flourish of domesticity, I added potato chips and a pickle to each plate. We rounded out the general wholesomeness with big glasses of milk.

"Let's take these to the dock." I gestured vaguely toward the lake. "It's too nice to stay inside."

She shrugged but followed me down the path and settled herself in a deck chair. Daphnia trotted off to investigate the shoreline.

"Do you like to swim?"

"I don't know how." Her eyes followed Daphnia. "He's not going to run away, is he?"

"Daph? No, he's not the roaming type. Too fond of petting and biscuits, as I think you've discovered." She blushed but continued to watch him. "I'll bet within fifteen minutes he's on your lap, wet paws and all."

We ate in silence for a time. All sorts of inane avuncular conversation starters floated through my mind: "What do you want to be when you grow up?" "What's your favorite subject in school?" "What do you do for fun?" I pondered and rejected each. The gulf between twelve and fifty-three seemed more than generational.

Finally, she asked, "So how long have you lived here?"

"Off and on all my life. My grandfathers built it." I looked up at the white house dominating the hill. "This is where I was happiest as a kid, so as soon as I could, I moved here permanently."

She nodded. "I thought you were the rich one."

"Oh. It might have been Sam."

She shook her head. "Nah, he's cute." She started. "I mean, not that you're not, but he's more—"

"—I know." I rescued her while trying to move with the punch. "I try to make up for it in charm." I didn't want to dwell on the nuances of her reasoning. "It would be a shame to live here and not swim. Do you want to take lessons at the Y?"

She shook her head. "Only babies take swimming lessons."

"Okay, what do you suggest?"

"You could teach me." She looked at me from under her lashes.

"But we'd need to go shopping for a bathing suit first."

I grinned at her. "It's bad form to go shopping more than once or twice a month. Fortunately I have a trunk full of my," I paused, sometimes my family structure is too difficult to explain, "my cousin Gillian's old suits. There should be something in there that fits."

She wrinkled her nose. "I'll look funny."

"I promise not to laugh." I set my plate down. Daphnia came barreling across the dock, jumped first on my lap, licked my chin and catapulted himself over to Ginger. "I tell you what. As soon as you can swim safely in water over your head, I'll buy you a swimsuit or two and we might even teach you to ski."

Her eyes opened wide. "Really? One of the other girls talked about tubing. She said it was wild."

"Someone from the foster home?" Maybe I could get her talking about friends.

She shook her head. "Nah, someone I knew." She paused for a moment and looked behind her at the boathouse. "Do you have a boat?"

I nodded.

She jumped up, dislodging Daphnia. Together they ran to the door. I followed more slowly, thinking, why didn't we sell the smelly old thing while we had the chance? On the other hand, the blast of an outboard at full throttle would absolve me of awkward small talk.

"You wanna ride?" I asked, pulling one of the smaller life jackets from its hook.

❧ ❧ ❧

Sam kicked open the door, a full bag of groceries balanced on each hip.

"You want help?" I stepped forward.

He pointed with his head. "There's another in the car."

When I brought the last bag into the kitchen, I found the counters covered with produce and Sam busy shuttling things into our refrigerator.

"These foods are raw." I picked up a potato. "What will we do with them?"

He turned to face me, holding a package of meat, which he waved for emphasis. "I have done many difficult things in my life. I earned a PhD, got a job in a saturated market, wrote a book, even found true love in a tiny redneck town north of nowhere. I can learn to cook a goddamned chicken." He slammed the package down on the counter.

"Great." I backed away so I wouldn't get splattered with more raw meat juice. I almost bumped into Ginger, who stood in the open doorway behind me. She deftly maneuvered herself to the side in time to avoid contact.

She surveyed the food. "What's for dinner?"

Sam brightened and pulled a small notebook from his pocket. "One of the grad students made me a list of simple dinners. She wrote down the directions. So tonight we're having," he consulted his notebook, "baked chicken thighs, mashed potatoes and steamed broccoli."

"Sounds good," she said. "Can I help? I'll wash the broccoli if you like."

He smiled. "Of course you can help, I'd love it." Looking again at his list he added, "It doesn't say you should wash the food first, but it does sound like a good idea."

I slipped back into the living room before anyone recruited me to peel potatoes.

જી જી જી

It was such a beautiful evening. I moved a small table and four chairs onto the screened porch, covered the table with an orange and red Mexican cloth and found several bright, mismatched cloth napkins. I thought about adding candles, decided against laying it on too thick, and stretched out on the old wicker couch to watch the lake.

The doorbell woke me. By the time I got to the living room, Sam had already introduced Maggie and Ginger. Maggie held a box from Front Street Bakery, always a good sign, and I hurried to help her find a place for it.

"Hey, Edward." She kissed my cheek and handed over the box. "Chocolate torte."

"You're a goddess." The box felt encouragingly heavy.

Ginger studied Maggie but didn't speak.

"So," Maggie turned to Sam. "What's for dinner? The whole science building seems abuzz with the news that you've taken up cooking."

He blushed. "That is the problem with students. They're a gossipy bunch."

She laughed. "I heard it from Professor Carter. Evidently someone is doing a very good imitation of you asking things like," she screwed up her face and scribbled with an air pencil, "sooooo, 350 degrees, is that Fahrenheit or Celsius?"

Sam rolled his eyes. "I would never ask that, do you know how hot 350 Celsius is?" Even Ginger laughed, although I doubt she really got it.

During dinner, Maggie asked all the questions I hadn't. It turned out that Ginger wanted to be a teacher when she grew up and her favorite subjects were science and art. I wondered how the answers would have differed if we'd been a family of lawyers. But I watched her slowly open to Maggie, unfurling small truths in an effort to please. She loved blue, had read all the Harry Potter books, and her favorite movie was something called *Matilda*. I could see Maggie warming to her. Ginger might not know she was at a job interview, that if Maggie liked her she'd be hanging with the rats all summer, but she seemed to be acing it naturally.

After dinner, which was surprisingly good if you ignored the unmashed bits of potato and added extra butter and salt, we demolished Maggie's torte and Ginger offered to do the dishes.

"You rinse and I'll load," I told her. "We'll leave these guys out here to talk shop."

We cleaned in relatively companionable silence and I let her escape to TV land. I brought decaf to Maggie and Sam on the porch where they were, predictably, engrossed in faculty gossip.

Since I really don't care what the dean said about the merit evaluation process, I asked, "How's your big secret drug company project going?"

Maggie smiled. "It's still early, but we're getting amazingly good results. If this continues through the summer, we should be able to get our report into a top journal and the drug company can go ahead with human testing."

"I know you can't tell us the details," Sam said, "but in general terms, what are you doing?"

She smiled. "Let's see if I can be appropriately vague. An unnamed pharmaceutical company has given us money to test the effects of a mystery drug on the DNA of rodents using their red blood cells. It's called genetic toxicity testing."

"Does it hurt the animals?" I felt a little queasy.

She shook her head. "You sound like Paul."

"Old, unattractive humanities types are all the same." I settled back in my chair with my coffee.

"I probably deserved that." She grinned. "We inject them with the drug and periodically draw some blood. If the chemical isn't mutagenic—in other words, if there's no discernible effect on the DNA, which seems to be the case this time—then no problem. If we do find mutagenesis, the drug never makes it to clinical trials and, presumably, volunteer lives are saved."

"Why don't they do these trials in the pharmaceutical labs?" I worked to steer the conversation away from my vision of tiny white rats in need of chemotherapy.

"Often they do. I guess this company wanted the credibility that comes with testing at an independent lab."

Sam kicked back in his chair and looked thoughtfully up into the pines. "Maggie, is it really an independent test if they give you the funds and train the lab tech?"

She took a deep breath. "I think so. After all, I'm doing the data analysis, they're my animals, I take the samples and oversee the whole process. I made them sign a form saying I can publish the results, no matter what they are. Lots of companies won't do that, but this one did." She shrugged again. "It's not a perfect system, but it would take an insanely complex scheme to falsify the results and, after all, things have to get tested one way or another. It might as well be through a grant to me."

We sat silently, watching the trees swaying in the wind and listening to a cacophony of horny frogs.

"I like Ginger," Maggie said after a while. "Do you know the plot of that movie she likes so much?" We shook our heads and she explained. "In kid movie terms it's an oldie but goodie, the story of a smart little girl with magic powers who manages to escape both a neglectful family and a brutal headmaster to live happily ever after with a sweet teacher in a big house." She smiled. "Do you suppose it was her favorite movie before this week?"

"She seems like a good kid." I leaned back in my chair. "But she works so hard to get us to like her that I'm thinking it will be a while before we know anything real about her."

Maggie nodded. "Here's the deal. She wouldn't be able to touch the rats. That takes a special license and she's not old enough. But I don't see the harm in her cleaning cages, refilling food and water and washing glassware. It would free up student time for other things and she might even grow to enjoy it. It can't be more than a couple of hours a day since I'd feel like I needed to be there with her. But if you'll bring her from say ten to noon weekdays, I'd be happy to put her to work."

"Thanks." I finished my coffee. "Anyone want a refill?" I took their cups with me to the kitchen. When I returned, the conversation seemed to have wandered onto more delicate ground.

"I'm just saying," I heard Sam's voice as I opened the porch door, "having a personal relationship with my postdoctoral advisor made things very awkward for a lot of years."

I started to make a quip about affairs with married men, but Maggie replied, "It's not like he's underage. He's twenty-five, for god's sake." I decided to keep my mouth shut and listen. I handed them coffee and sat quietly in my corner chair.

"Right. I was even older than that. It's about power, Maggie. My advisor had it and I didn't. Christ, even now when I see him at a meeting he tries to get me into bed." He flicked a glance in my direction. "I haven't taken him up on it in years, but up until I had tenure there was always this hint of threat that he could fuck up my career if I didn't put out."

Maggie shook her head violently. "I'm not going to fuck up anyone's career. Bill's a big boy. He came on to me, not the other way around. It's an affair, that's all. Don't worry about it."

Sam shook his head.

Shit, I thought. "It's getting late and we need to get Ginger to bed. Do you want to talk about the job with her now or should I bring her by in the morning?"

❧ ❧ ❧

As we got ready for bed, Sam asked, "Did you take a couple of twenties from my wallet this morning?"

"No, why?" I mumbled through my toothbrush.

He shrugged, climbing into bed. "I thought I had more cash. When I got to the grocery, I looked in my wallet and it wasn't there. No big deal—I wrote a check. I must have spent the money somewhere else and forgotten."

Turning off the lights, I slipped in beside him. I propped myself on one elbow so I could watch his face in the moonlight. "Would you still love me if I was poor?"

He opened his eyes. "Is there something I should know?"

I shook my head. "Just wondering." I settled my hand on his chest. He covered it with his own and thought for a moment.

"Let's see. If we were poor, I probably wouldn't drive a fancy car. Oh wait, I still drive my old Honda. I'd have to go back to work. No, I guess I do that now, too. I'd have to wear frumpy academic clothes. Hmmm, what would change? I might come home to a smaller house."

"No European vacations," I added.

"That would be a relief. I could get some work done." He picked up my hand and kissed it. "Is that what Ginger thinks—that I'm here for the money?" I nodded. He chuckled. "Well, whatever you do, don't tell her the truth—that I'm only in it for the sex." He pulled me into the kind of soul-wrenching kiss we hadn't dared in days.

SEVEN

*

I'd set my alarm for four and stumbled into my sweatshirt and jeans without turning on the light. Sam got up anyway and by the time I'd loaded my camera case, tripod and a backpack crammed with green canvas tarps and bug spray into the car, he appeared with a thermos of coffee and two pieces of toast with cream cheese and jelly.

"I was sure I bought bagels, but I can't find any. I guess this will have to do. Do you think it would be okay if I went for a run before she gets up?" he whispered as he handed me my breakfast.

"She hasn't gotten out of bed before nine yet. You might leave her a note in case."

"I'll stop by the store, too. We're out of everything. Funny, she doesn't seem to eat much but food is disappearing at a fast clip." He shook his head. "Probably seems that way because we're not used to cooking."

I opened the car door. "Thanks for taking over this morning. If you drop her by Maggie's lab, I'll stop by your office on my way to pick her up."

He nodded and kissed me goodbye. The whole scene reeked of domesticity. Maybe we could start our own twenty-first century sitcom, *Fathers Know Best? Three's More Than Enough?*

I'm not a morning person. That's sort of like saying Franco wasn't much for voting. I've been in meetings where people burbled on about how wonderful it is to greet the dawn sober. It seems to me that it's as miraculous to wake midmorning without a hangover or the shakes and, a bonus, well-rested. Be that as it may, there's no getting around the luscious wash of post-dawn light. As I barreled down the highway toward Neskame, slurping and spilling coffee out of the thermos cup, I wondered why I hadn't gone into computer programming or late-night talk radio.

By the time I'd parked in the back lot, the predawn sky illuminated the path enough to convince me to leave my flashlight behind. I shrugged on the backpack, slung my camera case across my chest, picked up the tripod, locked the car and trudged out across the boardwalk onto the bog. About half a mile in, I veered off the boardwalk onto a mound of high ground and started setting up beneath a stunted tamarack. I rigged the camera with a medium-length zoom lens and screwed it into the tripod, and cocooned myself in the tarps, a Cyclops blob peering into the wilderness as the sun rose behind me.

I slowed my breath and willed myself invisible. The stink of mold on the tarps washed out the fresh, wet green smell of the bog. As the sun rose, bird song blew up around me. I swung my camera toward each call, searching for the singer. At each sighting, my finger depressed the button before I consciously saw the bird, catching as many frames as possible before it flitted or flew away.

The sun rose higher and I was about to emerge from my nest and search out the plants. In Neskame I like the carnivores best – sundews and pitcher plants dissolving their insect prey. A red fox trotted across the bog, stopped twenty feet in front of me and turned to watch something in front of my left foot. I took a close-up of her sharp face and intent gaze, then zoomed out in time to get the pounce, the catch and a few shots of her trotting back home, mouse tail dangling from her jaws. Some days are pure magic.

I stripped down in the empty parking lot, threw my wet boots, jeans and sweatshirt in the trunk and changed into a dry tee shirt, jeans and sandals. Checked my watch—still time to make the ten o'clock meeting and have a leisurely coffee downtown before heading out to the university to pick up Ginger from her sixth day of work. Clearly, as long as I went without sleep and twisted Sam's arm until he agreed to stay home mornings with Ginger, I had the work/life balance thing licked. Poor Sam, on the other hand, he'd probably have to work on it. To compensate I bought him a giant skim latte with extra shots and carried it, along with my own double mocha extra whip, up the three flights of stairs to his office.

He wasn't there. A sign on the door said simply, "I'm in the lab." I peered through the glass window in his door and saw his perfectly clean desk and neatly ordered bookcase, but no Sam. Jogging back down to the ground floor, I only spilled a sip or two of his coffee. Mine barely sloshed, protected by a thick layer of whipped cream. I strolled down the hallway, approaching and then passing a scratchy baritone that boomed from one of the teaching labs. A few students passed me, dull-eyed. Nothing about summer school made me want to go back and finish my degree.

I poked my head through Sam's lab door, immediately accosted by the difference between office and lab. Where Sam's office whispers *feng shui*, his lab screams FEMA. Piles of boxes and plastic bins line the walls, overflowing with netting, waders, bags and funky-looking sampling mechanisms. There's a long steel pipe for soil sampling, an ice auger, giant clippers and PVC pipes duct-taped into squares. Benches in the middle hold microscopes, slides and stacks of papers and books. And everywhere there are jars and jars of pickled fish, bugs, whatnot. The place reeks of rubbing alcohol and rotting things. A student sat at one of the scopes. I couldn't remember her name—Jennifer? Ashley? Betty? – no, nobody was named Betty anymore.

When she saw me, she gestured toward the back. "He's in the gene room."

I took a couple of steps forward and watched him through the glass door window, handsome in his lab coat, secreted in another spotless room. He looked up and waved. I leaned against a lab table to wait.

"How'd it go this morning?" He closed the door behind him as he stepped into the main lab.

"Great." I handed him his coffee and wiped my hands with one of the ubiquitous brown paper towels. "A red fox caught a mouse right in front of me. Let's hope the camera gods smile and a picture or two turn out. How was your morning?"

"Fine." He glanced over his shoulder at the student—Megan? Lois? whose eyes seemed glued to the eyepieces. "I ran about ten miles and got back well before Ginger was up. Thanks for the coffee." He gestured with his cup. "I'll walk you up to Maggie's lab."

"Frosty in there. What was that about?" I asked as the door closed behind us.

He shook his head. "Nothing. I chewed her out this morning for messing up some gels, but it was my fault, really. I should have been here to supervise instead of home babysitting." I stopped walking. He stilled and faced me. "Yeah, I know you needed the time to work and that was out of line. Sorry, I'm in a crappy mood."

I took a deep breath and swallowed a resentful sentence about how parenting isn't babysitting. "I'm taking Ginger to the Rise and Shine for lunch. You want to come?"

He winced. "I'm not that hungry. Besides, I have to work. Thanks for the coffee, though." He touched my arm lightly and turned to go.

"You want to meet us at the Rabbi's office at four?" I asked his back.

He turned back with an apologetic smile. "Oh shit, I forgot. Sure, that's fine."

I caressed his shoulder. "Let's do pizza tonight. Ginger and I can rent a movie. I love your cooking and adore you for doing it, but maybe we all need a day off."

He smiled. "Good idea."

With fifteen minutes before I was due at Maggie's lab, I sat on a bench swigging the last of my mocha and letting the sun warm me. It felt wonderful after the artificial cool of the science building. A small group of young men tossed a frisbee to each other across an expanse of well-groomed lawn. I took slow breaths and practiced letting go.

As I entered the lab, Ginger greeted me with one of her asymmetrical smiles. "Edward, look—this one with the three black toes? I think he likes me." She pointed toward a cage near the end of a middle row. "See how he watches my finger?" She passed her hand in front of the cage and the rat followed with his eyes, nose, and whiskers twitching.

"He thinks you're going to feed him."

"I am." She laughed and poured rat kibble into the feeder before continuing down the row and filling them all. "I washed and filled their water jars. This is the last thing." She clucked her tongue at a rat in the bottom row who'd come to the front of its cage. "I think they're lonely. Maggie says they have to stay separate so she knows who's who and they don't fight or mate, but I don't think they like it. So I'm going to name them all and keep them company. This one," she straightened and pointed to a largish rat on the top row, "is Albert, and this is Berryface (see the little pink spot on its nose?) and Candy and David and," she looked at me sideways, "um, Ed and Frank and—"

"It looks like there are more than twenty-six of them. What about the ones down there?" I pointed to the bottom row.

"I haven't named them yet," she said with a blush. "I'm only to here." She pointed to a spot part-way through the top row. "Zena. I'm going to write a big list tonight. There are five hundred of them."

"We should stop at the store and buy a book of baby names," I suggested.

"Oh, can we?" She touched my arm briefly. "That's a great idea."

"Sure," I said, surprised by a wave of pure joy at this first gesture of affection.

Maggie stepped through the lab door. "Hi, I was down the hall and didn't see you come in. Ginger's doing great stuff here." She gestured to the cages. "They all thank her."

Bill appeared behind her. He smiled broadly and strode forward to shake my hand. "Edward, right? Your little girl is doing a bang-up job with the rats." He patted Ginger's head and she took a couple of quick steps back.

"Glad to hear it." I angled myself so I stood between him and Ginger. "If you're done with her for the day, I'm taking her to my favorite restaurant for lunch."

"She's all yours," Maggie said, with a tight smile that let me know she'd be speaking to Bill about boundaries after we left.

"Where we going? Is it fancy?" asked Ginger as we bounded down the steps.

"Nope. The décor is older than I am and so's the coffee, but they serve the best hamburgers in town and the pie's to die for."

"Cool. Milkshakes?"

"So thick you need a spoon."

❧ ❧ ❧

Over lunch I asked, "Hey Ginger, what do you think of Bill?"

She shrugged. "He's kind of fakey."

"He doesn't make you nervous or anything, does he?" I took another bite of burger and pickle. Onion and sauce dripped through my fingers. I licked off what I could and wiped the rest with what was left of my napkin.

She shook her head. "He's kind of creepy, but mostly he leaves me alone." She tore a small bite off her plain hamburger, popped it in her mouth, chewed, swallowed, and took a sip of chocolate milkshake. "I think he's banging Maggie, though."

I'd taken a sip of coffee and some of it caught in my windpipe. When I finished coughing I asked, "What makes you think that?"

She sipped her milkshake thoughtfully. "The way he looks at her and he's always touching her. She touches him back, so I guess she likes it."

I nodded, parsing the statements both for what they told me about Maggie and Bill and for what I could learn about the way Ginger viewed relationships. I looked up at the board, trying to decide between cherry and chocolate meringue pie.

"I like the other guy, though." Ginger bit into a thick crinkle fry. "The old one."

"Paul?" Why did everyone feel the need to identify him by age?

She nodded. "He's nice. Comes by almost every day and he thinks the rats look lonely, too."

"Sam thinks he likes Maggie." A little bit of gossip seemed to make the conversation flow.

Ginger looked at me like I might be dim-witted. "Obviously," she said slowly. She popped another fry and giggled. "You should see the way he looks at Bill. I don't think he likes him."

I smiled. We only think we're more sophisticated than we were in junior high. "You want some pie?"

❧ ❧ ❧

Sam, already ensconced in Rabbi Talia's office by the time we arrived, leaned against an overflowing bookcase, paging through a paperback. As soon as he saw us, he smiled and set it face down on one of the tall stacks that threatened to cascade across the floor. I glanced at the spine: *Jewish Adoption: A Guide for the Perplexed.* I caught his eye and smiled. He blushed.

Ginger strolled in behind me, looking around with a vague curiosity. She seemed to be taking the outing in stride. I'd expected more questions, surprise, maybe even argument when I told her we had an appointment with the rabbi, but she just said, "Okay."

I hoped it would go this smoothly next week at the dentist.

Rabbi Talia burst through the threshold. Although she looks more like Thelma from Scooby-Do, our wonderful rabbi might really be the result of a one-night stand in Brooklyn between Glenda the Good Witch and the Roadrunner.

She stopped before Ginger, a grin spreading across her face. Ginger returned her smile and I didn't blame her, I'd never been able to remain impassive before that beam either. "Hi, Ginger." She held out her hand to shake. "It's wonderful to finally meet you."

Ginger looked at me, then Sam, who smiled down at her and nodded. Reluctantly, she shook hands, her thin fingers resting in Rabbi Talia's for a second.

"Let's all sit." Rabbi Talia pointed toward the chair nearest the door. "Ginger, you sit there, and Sam and Edward can take these two." Ginger settled lightly in her chair. Sam and I took our appointed places. Rabbi Talia continued, "This is simply an opportunity to meet and get a chance to know each other a little bit. Is that okay with you?"

Ginger nodded.

Rabbi Talia smiled. "Your—what do you like to call them?"

Ginger shrugged. "Edward and Sam, I guess."

"Okay then, Edward and Sam are valuable members of our congregation. They'd like you to feel welcomed here, too."

Ginger shrugged again. "Okay."

Talia gazed at her for a long moment. "What's your religious background? Have you gone to synagogue or church before?"

"One of the girls was always talking about Jesus."

"A girl from the group home?" she asked.

"No, someone I knew. Nobody special." Ginger shook her head, her eyes focused on her tennis shoes. "Most of my foster parents made me go to church." She looked up, a teasing smile behind her eyes. "I've been a Baptist, a Catholic, a Methodist and one of the houses was Lutheran, but I didn't last there to a Sunday. Most of them gave up after a while and decided I was going to hell."

"Sounds like hell might be somewhere you've already been," Rabbi Talia said softly.

Ginger looked at her, blinked, and looked down.

"We're not big on hell here," the rabbi continued. "We tend to focus more on this life than the next." She leaned back in her chair. "I tell you what. I already know Sam and Edward. How about if you and I talk for a while? I promise not to try to convince you of anything, but I'll tell you a little bit about the synagogue and what happens here. We'll send the guys out and you can ask whatever silly questions you can think of. Does that sound like a good idea?"

Ginger looked uncertainly at me. I smiled. "I think you'll be safe. She's about the least dangerous person I know. And besides, you can always bolt. We'll be nearby."

She looked at Sam who said, "It's up to you."

Ginger turned back to Rabbi Talia. "I don't believe in God."

Rabbi Talia smiled. "Neither does half the congregation, and some of the brave ones even admit it."

Sam and I stood. "We'll be in the kitchen," Sam told Ginger. "It's down the hall, second door on the left, all right?"

Ginger nodded and we left. Rabbi stood and pulled the door to, but not quite closed, behind us. We walked together in silence to the kitchen.

Sam strolled over to the coffee pot. "You want some?" he asked, pulling a cup from the dish rack.

"Sure." I leaned against the counter and watched him fill both cups and spoon two heaping mounds of creamer into mine.

He handed it to me with a sad smile. "I'm sorry I was an asshole earlier."

I took a deep breath. "This isn't easy."

He pulled himself up onto the counter to sit beside me. "I'm not sure what I envisioned, but it wasn't this. I didn't think it would take so much work, or that she'd be so closed down all the time, or that I'd feel so torn between home and work." He paused and sipped his coffee.

It felt like there was more, so I waited.

"And I miss you. I thought this would bring us closer together, but . . ." He shrugged.

An ugly anger threatened. I could feel it stirring low in my belly. I wanted to yell that I was staying home and doing most of the childcare and that I'd asked for one frigging morning off so I could get some actual work done and—I willed myself into stillness. Resentful sentences sidled into my consciousness but I pushed them back down. God, grant me the serenity.

"We'll work it out." I swirled my coffee in the cup. "Things will settle down soon. It's only been a couple of weeks. Give it time."

Silence. I knew I should reach out and touch him, reconnect, but I couldn't make myself move. After a long moment, I asked, "So what are they talking about?"

Sam stirred. "I'm not sure. I talked with Rabbi earlier about Ginger and religious education. She said that conversion is a possibility, but probably not worth thinking about unless we adopt her, and only if Ginger wants to, of course." He played with his half-empty cup. "Meanwhile, there's nothing to stop her from going to religious school or hanging out with us during services."

"Sounds like she's used to shrugging into whatever religious overcoat her foster parents offer."

Turning toward him, I took the cup from his hand and set it on the counter beside mine. Taking both his hands in mine, I stepped closer. "Sam," I whispered. He looked up. "You and I will be fine and happy, no matter what we have to do to make that happen. It took me a long time to find you. I'm not letting go, no matter what."

He held my gaze and nodded.

Brittany Goldstein burst into the kitchen. "Rabbi wants you." She whirled back out before we had time to answer.

Sam raised his eyebrows, his eyes warm. "Guess we've been summoned."

Brittany leaned against the wall near the rabbi's chair. Ginger stood as we entered. Rabbi Talia said, "I know that Brittany's here to work with you this afternoon, Sam, but I thought maybe she could show Ginger around for a few minutes while you and Edward and I chat. I think Brittany's likely to have a better idea of what Ginger might find interesting." She smiled at Ginger, who nodded. Rabbi Talia stood and extended her hand again. "It was very nice meeting you. I look forward to seeing you at services."

This time Ginger shook her hand easily. "Nice to meet you, too." She followed Brittany out the door.

Sam and I returned to our seats. Rabbi Talia closed the door and sat again herself. "She's an interesting kid. Thanks for bringing her in. Now tell me how you guys are doing."

Sam shifted in his seat. I looked at him, then at my shoes. I sure wasn't going to be the first one to talk. Eventually, Sam said, "It's weird. She hasn't done anything wrong and I shouldn't complain, but it's like something's missing. There's no connection. It's harder than I thought. Most of the time I don't feel up to it. Edward's great with her."

I looked up, startled by his statement.

"It's like he gets her and I can see her warming to him, but not me." He shrugged. "I had this idea of myself as the perfect dad, like my dad, I guess, doing wholesome all-American things and Ginger's, well, she's not really into all that."

"Your dad disowned you when you came out." I was glad she'd said it, not me.

Sam looked at her for a moment. "Yeah, he did. That's a good point."

She paused, holding his gaze. "Sometimes the all-American dad isn't the right fit, either for dad or kid."

Sam closed his eyes and nodded.

"And sometimes," she continued, "it takes a while to push through all those stored images of who we think we ought to be, before we find our true fit." She reached over and patted his arm. "Give her some time, Sam. She's as new at this relationship as you are." She turned to me. "How about you? How have the last couple of weeks been for you?"

I sat back in my chair to think. "Actually, better than I thought they'd be." I paused, trying to find the right words. "And maybe too easy. Sam's right. She does all the right things and is being *uber* good and I keep waiting for the other shoe to drop. Still, I like Ginger. Maybe Sam's right and I understand some stuff about her. I don't know. Seems to me he's good with her, too. She's like a foreign country, though. I'm sure nothing either Sam or I have ever experienced comes even close to what she's survived. What's amazing is that, in spite of all that, she's still spunky. You gotta love that."

Rabbi Talia smiled. "I agree—she's got spirit. But that's not what I asked. How about you?"

Oh. Right. I took a deep breath. "Me. Well, I'm not getting enough sleep, or sex, but the food's better." I grinned at Sam. "I'm finding it hard to get any real work done, but I'm thinking that will change when we can leave Ginger on her own more or when school starts. So, I could be better, but basically, I'm fine."

She looked at each of us. "Here comes my standard new-parent lecture. In my experience, one of the hardest things for parents to do is to find time for each other. So you'll need to figure that out. You can't be there for Ginger if you're not together. If you don't do this as a team, you're sunk." She smiled. "Raising kids is hard. I see a lot of parents struggling to hold on to each other while their kids suck up their time. Some make it, many don't. So be good to each other."

She glanced at her watch. "Enough of that. I'm not going to take any more of your time. Sam, I know Brittany needs all the help she can get, and every minute we chat is one she doesn't chant, but I need to say this one last thing." She paused. We waited. "Most people don't get a money-back guarantee with their kids. You do. But, if you take too long before you claim the refund, you'll do serious damage. So, figure out how to be a couple and a family or send her back soon."

I blinked. Sam inhaled, nodded and stood. We all shook hands.

"Thanks," I mumbled.

"I'm here if you need to talk." She ushered us out the door. "Oh, Sam," she said suddenly, "I almost forgot. I got a call from a family who recently moved to town. Their daughter turns thirteen in September. She was scheduled to do her bat mitzvah early this fall, but her father got transferred and now they want us to fit them in before Thanksgiving." She grimaced. "She's evidently attended religious school for years, but frankly, I don't know what they did in those classes, because she's not ready. Her Hebrew is marginal and evidently she hasn't started learning her portion."

Sam's eyebrows shot up. "So she's supposed to learn it in a few months?"

"I know, I know. Maybe I can convince her parents to move the date, but I doubt it. The relatives have all been notified and I'm afraid poor Ora will be humiliated if we put it off too long. If I can't get the date changed, can you help her get up to speed?"

He glanced at me. I looked at my shoes thinking that we really didn't need to rescue another kid.

"Sure," he agreed.

I left them talking about it while I wandered off in search of Ginger. I found her in the sanctuary with Brittany, heads together, laughing.

EIGHT

ᴥ

We ordered pizza and watched a movie that Ginger'd chosen after wandering the aisles of the video store for what seemed like an hour. It was terrible. Stupid people did embarrassing things in ridiculous situations and the boy got the girl in the end. But she liked it.

Still plenty of daylight when the movie ended. I cleaned up while Sam and Ginger played a couple of rounds of gin rummy on the porch. They propped the screen door open so that Daphnia could run back and forth between Ginger's lap and the lure of deer-scented bushes out back. I watched from the kitchen window as he appeared and disappeared, stalking whatever through the tall grasses and shrubs covering the slope to the lake.

Grandpa Rosenberg always said he learned two important things from the Depression. First, trust your gut. He got out of stocks in early 1929. And second, preserve the soil. Almost on his deathbed, he'd made Gillian and me promise to leave wild the slope from our houses to the lake. So other than clipping the occasional sapling, we let it grow. We're a super green, sustainable example to the neighbors, and Daphnia, king of his own small wilderness, is the happiest dog in town.

Near the lake, the damp air in early summer suffocates. I've always balked at the idea of putting air conditioning in an old lake house, so we swelter through. By July we're usually used to it. But June can be hell. I could see the wilt in Ginger and Sam, and felt a rivulet of sweat dripping down my spine.

"You guys want to swim?" I called. Ginger looked at Sam, who shook his head.

"You go ahead. After I finish this game, I need to get some work done. I want to finish a first draft of my paper by Friday."

"Ginger?" I asked. "Want a quick swim before bed? I can wait until the game's over."

She nodded. "Okay."

I wandered upstairs, changed into my baggy surfer-style swimsuit and looked at myself in the full-length mirror. Not bad, not great, good thing I'm not single.

Downstairs I told Ginger, "Take your time. I'll do a few laps between our dock and the other." I pointed toward the neighbor's, where Bo Lin lay stretched out on a deck chair, reading. I didn't see Qian on the dock. Probably up in the house playing video games. Isn't that what fifteen-year-old boys do with spare time? Then I saw him kick out from the shallows on an inner tube. Heartening to see a young man enjoying nature.

Ginger nodded, intent on her cards. I glanced over her shoulder to gauge the hand's progress. Depending on Sam's cards, it could be a while. She was picking the game up quickly and with time, she'd learn not to pull to an inside straight.

Daphnia followed me down the trail. He ran behind as I loped across the dock, and skidded to a stop as I dove into the water. Not a frequent swimmer, he sat attentively watching as I launched into a slow crawl, plowing through the cool water in a way that felt sleek and graceful and made me forget my over fifty, less than perfect image. As I neared the far dock, I almost ran into Qian, sprawled in his inner tube, working one of those electronic gadgets that increase thumb dexterity. So much for my image of him as a nature boy.

"Hey." I switched into a sociable sidestroke. "How's it going?"

"Good." He looked away from the screen for only an instant, kicked twice and swooshed away. Clearly, I had a real gift for communicating with teenagers.

I touched the dock, turned onto my back and kicked. "Hi," I called to Bo, who looked up from her book for a moment, smiled, waved, and went back to reading. Really, mine's a more general social talent. I swam back to my own dock where Daphnia sat, expectantly watching the water, wiggling his entire body with joy as I neared.

"Hey, boy."

He turned and sprinted to greet Ginger as she picked her way down the path.

I swam to the ladder, hoisted myself up and crossed toward them. "Hey, Ginger, a quick dip or short lesson?"

She plucked at her baggy navy Speedo. "Anything to get me out of this."

"Right." I darted into the boathouse to grab the battered kickboard I'd found at the bottom of our bin of water toys. "Today you learn to kick. Let's hop in here where it isn't deep."

With her upper body plastered to the floating board, it took her no time to master the flutter kick. I swam beside her for three victory laps around the boathouse, before declaring the lesson over and bedtime near.

"When do I get my new suit?" she asked as we walked up the path to the house.

"When you can pass the swimming test."

"What swimming test?"

"The one my grandpa Wolf made me pass. Swim around the boathouse and back without stopping, tread water for one minute and do the dead man's float for three breaths."

She groaned and looked down at the ill-fitting suit. "That'll take forever."

"I doubt it. Now go change into pajamas and brush your teeth." I followed her upstairs, changed into dry clothes, waited until she emerged from the bathroom, and watched from the doorway as she crawled into bed. Daphnia leaped onto the bed, circled three times and curled on a pillow beside her head.

"G'night." I turned off the light. "Don't let the bed bugs bite. Roses on your pillow." I left the door open enough so the hallway could serve as a night-light.

I passed Sam's office. He sat up straight, gaze locked on his screen, fingers flying across the keyboard. I opened my own office door, flipped on the computer and while it booted up, dug into my camera bag for the memory card. I plugged in the reader and slipped in the card. As the images appeared, I paged through quickly, looking for the red fox. I found her and opened to full screen.

How had I not seen, and cleaned, that water spot on the lens? I flipped through all thirty of my red fox pictures and there it was, a large smudge in the upper left corner. The perfect image again eluded me. Discouraging, even though I knew I could Photoshop or crop it. Fake it. Improve on reality. I named, saved and backed up the files and logged out.

Much later—I must have been asleep for a while—I felt the bedsprings shift. The sheets rustled as he slid between them. We lay not touching, breathing the damp, dark air.

Ω Ω Ω

"What do kids usually wear?" Ginger leaned in the door of my study Friday afternoon.

I closed my eyes and tried to remember. What came up for me was Ben Ruben's bar mitzvah party. My mother, always impeccably dressed, had forced me to show up in the suit I'd worn to the synagogue. We arrived to find everyone else in shorts. Humiliating. "I can't remember. Let's call Sam. He's the guy who knows the middle school crowd."

"Nothing fancy. This time of year, mostly light summer dresses," Sam announced. "Often inappropriately skimpy, but don't tell her that."

"We didn't get any dresses," I complained.

Sam chuckled. "I might be able to get Taylor's phone number from the registrar. Will you be needing shopping intervention?"

"We'll manage."

Ginger watched attentively from the door.

"Put on some shoes," I told her. "We're going shopping."

She beamed.

❧ ❧ ❧

Our first official appearance as a family, I thought, as the three of us entered the sanctuary, Sam handsome, and me at least clean, in our chinos and button-down shirts. Ginger preened slightly in her new blue cotton shift, but wilted shyly when confronted with a roomful of staring strangers. Brittany appeared and Ginger smiled.

"Hi, Ginger, nice dress."

"Thanks," Ginger answered. "You look great."

I nodded my appreciation to Sam. The two girls looked perfectly matched, Brittany's lavender flowered dress a touch less stylish than Ginger's. Sam smiled.

"I gotta go sit with my parents," Brittany said. She nodded toward the Goldsteins. We all followed her gaze. Sam and I nodded hello to Vera and Bob. They nodded back. "I'll see you at the *oneg*."

We positioned Ginger between us as we scooted into our seats. After we'd settled, she whispered. "What's an *oneg*?"

"Hebrew for 'coffee hour,'" I whispered back.

"Hebrew for 'joy,'" Sam corrected. "But we call the coffee hour an *oneg*."

She looked from one to the other of us. I winked. Sam rolled his eyes. She giggled softly.

"This might be different from what you're used to," Sam whispered. "Follow us. If we stand, stand, if we sit, sit, but whatever you do, don't try to follow Edward's singing. He's flat."

She nodded, quietly scanning the crowd. Assimilating.

I looked around myself. Lacland isn't what you'd call a thriving Jewish population center. Most Jews living within a fifty-mile radius belong to the temple and we still only have maybe one hundred families. While I knew most folks from the holidays, this was not my usual crowd. Younger and noisier. Something else to get used to.

But I had to admit it was a fun service. More English, more music and much shorter. I missed hearing Sam chant, but loved the sound of him singing practically in my ear. Ginger mouthed the words. I think she spent most of the service checking out the handful of preteen girls scattered around the sanctuary. As soon as the service ended, she

wound her way over to Brittany, who stood at the center of a group of
girls. Sam and I joined the wine and juice line, figuring she'd find us
again in time.

"I hope she's ready for this," I whispered to Sam.

He nodded and was about to speak, but Erma Malamud appeared,
wanting to chat about the religious school. "Do you think we should
be doing something to protect the children from that awful man?"

"What awful man?" Sam stepped aside to let her cut in line.

"The one who steals children. Another disappeared in New Devon
last week."

"I'm sure our kids are safe," Sam assured her. "What could happen?
It isn't like we let them out for recess."

I looked for Ginger, newly cognizant of threats to her safety. She
hung at the edge of a group of girls. I watched as she mirrored one
of Brittany's gestures. The kid knew how to blend in. Good survival
skills for an unstable world.

Liv Bloomberg caught my eye from across the room. She smiled
and mouthed, "Beautiful girl." I grinned back my thanks.

Later, as we stood munching dry, store-bought cookies, Rabbi
Talia swept up, a compact, round-faced girl in tow, Pippi Longstocking
with glasses and braces.

"Sam," Rabbi Talia said, presenting the reluctant teen, whose
parents trailed a few steps behind. "This is Ora Lev. She moved
to town a few weeks ago. Her bat mitzvah is the third Saturday in
October. We've agreed she will lead the prayers and chant three verses
of *Haftorah* in Hebrew, after which perhaps you could take over?" Her
voice rose uncertainly at the end.

He nodded and smiled at Ora.

"Her parents, Josh and Vera." She introduced the couple standing
awkwardly behind Ora. Turning toward them, she continued, "At one
point in his life Sam studied to be a cantor. Now he teaches at the
university, but graciously volunteers to help our kids get ready for their
big day." Her eyes didn't smile along with her mouth. Evidently, she'd
lost the 'let's move this to the spring' argument.

Josh Lev stepped forward, hand extended. "Jewish Studies?"

"Um, no, biology actually." Sam shook hands. He gestured toward me. "This is my partner, Edward."

Josh's smile faltered slightly, then picked up again. Vera blinked twice, but smiled. They both shook my hand and we all turned our attention to Ora. It looked like that was about the last thing she wanted to have happen.

Sam smiled warmly. "Hi, nice to meet you."

She returned his smile shyly. Shit, I thought, there goes his spare time.

"Hey, Edward, Sam." Ginger appeared beside us.

"I'd like you to meet our daughter, Ginger." I gestured toward the little cluster of Levs. "This is Ora and her parents, Mr. and Mrs. Lev."

"Oh, hi." She quickly scanned Ora, who looked hot and overdressed in her Sabbath best. Perhaps in her approach to preteen fashion, Vera Lev had something in common with my mother.

"Hi." Ora appeared fascinated with her own shoes.

"Um." Ginger looked uncomfortable.

"Excuse us." I steered her away from the group. "What's up?"

"I didn't want to say anything in front of that other girl, but Brittany asked me to sleep over next Saturday. Can I?"

"I'll check with Sam to see if we have anything planned, but otherwise I don't see why not."

"It's just that," she tapped the floor with the toe of her sandal, "they have a pool."

"Oh, I see." I rubbed my chin in what I hoped was a thoughtful, paternal gesture. "I guess you'll have to work hard at those swimming lessons between now and then."

"Edward." She dragged it out into three syllables.

"Pass the test or you'll be wearing that old baggy tank in Brittany's pool."

She sulked for a moment, looked around for Brittany, who was heading out the door, and darted over to say goodbye.

I wandered back toward Sam, who'd already been captured by yet another set of anxious parents.

❧ ❧ ❧

Sunday morning I answered the door to find Henry standing on my steps, coffee cake in hand. A slight breeze brought the rich smell of cinnamon. "Is that homemade?" I asked.

"Good morning to you, too." He grinned. "I thought I'd make myself look good by visiting at least one of my foster placements at home this week. The coffee cake was Fran's idea."

"Come on in." I waved him through the door. "Ginger's still asleep and Sam's gone in to work, so I'm all you've got for the moment."

"You have coffee to go with this?"

"I sure do. Let's take it out to the porch."

"So how's it going?" Henry asked, settling into a chair. I handed him coffee and a slice of the cake.

"Are you asking as Ginger's caseworker or my sponsor?"

He thought for a moment. "I've been thinking about that. At first I was worried that maybe it was a conflict of interests, but it isn't really. If you were to really mess up, as your sponsor, I'd have to call you out on it, right?" I nodded. "As Ginger's caseworker I'd have to call you out and pull the placement. On the other hand, if you're having problems, well, the same principle applies. Either way, my responsibilities are the same: protect Ginger and call you on your shit." He sipped his coffee and looked contentedly out at the lake.

I lowered myself into the chair next to him. "Fair enough." I took a bite of Fran's coffee cake, cinnamon so strong it bit back before the butter soothed it all away. "Oh," I groaned involuntarily.

"I know," he said, fork poised. "She's quite a baker."

"Sam's been learning to cook. He's come home almost every night with a new recipe. He's not ready for the cooking shows yet, but he's determined and I think it's getting better all the time."

"Good for him." Henry chewed thoughtfully. "About time one of you quit acting like a frat boy."

I grinned. "I used to like frat boys in my younger days."

"I bet you did. You used to like a lot of things that weren't good for you."

We ate in silence.

"Did you answer my question about how you are?"

"I'm surviving. This parenting stuff is a lot of work but she grows on you." I resisted the temptation to lick my plate and instead cut myself another piece.

"How's she behaving?"

I savored the taste of buttery cinnamon. "She's very helpful and eager to please—like she's on probation."

Henry laughed. "That won't last."

I licked my fork. "I know, but at least for now the only thing we have to deal with is time management. Except for the few hours she works every day, someone needs to be home with her. Makes it hard to get anything done."

Henry ran his fork along his plate, gathering the last crumbs. "I expect it will get easier come September. Meanwhile, you'll have your hands full, especially when she quits being on her best behavior." He paused, eyes on the horizon. "And Sam's a busy man."

"He's not so good at saying no," I admitted.

Henry raised his eyebrows. "Meaning?"

"Meaning between work and teaching Hebrew, there's not a lot of time left over." I took another huge bite that I barely tasted. "He's got a new kid, a Hebrew emergency. That's why he's gone into work this morning, so he can spend more time with her this afternoon."

Henry started to speak, but Ginger appeared in the doorway. Daphnia sprinted past her, leaped into Henry's lap and began licking his face frantically, hind legs planted firmly in the poor man's crotch.

"Stop, Daphnia." I swooped him out the door. "I'm sorry about that. He's not what you'd call a well-mannered dog."

Ginger defended him. "He gets excited. You can't blame him for that."

"Hi, Ginger." Henry smiled. "I came by to see how you are."

"And to bring us some great coffee cake. Try some."

She shook her head. "Maybe later. Can I use the phone? I promised Brittany I'd call."

"Sure, but don't forget to eat something."

She nodded and disappeared.

"Brittany?" Henry asked.

I shrugged. "It appears Ginger's made her first friend. She's having an overnight with her next weekend. I guess I'm supposed to check in with you about that?" He nodded, and I continued, "Brittany is one of Sam's bat mitzvah girls. She's Bob Goldstein's daughter, you know, the optometrist? I wouldn't have expected the two of them to bond. She's always seemed so preppy to me. Of course, I don't really know her that well. I've never liked her folks, but if Ginger likes her I'm not going to complain."

"Hmmm, sounds safe enough." Henry nodded, watching the lake. "He the one who stopped taking Medicare cases when the state cut reimbursements?"

"Probably," I said. "He's a big donor to the synagogue but always needs to have his name attached to the gift."

"Is that the same synagogue with the spectacular Rosenberg library?"

"That was my mother's doing."

"Uh-huh. You want to cut me another piece of that cake before it's gone, Mr. Humility?"

ॐ ॐ ॐ

"Let's try it with this." I held out an old water-ski belt. "Put this around your waist. It should keep you from drowning while you attempt the breast stroke."

"It should keep me from drowning? What if it doesn't?" Ginger looked skeptical but allowed me to help her with the buckle and pull the straps as tight as they'd go. Still the foam belt rested loosely on her hips.

"In that case you'll either have to be smart enough to stand up or hope I haven't gotten distracted watching the muskrat. Look." I pointed. We could see the head and upper back as the animal plowed through the water on its regular route to the next dock.

Ginger looked around. "Are there more of them in here?"

"Nah, they're solitary animals. You're safe. But if you stand still too long like that, fish are likely to nibble your ankles."

"Gross." She kicked up both legs. The motion sent her sprawling onto her front. The belt held her afloat and she started to thrash.

"Remember the form we practiced on the dock," I shouted. I

might have to rescue her after all. Her head popped up and her arms started sweeping arcs. She even almost got the frog kick.

"Hey, you're swimming."

She grinned.

"You're a quick study." I handed her a towel as she waded toward the dock. "Keep it up and you might actually pass that swim test by Saturday."

"I want a bikini," she said, sitting on the edge of a chair with Daphnia settled behind and the towel draped over her shoulders. She fingered the worn lycra of her tank suit. "Bright blue to match my tattoo."

"You have a tattoo?"

She nodded and pointed to a spot low on her belly, inside her left hip. "An eye, right here. We all got them."

"Who all?"

She looked at me for a long moment and shrugged. "It's blue. Well, the eye is blue, the lashes and stuff are black and the inside is, you know, white."

"Why an eye?"

She shrugged.

I waited, but nothing came. Finally I told her, "If it's where you pointed, your swimsuit bottom will cover it."

She looked down. "No, it won't."

"Yes it will. Maybe you should get a black suit to match the tips of the lashes. That'll be all that shows." I stretched out in my chair to let my legs dry in the sun. On the next dock, Bo Lin appeared and dove smoothly into the water. They'd be leaving soon. I needed to get those photos over to her.

Ginger pouted for a minute. We heard Sam chant a short line of Hebrew, his voice like an undulating ribbon through the still air, followed by a thin soprano echo, frail but on key.

"What do you think of Ora?" I asked to change the subject.

Ginger shrugged. "She's all right, I guess. Not very pretty."

"I'm not sure that's the best measure of a person." It came out more didactic than I'd hoped. A boat whipped by and within seconds the wake slapped loudly against the shore.

Ginger shrugged again. It's an elegant language, these shrugs, I thought. There's the quick conversation stopper, the angry "get away from me" hunch, and this languid "there is no way you can understand me, but I will indulge you" shoulder roll. I experimented with my ankle to see if I could come up with my own emotional body language.

"What are you doing?" she asked, watching my foot gyrate back and forth.

"Nothing." I stopped. "You hungry? I could go for a sandwich. I'm thinking of a peanut butter and banana sandwich with frosted flakes for crunch. Interested?"

Her face scrunched. "Frosted flakes in a sandwich?"

I grinned. "Frosted flakes are good with anything. Try it, you might like it."

"Maybe something normal like peanut butter and jelly?"

"If you must. Come on." I jumped up and sprinted toward the house. Daphnia followed first but soon Ginger passed me, towel flying behind her like a cape.

❧ ❧ ❧

I printed several copies of those last few shots with Qian gazing over his mother's shoulder and smiling at something in the distance, then burned a CD with all the images and stuck everything in a big envelope. While Ginger and Daphnia watched TV and Sam rehearsed Ora, I walked the package next door.

Bo opened the door, her hair a sleek wet blanket down her back. I could see a neat stack of boxes behind her. "Edward, how nice to see you."

I held out the envelope. "Sorry this took so long. We've been busy getting Ginger settled. I hope you like them."

She pulled out one of the pictures and smiled. "These are lovely, thank you. Would you like to come in? I'll make tea." She led me into the kitchen. "Please excuse us. We leave Monday."

"I understand. Packing is hard work." I sat at the kitchen table while she poured water into a kettle and shook tea leaves into a porcelain teapot. "Do you need any help?"

She shook her head. "There's not much more to do. I'm afraid I've packed everything too early, but it's hard to gauge these things." She shrugged.

"We'll miss having you next door, but I expect you're getting homesick. I know that by the time we left Amsterdam I felt ready to go home." I looked out the kitchen window, following the path of a heron as it swooped along the shoreline.

"It will be nice to be back with my husband." She filled the teapot with boiling water and retrieved cups from the cupboard. "And Qian needs to be home. It has been good for his English, but lonely, I think."

I nodded. "I know how he feels. Those first few months in Amsterdam were tough even though almost everyone there speaks English."

She brought the teapot and cups to the table and sat across from me. "And how is your new daughter, Ginger?"

"We're all still getting used to each other, but I think it's working out."

"I see her all the time in the water. She must love to swim."

I laughed. "I promised her a new suit if she learned how. She's determined."

Bo poured the tea and handed me a cup. It smelled like newly chopped wood and tasted like bark.

"It's amazing how quickly she's learning, really. And tough? The kid's so skinny she floats like a rock but she keeps fighting her way back up to the surface."

Bo smiled. "Perseverance is good."

"She's got that, all right."

"You're a good man, Edward." She patted my hand. I started to contradict her but stopped. Why not let someone think of me as the good guy, for once.

NINE

❦

"Why does it have to be the Goldsteins?" I asked Sam when he brought me coffee in bed.

"Who cares who it is?" He rested his hand on my thigh. "We get a night out together."

"But I worry about her soul with those people. They're so all American." I sipped my coffee. I love seeing Sam all dressed up of a Saturday morning, sparkly clean, smelling of shampoo and soap. "Who ever heard of a Brittany Goldstein? What's wrong with Ruth, Ester, Miriam, Zipporah, for god's sake?"

"So now you're Mister Anti-Assimilation? Did I miss the use of the name 'Edward' in the Torah? Aren't you the guy who used to live on shrimp cocktails and bacon? Don't worry, one night in *Leave it to Beaver* land never killed anyone." He slid his hand higher. "Think of it, Edward. You're taking me out to dinner at the best restaurant in town."

"Such as it is," I mumbled into my coffee.

"Focus." He slipped his hand under the covers. "We'll have a nice dinner and then come home and . . . are you getting the picture?"

"You're right. Who knows, a night away might even be good for her." I reached for him, but he jumped up laughing.

"I gotta run, but hold that thought. No, not literally, you need to maintain your strength for later." He waved once and darted out the door. "See you soon."

❧ ❧ ❧

A few years ago, Sam dragged me to an Orthodox service when we were on vacation in New York City. I couldn't follow the Hebrew, so I mimicked him and pretended to be an anthropologist. It was a very long morning. We'd gone dancing the night before and I still had the visceral memory of sweaty male bodies gyrating in rhythm. That morning, standing and swaying, wrapped in prayer shawls and hunched over our books, served as an interesting counterpoint, except for the creepy feeling of women watching from behind the lattice wall.

The one really useful thing I got from that service was permission to be late. Those guys straggled in whenever. So I felt safe within an ancient tradition as I dawdled over breakfast and Ginger scrambled to pack her things.

"How long are you planning to stay?" I asked when she flung her bulging overnight bag onto the back seat. The bag pulsed with newness, collateral damage from our Friday afternoon shopping expedition (three bathing suits, the bag, new sandals, a robe, sunglasses and a plethora of other crap).

"I brought a few things I might need, just in case." She slumped in the passenger seat and shrugged. "Besides, I like to have my stuff around me."

"Fair enough. Buckle up, I'd like to get there in time to hear Sam chant the *Haftorah*." I coaxed the car into reverse and backed out of the garage.

"That's the big, long Hebrew thing he does near the end, right?"

"Uh-huh." I love the feel of driving through town in a convertible, wind swirling around me. Ginger clutched at her hair. I stopped to put up the top.

"It's pretty," she said when we started again. "That's what he teaches kids, right?"

"Yeah. There aren't many Jews in town, but you'll see those of your classmates who are wandering through the house on Sundays next year."

"But Ora's starting now, in the summer?"

I nodded. "Usually they begin a year or so before the big event, but for some reason Ora didn't. So now she's doing double time." I looked over at Ginger, who had her feet planted firmly on the dashboard. "She has a nice voice, don't you think?"

Ginger nodded. "Will Brittany come over every Sunday, too?"

I shrugged. "Once school starts she probably will. She did last year."

After a while she asked, "So did you do one?"

"A bar mitzvah?"

She nodded.

"Sure. My dad had a job in Chicago that year, so it was at one of those great big places where they have so many kids they need to double up. All I had to do was stumble through a few lines of the *Haftorah*. Still," I smiled at her as I took a left into the synagogue parking lot, "I was terrible. My mother was mortified. I think even my dad was embarrassed. Of course, my grandfathers told me I was great, but I don't think even someone like Sam could have fixed me."

Ginger nodded thoughtfully. We ran to the door, a little over an hour late.

At the *oneg*, we exchanged pleasantries with the Goldsteins and transferred Ginger, bag and all, to their care. "Be good," I told her.

She rolled her eyes and turned toward Brittany, gracefully excluding the rest of us.

Sam and I strolled toward our cars. He grinned and winked.

ᘓ ᘓ ᘓ

"I walked in on Maggie and Bill in the office supply storeroom yesterday." We lay side-by-side holding hands, our sweat drying slowly in the breeze from the overhead fan.

I propped myself onto one elbow. "Really? What were they doing?"

He gave me his slow-student look. "Are you asking about positions?"

I thought for a moment. "You're right. I don't care what she was doing. But could you tell if he's that well-defined everywhere?"

"Yes, but you're missing the point." Sam sounded exasperated.

"Yes, you could tell, or yes, he is?"

He looked at me sternly.

I pushed back a curl that had fallen across his forehead. "The point is, she shouldn't be screwing her student, right?"

He snorted. "Right. I'm worried about her. She thinks she's immune because she brings in tons of grant money and out-publishes the whole department, but what she can't get is that that's the problem. We have colleagues who don't like being shown up by a girl. Schtupping her students is about the only way for her to get fired."

"It wouldn't come to that, though, would it? It's not like Bill is some frail freshman. He looks like the kind of guy who could take care of himself."

"All the more reason for Maggie to be careful with him."

I looked down at my lover, beautiful in his glistening skin. Of course, I've known lots of good-looking men and in the end that's not what counts. Good thing Sam's insides match his outsides. "You're right. Come on," I tapped his belly, "let's eat some lunch."

❧ ❧ ❧

"Good evening, Mr. Rosenberg, Professor DeCosta." The maitre d` led the way to a window table with a view of the sun setting across the lake. As I crossed the dining room, I felt loose-limbed and relaxed. It had been a very long time since Sam and I had spent an entire afternoon in bed. Maybe he'd been right and parenthood could be sexy. Had my own parents performed bacchanalian rites whenever I was away? Maybe. Hard to imagine Evelyn and Stan naked, much less tangling in sweaty bliss.

"Can I get you something to drink?" The young waiter hovered.

"Sure, diet whatever."

Sam smiled. "Water's fine, thanks."

"You know, you could have a glass of wine," I told him once the waiter had disappeared.

"I know. Sometimes when you're not around I'll have a drink with Maggie, but when we're together it feels sort of, I don't know, wrong." He sipped his water. "Besides, it's no fun to drink alone."

"There's no way I'll ever understand how you can take it or leave it." I smiled. "Personally, it's leave it or let it take me."

He shrugged and picked up the menu. "It's nice to be out like this."

"It is." I scanned the menu. "I think I'll have the prime rib."

Sam laughed. "Why do you even bother to look at the menu? You always have the same thing. Do you think maybe you'll have the chocolate torte for dessert?"

I made a face. "I can change. Wait and see."

The waiter reappeared with my drink. I didn't recognize him—must be new. "Are you ready to order?"

"How's the poached whitefish look today?" Sam asked.

"Good, fresh."

"I'll have that with rice pilaf and a green salad, house vinaigrette."

"Excellent. And you, Sir?"

"Prime rib, rare, baked potato and a salad with," I paused, looking significantly at Sam, "ranch."

He laughed. "He's kidding. Make it bleu cheese."

The waiter looked at me. I grinned. "Actually, bleu cheese does sound good. Thanks."

After he was gone, I winked at Sam. "But I'm going to really mix it up with dessert."

He smiled. "You don't have to. I worry that your diet might give you a heart attack or diabetes, but I like that there's something predictable about you."

"Are there things that aren't?"

"Almost everything. Look at you." He started ticking them off on his fingers. "If I only knew about the money, I'd think you should be a spoiled playboy. But you spend all your time knee-deep in swamp muck. And you're about the worst-dressed gay man I've ever met. If all I'd heard was your sordid past, I'd expect you to be tough and street-smart. Instead you're this sensitive, kind marshmallow man."

"I'm street-smart," I protested, and looked around the restaurant at the small-town families out for a special meal. "But Lacland doesn't have those kinds of streets."

"All I'm saying is that you don't have to try to fake me out with meals, you're already unexpected and I love that." Sam smiled, his dark eyes warm in the candlelight.

"Thanks, I guess." I picked at the fingernail of my right index finger. Then I remembered. "Hey, guess what? I checked my email while you were in the shower. Kathy found an editor who's interested in my book."

Sam's smile broadened. "That's great news!"

"She wants me to fly out to New York for a meeting."

"That's weird. Can't they do everything electronically?"

I shrugged. "I don't know. I've never sold a book."

"I have, but it was an academic press, so that may be different." He held out his water glass. "To your book. I still think you should call it *Cosmopolitan Pigeons*."

"You don't like *Old World Urban Wildlife*?" We clinked glasses.

He shrugged and sipped his water. The waiter appeared with our salads. He ground pepper over them and disappeared. Dressing filled a little cup on the side of my plate. I should have asked for extra. I scooped it all onto the lettuce, smeared it around and took a giant bite, creamy and tangy, the lettuce forming a nice texture underneath.

Sam smiled sadly across the table, as he sprinkled small amounts of vinaigrette onto his salad.

"Hey," I protested, "my cholesterol is fine, and as long as I hit the treadmill every day I keep myself to less than twenty—okay, thirty—pounds overweight. What's the problem?" I took another bite. "I've got great genes. My mom's eighty and still spry enough to be marrying again."

"What about your dad? Didn't he die at about seventy?"

"Seventy-two. But remember, he lived with Mom for nearly fifty years. It's a wonder he didn't die sooner."

"That's terrible." Sam forked salad into his mouth.

"Yeah, isn't it? Poor guy."

The waiter brought our dinners, Sam's plate a wash of white decorated with delicate green sprigs, mine a dripping pool of blood and sour cream. I grabbed the saltshaker and enthusiastically sprinkled the meat.

Sam shook his head and picked off a flake of fish. "If I figured out how to make this, do you think Ginger would eat it?"

"I don't know." I sawed off a hunk of meat. The rich prime rib almost melted in my mouth. "She's not exactly a picky eater—no matter what you serve, she doesn't eat much."

"You're so good with her." Sam poked at his rice. "That's another thing I didn't expect."

I looked at him. "What do you mean?"

He tilted his head, watching his plate. "You guys connect. I guess I think of myself as the one who's good with kids, particularly that age. But she's different. I can't figure her out and I can't seem to get through. And like you said, that other shoe could drop anytime and she'll start acting out."

"She's not so different underneath, I think. Give her time, once she gets comfortable . . ."

"Who knows what she's like underneath that fake goody-goody veneer?" He shook his head and took a bite. "Maybe I'm more conventional than I imagined. I had this image of you and me and baby makes three, hanging out, laughing, bonding, playing football."

"I hate football."

"Soccer, baseball, catch, Monopoly, whatever."

"You play gin rummy." I sliced another piece of meat.

"Yeah, but it feels more like inmates passing time together than a family. Sorry."

I shook my head. "No, I get what you're saying. Of course, spending time with my family was—never mind. You've heard that story enough." I set down my utensils, folded my hands and looked at him. "She'll warm up once she figures out that we're safe, we don't want her to do anything horrible, and we're not throwing her back." I shrugged, picking up my fork and starting on the potato. "Until then, we need to let her unfurl."

"I guess." He took a bite of fish.

Paul Johnstone appeared by our table. "Sam, how are you?"

"Good. You remember Edward?"

"Of course." We shook hands. "Where's your perky daughter, my rat-loving pal?"

"She's at a friend's for the night."

"Oh, so I'm interrupting." He started to back away.

"No," Sam said, "you're fine. Are you alone?"

Paul blushed. "I was supposed to meet someone here, but it looks like she isn't coming." He glanced around the room.

"We're about to order dessert. Would you like to join us?" I suggested.

He smiled. "Are you sure I'm not interrupting?"

"No, no, of course not."

He pulled up a chair. The waiter appeared with a place setting and took his drink order. "This is very kind of you." Paul waved his hand so we'd continue eating.

"Do you want to talk about it?" I cut my last chunk of prime into two bite-sized pieces.

He sat back and crossed his legs. "It was stupid, really. I thought I'd try an internet dating service, but clearly that didn't work out either."

"Being single is hard," Sam said before finishing his fish.

Paul nodded. "I had hoped—but never mind. Things don't always work out the way you plan."

"Things rarely work out the way I plan." I used my potato skin to sop up the juices. "I've had to give up planning entirely."

Sam contemplated Paul. "It's going to pass, you know. If nothing else, he'll graduate."

Paul smiled sadly, gazing at his hands. "I know. And Maggie's a wonderful, vibrant woman. She has a right to be with whoever she wants." He paused. "Still, I can't help but think this particular choice may be unwise." He looked up at us. "I'd do anything for her, you know."

He looked on the verge of tears, so I asked, "Paul, I don't know what you study—history, right?"

He perked up immediately. Academics are so easy. "I'm interested in the British East India Company, mostly the early years, the transition between when they were primarily a commercial venture and then morphed into a colonial government. It has vast implications for our own multi-national industrial pseudo-governmental complex." He stopped, embarrassed. "Sorry, I get carried away."

"It's okay, I live with an academic. I'm used to it." I signaled the waiter. After he'd taken our plates, dessert orders and a to-go order for Paul, I said, "So, go on, I'm interested."

Later, as we climbed into the car I told Sam, "Paul must be one hell of a lecturer. If there'd been more like him way back when, I might have stayed in school."

Sam smiled. "The students love him. Faculty in his department aren't so sure. He's a bit of a gadfly, always pushing them to reconsider their prejudices."

"He seems like a great guy. Maybe Maggie should take a second look."

Sam shrugged. "Never underestimate the pull of a pretty face."

I looked at him, one eyebrow cocked. "Good thing for me you don't really believe that."

He laughed. "It was nice of you to let him join us. I think he felt better by the end."

"Hey, he was interesting. I'll never look at curry the same way again." I turned the key and started out of the parking lot. "Besides, we have all night."

We heard the music from half a block away. As I pulled the car into the drive, I could feel the rap beat pounding deep into my bones.

I glanced at Sam. "It sounds like the honeymoon is over."

He nodded, looking pale and worried in the moonlight.

The front door stood slightly ajar. I pushed it open. The gyrating bodies on the television drew me first, but then I saw the tangle of limbs on the floor, his pale bottom and her thin legs bluish in the light from the screen. I felt Sam come up behind me.

"Hey," I yelled, and Qian scrambled off my daughter, grabbing at the jeans bunched around his knees. She pulled a pillow from the couch to cover herself. As Sam stepped out of the doorway and into the room, Qian bolted past him and disappeared.

Ginger started to cry.

"Shit." I found the remote and flicked off the TV. The room settled into quiet darkness for a moment before Sam turned on the overhead. I looked around. Two half-full glasses and a bag of chips sat open on the coffee table. Ginger huddled on the floor in front of the TV. Her new overnight bag sat beside the couch. Otherwise, nothing had changed.

"Where are your clothes?" I asked. She pointed to the filmy cover-up we'd bought to go over a bathing suit. I raised my eyebrows. "That's it?"

She nodded.

I looked at Sam. He stared at her.

"Come on," I said. "Let's get you into some clothes."

Her bedroom door was closed. When I opened it, Daphnia leaped against my thighs, wiggling and panting. I picked him up and looked at Ginger.

She shrugged, still clutching the couch cushion. "I didn't want him to watch."

Daphnia coughed once and threw up on my chest. "Christ," I muttered.

"I'll take him outside," Sam offered. I handed him the dog and pulled off my wet shirt. Ginger scampered past me, grabbed a pair of sweat-pants and a tee shirt from the floor and pulled them on. She pulled a pillowcase off one of the bed pillows and began stuffing it with clothes.

"What are you doing?" I asked.

"Packing." She didn't look up. "I'll send back the pillow case whenever I get to the next place."

"Stop that. You're not going anywhere, at least not right now. What's all this?" A trail of broken bagels and torn plastic littered the floor to one side of the bed. I could see the corner of an overturned cardboard box poking from under the coverlet.

Ginger froze. I pulled it out and surveyed the jars of peanut butter and jam, packages of cookies, some candy and a gnawed open bag of bread and bagels. Sitting back on my heels, I pulled out the tea tin we'd been missing for the last few weeks. It rattled. I glanced at Ginger. She looked at me. Her eyes dropped.

"How much is in here?" I asked.

After a long pause she whispered, "Ninety-three dollars and fifty-seven cents."

Sam appeared in the doorway holding Daphnia. I watched him

take in Ginger, me, the jumble of food and the tin, which I'd opened to show neatly folded bills atop a mound of coins. He stared at her. "You've been stealing from us?"

She stared at him, her face pale and eyes filling.

He turned and left. A moment later, I heard the slam of our bedroom door.

I pointed toward the bed. "Get in. We'll talk about this later. Do not leave this room. Do you hear me?"

"What if I have to go to the bathroom?" Her face remained impassive despite the tears leaking down her cheeks.

She looked so frail and afraid that all I wanted to do was to hug her close. Instead, I nodded. "You can go to the bathroom, but come right back. I don't know what we're going to do, but I promise it will be much worse if you leave."

She nodded and climbed into bed. I turned off the light, turned on the hall light, ran downstairs, locked the doors and flipped on the security system we never use. The last thing I wanted was to spend half the night searching the streets for a terrified little girl.

By the time I opened the door to our room, Sam was sitting in bed, cradling Daphnia in his arms. He looked up at me. "I can't do this."

"It's okay, I'll deal with it." I crossed to flop beside him on the bed. Daphnia wiggled out of his arms, threw himself on my chest and licked my chin, his breath an unpleasant mix of bagel and dog vomit.

"No, I mean I can't do it. Maybe the rabbi is right and we need to send her off now." Sam picked at a loose thread in the cover. Daphnia wandered to the end of the bed and curled up by his feet.

I propped myself on an elbow and looked at him. "Rabbi Talia said we should send her away?"

He smiled tightly at me. "You were there. She said that if we weren't going to keep her, we should get it over with now. And I don't think I can deal with this."

I looked at him for a long time while he continued to fiddle with the blanket. My chest felt tight. I took a deep breath, closed my eyes and willed myself to relax. "I think you're overreacting."

"She was fucking the neighbor boy on the living room floor." His voice rose. Daphnia perked up his ears but settled back down.

"I doubt she caused him irreparable harm," I said, trying to lighten it up.

"That's not the point."

"So what's the point?"

He glared. "Look. I know she's been through a rough time but maybe that's the problem. Maybe it ruined her and she'll never be normal. How are we supposed to deal with this? We can't have her sleeping with everyone who drops by."

I could feel the anger rising. I tried to breathe through it and let it go, but it kept coming. "Do you hear yourself?" I snapped. "Ruined? Is this how your father talks? All about what's normal and what we can't have? We're such paragons of sexual virtue that we have to toss out a damaged kid because she made a mistake?"

"What about the stealing? Or what if Daphnia had choked on that plastic bag he chewed open?" His eyes flashed.

"What, you think she's hoarding food and money because she's a bad kid? She doesn't feel safe, thinks maybe we might kick her out. And I guess she's smarter than I am, because I didn't think that was possible." I stalked off to the bathroom to pee.

When I returned, Sam lay curled on his side at the edge of the bed. I squatted in front of him. "Look. Sam. I'm sorry. I shouldn't have yelled. I know this isn't easy." He grunted. I took a deep breath. "Give her a little longer, please? I've grown fond of her and I think we could make a difference in her life."

He uncurled slightly. "I'm not the person I thought I was, Edward. Maybe I'm less Bohemian than I'd like to believe."

I smiled gently at him. "I don't know who you thought you were, but you're the man I plan to love for the rest of my life. If you want me to choose between you and Ginger, of course I'll choose you and we'll send Ginger packing. But I think that would be the wrong thing, for Ginger and for us. Let's at least follow through with our original agreement to keep her through the summer. If you still feel the same way at the end of August, I promise not to fight."

He lay silent a long time. I began to think he'd fallen asleep. Finally he murmured, "August fifteenth."

I sat back. "It's a deal." I crawled into bed beside him and turned off the light. I'd won Ginger six weeks. Of course, if she couldn't pull off a miracle by then, I knew she wasn't the only one who'd pay a heavy heart price.

TEN

I got up a couple of times during the night, tiptoed down the hall and pushed open Ginger's door to check on her. I figured the odds of her bolting at about fifty percent. That might tip Sam over the edge, deal or no deal. But she stayed put, curled in a little ball, blanket pulled so tightly around her chin that I sweated for her as I watched. I finally convinced myself she wasn't going anywhere and fell asleep.

The sun blazed hot by the time I woke. The only sign of Sam was his running shoes by the open bathroom door. I slid into shorts and a tee shirt, checked on the still-sleeping girl and walked downstairs to the kitchen to find some coffee. A note on the table told me Sam had gone in to work. He'd left coffee and fresh muffins, which I took as a good sign.

The coffee had cooled, of course, but Sam wasn't there to cringe when I stuck a cup in the microwave to heat before I carried it to the sun porch to think. Daphnia followed and I opened the screen door to let him out for his morning tour of the backyard. The light, already white enough to flatten everything, bounced blindingly off the wave crests. A light breeze moved hot air around the porch.

If this were any other conundrum, I'd call Henry, but I wasn't sure how the social work fallout would go, especially for Qian. I could picture him apprehended at the airport, detained indefinitely as a foreign national accused of defiling our native siren, his acned visage staring from a newspaper photo, having lost face and virginity in the same instant. I knew that wouldn't be what Henry would want to have happen. I wasn't sure how much control he'd have over what he did or didn't report.

I picked up the phone and called another sober drunk, as always amazed how talking about the feeling of my crisis without giving details helped unknot my gut. I called another, and by the end of my third conversation felt calm enough to face the day. How Sam can survive without support like that is beyond me, but then so is his ability to sip a single drink. Hauling a cooler into the kitchen, I filled it with the muffins, some cheese, juice, and soda, threw in a bag of chips and a package of cookies because they were there, and made another pot of coffee. While I was waiting for it to brew. I called Sam.

He picked up on the second ring. "Hi."

"Hi, thanks for the coffee and muffins."

"No problem. Sorry about last night."

I waited for him to say more, but when he didn't, I said, "No problem. If you need me, call the cell. We might be out all day."

"Okay." And that was it, no questions, no nothing. Guess it wasn't all fixed yet.

I poured the coffee into a thermos and ran upstairs to Ginger's room. "Hey."

She rolled toward me and blinked.

"Get up, we're going for a boat ride." I found a bathing suit on the floor and tossed it to her. "Put this on under your clothes." She stared at me, confused. "Just do it." I left, sprinting into my own room to change and find the sunscreen.

Eventually Ginger appeared downstairs wearing shorts and a tee shirt, her hair tied back in a high ponytail. She looked remarkably like a twelve-year-old girl. She shifted her weight from one bare foot to the other, watching my face. I handed her two towels and the thermos, lifted the cooler and charged through the door, whistling and calling for Daphnia. He came bounding up, jumped once on me, and leaped toward Ginger. Halfway down the hill, I turned to see him running circles around her legs and nipping at her feet with every step.

In silence we opened the slip gate, loaded, and started the boat. After a few minutes, I threw it into reverse and backed out. Ginger sat beside me holding Daphnia and staring stoically ahead like Lady Jane Grey on her way to the scaffold.

I hit the throttle and we flew across the lake, wind filling our ears and flapping the edges of our towels. Still relatively early for a Sunday morning, not much traffic on the lake, only a few fishing boats and the Petersons practicing slalom turns in Pinecone Bay, but evidence of occupation scattered across most cabins. People had arrived in preparation for the Fourth. I glanced at Daphnia, blissfully perched on Ginger's lap, sniffing the wind, unaware of the firecracker torture coming his way.

At the far end of the lake, I turned into a secluded bay, slowed and cut the motor. Quiet enveloped us, the only sounds water slapping the hull and the distant squawk of a hungry eagle. Daphnia jumped down and trotted to the stern bench where he could curl up and nap.

"We call this Loon Bay because there's a reliably successful pair who nest here. Most years you can see a chick or two." I scanned the shoreline. "In the spring you sometimes catch the chicks riding on their parents' backs, but by now they'll be little fluff balls floating near the shore. It's cool to watch the parents teach them to fish."

Ginger turned to look at me. She arched an eyebrow. "You brought me out here to look for birds?"

I stood, hit the seat lever and swiveled my chair to face the stern. "No, I brought you here because I thought we should talk and didn't want to be disturbed. Besides, it's peaceful." I pointed under her chair. "The lever's right there if you'd like to turn around. You want some juice? Sam made blueberry muffins. Here, put on some sunscreen so you don't burn."

She took the tube of lotion and held it, watching me. I could see her mentally paging through potential attitudes, scanning for the right look. Ah, to be young again.

"Look, Ginger," I poured myself some coffee, "it's just you and me in a boat eating breakfast. I don't plan to drown you or yell at you or throw you a bunch of shit. Can we be real for a while?" I leaned back in my chair, still idly scanning the shoreline for loons. "I had a bad night last night and I'm guessing you did, too."

I heard the pop of the lever and a squeak as she swiveled her chair. I offered her a juice bottle, but she shook her head. We sat silently for a long time. Finally, I asked, "So what happened with Brittany last night?"

"She's stupid," Ginger murmured.

"I don't doubt that."

Ginger looked at me sharply.

I shrugged. "Sorry, but I've met her parents. I've never liked them and I know I probably shouldn't tell you that but, like I said, it's you and me being real this morning. I'm too tired for anything else. So anything happen over there last night?"

She was silent for a long time. "We kind of had a fight."

"What about?"

She shrugged and took a deep breath. "It was okay at first. Mrs. Goldstein made us turkey sandwiches and gave us some awesome chocolate chip cookies for lunch. We didn't even have to clean up. Then Brittany showed me her room. It's pink with lots of dolls and stuff and she's even got a TV right in her bedroom." She paused and glanced at me.

I nodded sagely. "That explains at least some of her stupidity. Go on."

Ginger wrinkled her nose. "She has a CD player in her room too, but I don't like the music she likes. It's kid's stuff."

I nodded. "I can see that." I handed her a muffin. She took it and started peeling back the paper cup. "What did you do then?"

She shrugged and bit into the muffin. "Played a couple games, talked, you know. But then—" She stopped and stared down at her muffin.

"Then . . ." I prodded before biting into my own. It was packed with blueberries and not too sweet. I tried not to let the pure ecstasy in my mouth show.

A gull swirled overhead. Ginger broke off a piece of muffin and flung it into the water. The gull swooped down and scooped it up. Ginger methodically tore the muffin into small pieces and threw them overboard. "So then Brittany asked if I wanted to go swimming and I said, sure. And so we changed into swimming suits. I put on the yellow two-piece with red flowers?" She looked at me and I nodded. "And my cover-up. They have a pool in their backyard, which is sweet because it doesn't have any fish or anything, but I think I like the lake better."

"Me, too. Never been much of a pool guy."

"So anyway, we were playing this game, kind of like catch only with a big beach ball that you throw up into the air and the other person has to hit it back?" She looked quizzically at me and I nodded. "We were in about this deep." She motioned flat-handed to her hip. "I jumped up to catch the ball and my swimsuit bottom started to slip down. I pulled it up really fast but suddenly Brittany goes, 'What was that?' and I say, 'What?' and she says, 'Is that a tattoo?' and I say, 'Yeah you wanna see?' and I show her and that's when it started."

"What started?" I picked up another muffin, but didn't offer one to the gull feeder.

"So she says, 'You'll never be Jewish—Jews can't have tattoos.' and I say, 'Why not?' and she says, ''Cause we can't—don't you know anything?'" She looked at me.

"Go on with your story and we'll talk about Jews and tattoos when you're done." The sun felt hot against my skin. I picked up the sunscreen she'd dropped on the deck between the seats and started slathering it on, hoping to lead by example.

She nodded. "So I said, 'Maybe I don't want to be a Jew' and she said, 'Maybe we don't want you, and besides you can't,' so I said, 'I can too if I want to.' Then I say, 'If you don't want me, then why invite me over?' and she says, 'My mom said I have to be nice to you, but that it's okay because you won't be here long anyway.' She gets this real sneery look on her face and says, 'Mom says as soon as those homos get tired of playing house they'll toss you out.'" She sputtered to a stop.

I wanted to reach out and unclench her fists, wanted to promise we'd never abandon her, but thought about Sam and his six weeks. So before I spoke, I unfurled the awning and we were engulfed in shade.

"That sounds ugly. What happened next?"

She looked down at her lap. "She started saying stuff about you."

Damn Vera Goldstein. "What did she say?" I asked when I could be relatively sure it wouldn't come out as a growl.

She looked up, scanned my face for a moment, took a deep breath and said, "That you're a disgrace to your family, a drug addict and a criminal, and she only invited me over because everybody feels sorry for me having to live in your house. That's when I hit her."

I tried, but failed, not to smile. "You hit her?"

Ginger nodded.

"Did she hit back?"

She snorted. "She fights like an idiot."

"I bet she does. So what happened then?"

She shrugged. "Brittany starts crying and screaming and Mrs. Goldstein comes out and starts yelling for Mr. Goldstein. He comes running around the side of the house, jumps in the pool and pulls us apart. He grabs my arm and hauls me out. He tells Mrs. Goldstein to get my stuff because he's taking me home. She says she has to take care of poor Brittany, so he tells me 'Stay there.' and runs into the house. Brittany's crying and screaming and Mrs. Goldstein keeps staring at me with this evil look until he comes out with my bag. She says, 'Don't forget to put towels down or you'll ruin the leather seats.' He grabs a couple towels and marches me out to the car, holding my arm so tight it hurts. When we get home, he opens the door and says, 'I don't want to see you around my little girl again.' I get out and he drives off." She shrugged. "I don't know why they made such a big thing of it."

"So he left you standing on the street without knowing if you could get into the house or anything? The doors were locked. How'd you get in?"

"The kitchen window was open so I crawled in."

"And Qian?"

She shrugged. "I wandered around in the house for a while. Played with Daphnia. Then I saw Qian in the backyard so I went out to see if he wanted to come over."

"Let me make sure I have the whole picture." I leaned back in my chair and watched the light bounce across the waves. "You saw Qian in the backyard so you changed out of your suit and put on that transparent thing. Did you walk out into the yard or call to him from the door?"

"The door." She stared at her feet.

"So you weren't inviting him over for a game of Monopoly or to watch MTV?"

She shrugged.

I opened the bag of cookies and offered it to her. She pulled one from the bag and began to nibble around the edges. I popped two, chewed and swallowed before speaking.

"Did it help?"

She looked at me.

"You felt bad so you seduced Qian. Did it make you feel better?"

She shrugged. "A little." I waited. Finally she said, "It felt good for a while, but then it didn't."

"When we came in?"

She shook her head. "No. I was hoping he'd finish by then."

"That sounds like fun." I watched her shrug again. "I didn't find any used condoms around this morning."

She blinked. "I didn't have one."

I nodded and offered her another cookie. She took a couple. "Thanks for telling me all this. You want some juice?"

"Aren't you going to yell at me?"

I shook my head. "No."

"Are you going to tell Henry and the counselor?"

"Eventually. Probably tomorrow."

"What will happen then?"

"I don't know."

"Are you gonna send me back?"

I took a deep breath and let it out slowly. The boat rocked slightly. We were drifting slowly toward the western shore. "Not right now. But I don't know what's going to happen in the long term, Ginger. I guess it depends on what you do and what we can handle. If you go looking for our breaking point, you'll probably find it. We're not bad guys, but we're not perfect either. Nobody is. Do you want to stay?"

She looked at her feet, twisted her hands together and bit her lower lip, blinking rapidly. She nodded.

"Good," I said. "I'm glad. I'd like you to stay, too. So now we have to figure out how to make that happen. I need you to promise me a few things."

"What?"

"No more hoarding. I promise we'll feed you, and if things don't work out, we won't send you away hungry. Storing food in your room invites in rats or squirrels and I don't think you want those under your bed, right?"

She nodded.

"Also, no stealing. If you want something, ask. We can even set up an allowance, but don't rip us off—it feels crappy." I lifted my eyebrow. She looked down and nodded. "I think we had this rule before, but it seems to need repeating. No sex. I know you're not a virgin, but you're still twelve and that's too young for sex. It's illegal. Got it?"

She nodded again.

A long pontoon boat passed us, its wake pushing us closer to shore. I checked my watch. Soon churches would be letting loose the faithful and the rest would be pulling their hung-over heads off the pillow. I stood and pulled my shirt over my shoulders. "You want to take a quick dip before the lake starts getting crowded?"

Ginger nodded and peeled out of her shorts and tee shirt. I gestured for her to go first. She looked at me a long moment. I could see her weighing the thought that I might take off once she'd jumped. We were going to have to learn to trust each other sooner or later, so I waited. She climbed out onto the ski platform, plugged her nose and leaped in. Daphnia woke and stood on the transom watching her. I dove deep into the cool water before surfacing a few feet from where Ginger dogpaddled behind the boat.

I let her swim for five minutes or so, then hoisted myself onto the ski platform and gave her a hand toward the ladder. Handing her a towel, I pulled binoculars from the glove box and scanned the shoreline. As soon as I'd spotted the loon babies I passed the glasses to Ginger and pointed. "See those two little fluff, well really feather, balls bobbing on the surface?"

After a moment, she nodded.

"Juvenile Common Loons. How about if we come back next week and see how they've grown?"

"Cool." She peered at the birds. "We could keep track, write down what we see."

She lowered the glasses and looked at me. "Like they do in the lab."

"Great idea. You really like working there, don't you?"

She shrugged. "It's pretty sweet. I'd like it better if I got to play with the rats. Or if they didn't change all the time."

"The rats change?"

She nodded. "And Bill's kind of creepy. I don't like how he keeps watching me." She responded to my look with, "Not like that. Like he thinks I'm going to steal them or something."

"He's probably worried about his data. Scientists are like that. Are you hungry? 'Cause I haven't fed you any real food yet."

Ginger smiled. "There's chips."

"Are they real food?"

She shrugged. "Can't we stay out a little longer? I don't want to go back yet."

"Okay. But I should warn you. I have a lecture prepared and you're going to have to hear it sometime."

She wrapped her towel more tightly and shrank into her seat. "So go ahead."

I took a deep breath, looking down at her, folded up tightly in the chair. "All right. Let me start with a couple of things I thought of while you told your story, okay?"

She nodded slightly.

"First, in the Torah, the Hebrew Bible, there are rules against Jews getting tattoos. Probably part of the whole 'don't be a pagan' set of laws. But who knows? Some of the rules seem arbitrary. Like, there are also laws against eating shrimp and wearing cotton-wool blends. So outside the Orthodox world most of us do some picking and choosing. Still, tattoos aren't always a great idea. For example, here's mine, or at least some of it." I turned around and pulled down the edge of my suit to show her the top of the black blob that covers my left butt cheek.

She grimaced. "What's that?"

I twisted to see it. "I think it was supposed to be a tiger, but the guy who drew it was almost as wasted as I was, so it doesn't look like much of anything, except a mess."

"Can't you have it removed or something?"

"I could. But it's a good reminder of all the stupid things I used to do." I hitched up my trunks and flopped into my seat. "Which brings me to the second thing. Most of what Brittany said about me is true. Not the part about bribing social services, but I did do drugs and drink too much. One night I drove drunk and someone got hurt, so I went to jail." I ripped open the bag of chips and held it out to her. Daphnia perked up at the sound. "You sure you don't want some juice?"

She looked at me a little wide-eyed, but reached into the cooler and pulled out a bottle of orange juice before taking a handful of chips. I ate a couple myself before going on.

"All that brings me to the stuff I've been thinking about since last night. It seems that for lots of us there are these turning points in life. Whether you recognize or use them or not is up to you. For me, I had to wake up one morning in jail, my head hurting from whatever I'd taken the night before, and my butt cheek stinging like crazy from becoming some other junkie's masterpiece. I was almost forty years old. Zach, the kid who got hurt, was still in the hospital. I'd wrecked his life and disappointed everyone I knew. It was a truly crappy morning." I reached for the cookies. They tasted like sweetened sawdust, but I didn't care.

"Why were you in jail?" Ginger reached for more chips. Daphnia bounded to her side, watching her every bite.

"Driving while intoxicated, vehicular assault and reckless endangerment. The judge was a friend of my mom's. She encouraged him to 'deal severely with me.' I didn't speak to her for a long time after that. Really, it was probably the nicest thing she ever did for me. It got me to change direction. Since I got sober, I've met some people who did worse stuff before they turned around. I've also met some people who figured it out a lot earlier."

Rummaging in the cooler, I found the cheese. I cut it into chunks with a pocket-knife. Ginger took one, I popped another, followed it with chips, and found a soda in the cooler. "Anyway, it seems like you're at one of those turning points now."

Ginger started to feed a chip to Daphnia but stopped at my frown. I handed her a muffin instead. Probably as bad for him, but the blueberries made it look healthier.

She said, "So you think I'm a bad kid and should change?"

"No." I shook my head. "I think you're a good kid who's had some really bad luck and some awful experiences. But in the end, I don't think the past is what matters, or at least it doesn't have to control your future. What I do know is that if you keep going on this particular path, the one you were on last night, it's only gonna get worse. Right now, here in Lacland, at this moment in your life, you have a chance to change course, invent a new Ginger who isn't tied to everything that happened to the old Ginger."

"So, like I should pretend I'm someone else? What about Brittany? She'll talk about me to everyone." Ginger signaled with her hand and Daphnia sat on his haunches, lifted his front paws and begged. She gave him a bite of muffin.

"Hey, that's good. When did you teach him to do that?"

She grinned. "We've been working on it all week. He can do other tricks. Wanna see?"

"Yeah, but later. Let's finish this first."

She nodded and settled back into her chair. Daphnia leaped into her lap and licked her chin.

I continued, "It's not about pretending. It's about doing something different. Just because you did something in the past doesn't mean you need to keep doing it. And I wouldn't worry about what Brittany says. Once other kids get to know the new you, they'll probably think she's a bitch for talking garbage."

We were drifting close to shore. I turned on the engine and backed up. "Think about it," I yelled. "We'll talk more later." I hit the throttle and headed for home.

❧ ❧ ❧

We'd been back about an hour when the international moving truck pulled up next door. Ginger and I watched from the front window.

"Are you going to miss him?" I asked as a couple of guys carried out the first few boxes.

"I didn't really know him." Ginger played with the curtain. I looked at her. She blushed slightly. "Well, I didn't."

I nodded. "They leave tomorrow. If you want, we can go over and say goodbye together."

She shrugged, walked back to the couch, and flipped on the TV. The unrelenting beat of a rap video pounded me out to the back porch.

❧ ❧ ❧

Sam got home right before Ora Lev arrived for her lesson at three. Ora greeted Ginger with the shy, awkward smile she always wore in our home. Ginger nodded and returned her attention to the TV. Sam led Ora upstairs and for the next few hours we heard the same three lines over and over, first in a clear tenor then in a sweet but uncertain soprano.

"Move on, already," Ginger muttered at one point before turning up the TV sound. I grabbed a novel and retreated to the back porch. After a while, the TV went quiet and Ginger and Daphnia streaked past me into the backyard. Around five, Ora's parents arrived to pick her up and the house went quiet. I wandered back inside as Ora clumped down the stairs. Sam patted her on the back and murmured something. She nodded and disappeared. He sighed and turned to me with a shrug.

Sam cooked salmon with asparagus for dinner. Ginger made a salad and I set the table. As we carried our plates out, she turned to him. "Would you teach me to run? I think I should try out for that running team you talked about."

He looked startled. "Sure." He looked at me. I shrugged. "So when do you want to start?"

"Tomorrow morning?" she asked, setting her plate on the table. "But you might have to wake me up."

"Okay," he said slowly. "I'll come back and get you for my cool down, at about seven?"

She smiled. "Great."

He blinked and sat down. I smiled as I unfolded my napkin. Sam looked from Ginger to me and back again. He smiled. "My marathon is about a month away. There's also a 5K and a mile fun-run for kids. Maybe you both want to train with me?"

Ginger grinned. "Sweet."

I groaned. "I don't run outside." They both stared at me until I folded. "All right, I'll do it, but only if Ginger and Daphnia show Sam their tricks after dinner."

"Daphnia does tricks?"

Ginger nodded. "He's really smart. He can lie down, sit, beg and play dead. You'll see."

Sam looked down at Daphnia, who was sniffing around our feet for crumbs. "So it's true, Daph, you can teach an old dog new tricks?"

"Ouch, that was awful," I said. "Don't be getting ideas. I don't want you trying out behavioral conditioning on me. Some old dogs don't change."

After Ginger went to bed, Sam and I walked down to the dock. A cooling breeze blew off the water. We settled in deck chairs, watching the moonlight and the lights from cabins across the lake. He listened quietly as I told him about the morning.

"So that explains the running thing," he said when I'd finished.

I grunted assent. "But it was her idea. I was as surprised as you."

We sat silently. "Maybe the three of us can work it out," he said after a long moment. "But let's not get our hopes up. Change is hard for everyone."

I nodded even though I knew he couldn't see me in the dark.

ELEVEN

I felt Sam sit up in bed and opened my eyes to see the palest of pre-dawn light filtering through the east window. "What time is it?"

"About four. Go back to sleep. I'll be back for you guys at around seven. Do you want me to reset the alarm?"

I must have nodded because the radio blare forecasting sunny and hot sliced through my sleep a few hours later. A note in the bathroom said, "Eat something and drink some water, not coffee. Love, S."

I stumbled into my clothes and shuffled down the hall to Ginger's room. Pushing open the door, I saw her still asleep, curled around Daphnia, who looked up at me and yawned with a long stretch.

"Morning, Runner Girl." I opened the blinds so sun flooded across her face. She blinked, looked at me and nodded. "Get dressed. I'll meet you downstairs."

On the counter sat two small plates piled with a banana and a muffin. Empty water glasses sat beside each plate. I filled a glass with water for Ginger and made myself coffee. Dehydration be damned, I wasn't facing the morning without. Ginger appeared.

"Morning." I handed her the glass.

"Morning." She surveyed the food. "It's hard for me to eat this early."

"How about we split a banana?"

She nodded.

We quietly chewed our fruit. I ate my muffin. The coffee finished brewing and I poured myself a cup, reaching for Ginger's muffin as I sat back down. "This is a good thing you're starting. I'm proud of you."

She smiled. "Thanks."

The door opened and a sweaty Sam galloped into the kitchen. He scowled at the coffee pot but smiled at us. "You guys ready?"

First, he led us up the hill "to warm up" and I remembered why I hate natural topography. But once we'd reached the top and the road leveled out, I couldn't deny that the vista across the lake inspired. I sucked in the still cool air and tried to keep up as Sam led Ginger through a series of sprints and jogs. After about a mile, he turned us back toward home. That's when I remembered that hills can be your friend, at least on the down slope.

After the run, Sam had us sprawling, lunging and stretching on the front lawn for what seemed like half the morning. Finally, he asked, "Who wants pancakes?" and we trailed him into the kitchen.

Coach Sam appeared again over breakfast. "You've got a nice natural stride, Ginger." He doused his plate with maple syrup in large loopy circles. "But we need to get you some better shoes. How about if I check my email and call the lab after breakfast, make sure there aren't any emergencies, and we go shopping? I could drop you off at Maggie's lab on my way in." He raised his eyebrows at me.

"Sounds good to me." I spread peanut butter and syrup on another pancake, rolled it into a log and took a big bite. "You want me to pick her up at noon?"

"There's a going-away party then for Bo Lin and Qian in the commons." Sam smiled a little sadly at Ginger. "Do you want to go?"

She shook her head. "No. I mean, I don't want to, you know, see him."

"It's okay." I slurped coffee, washing away the peanut butter stuck to the roof of my mouth. "Sam and I'll go. You hang out with your rats and I'll pick you up after."

"Thanks," she mumbled, painting circles in the syrup with a forkful of pancake.

Sam watched her thoughtfully for a few moments before starting again with his coaching spiel, talking animatedly about interval training and sprint trials. I tuned out and stood to wash the dishes, already planning my suddenly free morning. I still needed to iron out a schedule for the New York trip and work up a fresh set of prints to take with me.

∞ ∞ ∞

I showed up at Sam's lab a little before noon and found him bent over the scope with the same young woman I'd seen a few weeks before. He'd probably introduced us at some point but I can't ever remember their names. My informal survey of faculty spouses shows that when it comes to the graduate students, we vary from cookie bakers and shoulder lenders to oblivious oafs. Since I rarely recognize them outside the lab, it's clear where I squat on that spectrum. The student and I nodded to each other, engaging in a barely conscious battle for Sam's attention. I won and whisked him up the stairs to the second floor faculty commons, an internal room with no windows, two vinyl couches and a long conference table surrounded by black metal chairs.

Ruth, in her official capacity as departmental program assistant, and her assistant, Sally Noonan, had done their best to make the room festive with balloons, a long folding table, covered in bunting and set with coffee, juice and a blue rose-decorated cake. We were early. Bo Lin stood chatting with Ruth and a couple of chemists. Ruth gave us a curt nod before returning her attention to Bo Lin, who smiled and waved.

Sam pulled me over to the side table and, while pouring us both coffee, muttered, "Do you suppose we should have told her?"

"No," I whispered back, smiling over his shoulder at the group. "Not unless Ginger's STD tests come back positive."

He looked up sharply, jerking as he did. Coffee spilled over his hand. "Shit."

Sally bustled over. "Are you all right?"

She grabbed a couple of napkins and began dabbing Sam's hand.

"It's fine," he said. "Nothing, really. Just clumsy."

Looking up, I spotted Qian staring at us from a chair tucked into a far corner of the room. Our eyes met for a moment. He blushed deeply and looked away.

"You've both done a great job," I said to distract us all.

Sally stopped patting Sam's hand and smiled. "Thank you, Edward. That's very nice of you to say. She is such a sweet young woman. We should have done this earlier—her plane leaves in a few hours, you know—but with summer school starting last week . . ." She trailed off with a shrug.

"I'm sure she appreciates it now." I watched Qian from the corner of my eye.

People were trickling in. Sally moved to greet them. Sam refilled his coffee cup. He started to speak and stopped.

I nodded, whispering, "Later."

The loquacious Dr. Carter arrived. Before he could spot me, I strolled nonchalantly toward the corner and swung into a chair beside Qian.

"Hi," I said, looking straight ahead.

"Hi," he mumbled.

"I brought you something." I pulled a manila envelope from my bag. Across the room, Bo smiled at me and I waved back. "It's some pictures of the place, the town, a couple of you, some of us."

He pulled the prints from the envelope. A five by seven of Ginger topped the stack. His hand shook slightly as he held it.

"What you did was not right." I spoke very softly. "I know you didn't start it and I saw the way you looked at her, so I know that you care about her. But she's too young and so are you. It's over now, right?"

He nodded, still staring at her picture. "Thank you for not telling my mother," he whispered.

"Don't write or text or email Ginger. Let it go. I know she seems more like a woman than a child, but she's not. Okay?"

He nodded. I patted his shoulder, stood, and wound my way through the crowd to Bo Lin.

"What did you give him?" she asked as I walked up.

"Some pictures to show his friends." As I said it, I winced internally, hoping he wouldn't.

"I hope you gave him a picture of your daughter. I think he has a crush on her."

"Yeah, she's in there." I held out my hand. "It's been wonderful having you next door."

She pulled me into an awkward hug. "Thank you for everything."

"Yeah, um, you're welcome."

With a nod to Sam, I made my escape. I bounded up the steps to the fourth floor. Opening the stairwell door, I ran into a flushed Maggie emerging from an empty classroom.

"On your way to the party?" I asked. She blinked and slowly nodded. I followed her gaze and saw the broad-shouldered back of a big blond turning the hall corner. "Maybe you want to stop by the ladies' room on the way."

Her hand flew to her hair. "Why? Do I look awful?"

I laughed. "No, actually you look quite beautiful. But your shirt is buttoned crooked and your chest is very pink. Didn't I read somewhere that some women get that after orgasm?"

Maggie flushed. "It shows?"

I couldn't help grinning as I nodded. "Better to skip the party than to arrive looking quite so well, um, taken care of."

"Crap." She turned around and began unbuttoning and re-buttoning her shirt.

"Uh, Maggie, I know I'm old and out of touch, but I've heard that many people have sex outside of business hours. They find it more convenient."

She turned back to me with a grimace. "Bill's not available nights. He's taken some sort of part-time job. I guess he has an ex-wife, alimony, all that stuff, and can't make it on a grad student's salary."

"Isn't that sort of unusual? I mean, it seems like none of Sam's students have time for extra jobs." I leaned against the wall.

Maggie shrugged, tucking her blouse into her skirt. "He gets his work done. That's all I can ask."

"Obviously not quite all." I smiled. "However, discretion is usually a good idea. Of course, you can deny everything, long as there aren't pictures."

She didn't look at me. She smoothed back her hair.

"Don't tell me there are." I frowned.

She blushed. "A little sex play."

I stared at her. "After which you deleted them from the camera, right?"

"Look, do we need to talk about this right here, right now? Much as I love discussing my sex life, don't you think I should trot off to the bathroom and see if I can make myself presentable? Unless, that is, you want to start rumors about the two of us."

I laughed. "That'll be the day. Come to think of it, it would probably be good for Sam's career. Could start talk about does he or doesn't he? Only his hairdresser knows for sure. Actually, scratch the hairdresser idea, I've some experience with philandering mates and hairdressers."

Maggie rolled her eyes.

"Sorry. Go fix yourself up. But try to be more careful."

She gave me a little wave and walked purposefully down the hall.

I found Ginger sitting on the floor in Maggie's lab, writing in a loose-leaf binder. When I opened the door, she quickly closed her notebook and slid it into her backpack.

"Ready?" I asked.

She nodded and jumped to her feet. "Can we go out for lunch?"

"You're on. Race you to the car." Of course, she won.

❧ ❧ ❧

On the way home I told her, "I put a box of condoms under the sink in your bathroom. Do not have sex. You're too young. If you do have sex, use a condom. But do not have sex. Is that clear?"

Ginger held her hand out the window and played with the wind. "Not really. If I'm not supposed to have sex, why did you get me condoms?"

"Because I'll be incredibly mad if you have sex and I'll kill you if you do it without protection. Really, Ginger, you're too young for all this. When we get home I'll show you how to put a rubber on a banana."

"What?" She looked at me open-mouthed.

"It's an important life skill. In case you do what you are really,

really, really not going to do for several more years." I turned into the driveway.

Ginger sat in the car for a few minutes before meeting me in the kitchen. It only took a couple of tries. She's a quick study.

❧ ❧ ❧

Bo Lin and Qian's plane was scheduled to take off at five, so I waited until seven to call Henry. "We had an interesting weekend."

"Everything okay?"

"I think it will be, but you tell me." I told him about catching Ginger with Qian on Saturday night.

"You do know this is Monday evening, right?"

"Yes, and by now the deflowered boy is on his way to China. I thought that might make things easier." I paced my office, watching Daphnia and Ginger playing some intricate game in the backyard.

He sighed. "It does, but you're not supposed to make those decisions. You're the foster parent, I'm the case worker."

"I know." I leaned against my desk. "And Sam's freaked out. He's only guaranteeing to keep her through the middle of August."

"And you?" Henry's voice rumbled in my ear.

I picked up a pen and began making tight swirls on a piece of scrap paper. "I don't know, Henry. I'm all messed up. Somehow this has left me feeling more like Ginger's dad but less like Sam's partner. The thought of letting her go feels like having parts ripped out. Of course, the thought of losing Sam, I can't even start to tell you what that feels like. It's not good."

"Does Ginger know about Sam's timeline?"

"God, no, but I think she knows she has to make it up to him. She's asked him to coach her running."

Henry chuckled. "I told you she was a smart girl." He paused and I shifted on my desk. "Look, we're going to have to deal with this officially. She'll need to be evaluated by her counselor. I might have to talk with the police. How old did you say the boy was?"

"Fifteen."

"Thank God for that, any older and we'd definitely have to contact the police. As it is, I'm going to have to pass it by my supervisor."

"I thought this sort of thing had happened before with Ginger."

"It did." Henry cleared his throat. "But there were no witnesses. Ginger denies everything and so do the perps. The only thing we've been able to do was pull one guy's foster parent license. But in this case, both you and Sam saw the actual incident." He paused. "So how is she?"

I looked at her running across the yard with Daphnia at her heels. "Well, she didn't want to see Qian before he left. And now, she's being superkid again. She baked cookies and cleaned up after herself this afternoon. My best guess is that she's feeling embarrassed and scared. But other than that, I can't tell."

"Bring her over tomorrow afternoon and we'll start the inquiry. And I certainly hope I'll see you at St. Sebastian's tomorrow morning."

"Yes sir." I signed off and went to find Sam. He stood in the kitchen looking out the window. I wrapped my arms around him and we watched together as Ginger made Daphnia roll over and over and over.

Sam leaned back against me. "She's good with him."

"Yeah, she is," I whispered into his hair.

❧ ❧ ❧

Sam tortured us for an hour again in the morning, took a quick shower, spread cream cheese on a bagel and lit out for work, leaving Ginger and me to a more leisurely breakfast. As she started toward the living room with her cereal bowl, I pointed her to the chair next to me.

"We need to talk." I took in a spoonful of frosted flakes, savoring what was left of the crunch.

She set down her bowl and spoon and sat.

"We're going down to Henry's office this afternoon."

The color drained from her face. She nodded, blinking rapidly and stood.

"Where're you going?"

"To pack," she said softly.

"Oh, Gingersnap, no." I put my hand on her arm.

She looked down at me, her nose starting to redden. "You're not sending me back?"

I shook my head, my own throat tight. She collapsed against me, wrapping her arms around my neck. I was so startled, I sat there for a moment before resting a hand on her thin, shaking back.

"Shhh." I stroked her hair. "It's all right. They just need to talk with you. It'll be okay." My own vision blurred. I pulled her closer, hoping I was right.

સ્ર સ્ર સ્ર

Sam, Ginger and I ate lunch in his office. She didn't speak, barely touched her burger and picked at her fries. If it weren't for the strawberry shake she wouldn't have had any nutrition at all.

"I booked a flight to New York next Monday." I bit into a fat hamburger, hoping Sam wouldn't notice the bacon and cheese oozing out from under the bun. "Can you guys manage without me for a few days?"

"What's in New York?" Ginger dipped a fry in her shake.

"He's meeting with someone about publishing his book." Sam scowled slightly at my burger while nibbling his own fish sandwich. "Make him show you sometime. See that?" He pointed to a framed copy of the picture of a swarm of feral cats sunning themselves along an interior Coliseum wall. "That's one of the photos, right, Edward?"

I nodded and stuffed the last of the offending burger into my mouth.

Ginger gazed at the image. "Sweet."

"We'll be fine on our own," Sam said brightly. "Won't we, Ginger?"

"Sure." She looked at him and back at me. "Great. Have a good time."

સ્ર સ્ર સ્ર

Even in this small town the local child protective services office, in a back room on the third floor of the courthouse, tends toward chaotic and institutional. Everyone looks overworked. A couple of years ago, they repainted the walls dull beige to cover the old diarrhea green. Ginger and I sat in adjacent orange molded plastic chairs waiting for Henry. I read the wall posters. Ginger picked at her nails. Eventually Henry appeared in the company of two uniformed officers, young guys I didn't know. Ginger stiffened until Henry escorted them to the door, everyone shook hands and the officers left.

"Ginger, Edward," he acknowledged. We stood and followed him down the hall. Stopping in front of a closed office door, he turned to Ginger. "I'm going to have you talk with Mrs. Briggs for a while."

She nodded. Henry rapped on the door and a pleasant female voice called, "Come in."

Ginger looked up at me. I gave her a thumbs up. She nodded and slipped into the room. Henry closed the door and with a gesture led me to his tiny office. He lumbered to his chair. I took a stiff wooden seat across the cluttered desk. He ran a hand through his hair and pointed to a coffee pot perched precariously on a side table. I nodded and he poured two cups.

"What's with the cops?" I asked as he handed mine to me along with a giant plastic jar of dried creamer.

He leaned back and took a sip of coffee. "There's been another abduction. The police were here trying to find out if the kid had any history with us."

"And?"

"She did. Mother's been in and out of rehab. But she's been clean now a while, regularly goes to meetings."

"Anyone I know?"

"Probably. But can you tell me what that second A. in N.A. and A.A. stands for?"

"Right."

Henry took a deep breath, another swig of coffee, and shifted forward in his chair. "Now, I assume we are clear that as long as you are Ginger's foster parent you will not be withholding things from me again, am I right?"

"What would have happened to Qian if I'd told you about this earlier?" I crossed my legs, trying to get comfortable.

"I'd have had to bring both of them in for questioning. Sex with a twelve-year-old is illegal, you know." He rested his arms on the desk.

I took another sip of the incredibly bitter coffee and added even more creamer. "I know, but would that have helped Ginger, Qian, or anyone else?"

He sighed. "Probably not, but you don't have that authority, Edward. Ginger is a ward of the state."

"So what happens now?" The creamer formed little clumps floating on the surface of the coffee. I set the cup down.

He shrugged. "Not much. In a few weeks, we'll get her in to a doctor, check for STDs and pregnancy. Do you know if she menstruates?"

"Hadn't thought to ask."

"Hmmm." He looked through his stack of papers and extracted a file. "Not as of this spring." Leaning back in his chair, he groaned. "My God, it's an ugly business. Bad things must have happened to that girl in the past. And you know, she's likely to put us through this all over again. Do you think Sam can handle it?"

I took a deep breath. "No."

There was a sharp knock on the door and a short, dark-haired woman appeared. She glanced sideways at me and asked Henry, "Can you come here for a minute?"

I started to get up, but Henry motioned for me to sit. "Wait."

I waited. After several minutes, Henry strode through the door, slamming it behind him.

"You showed Ginger your ass?" He stood, glowering down at me.

I blinked and thought a moment. "I showed her my tattoo, is that what you mean?"

"Show me," he growled.

"Excuse me?"

"You heard me." He crossed his arms and stared.

I stood and started to unzip my shorts. "Shit. I was wearing a swimsuit. This is—"

"Show me exactly how much flesh you exposed to your twelve-year-old foster daughter."

That's when I got mad. I rolled my shirt over my head. "Well for starters, I wasn't wearing that." I yanked down the edge of my pants to show him the top of my tattoo. The breeze from a ceiling fan cooled my skin.

He leaned down and snorted. "She's right. That is the ugliest tattoo I've ever seen." Shaking his head he said, "Put your clothes on. That's the way she told it."

"So why did you go all Robocop on me?" I pulled up my pants.

"Because she likes you and I needed to know she wasn't covering." He leaned against his desk. "I was reasonably sure she's not your type, but I've been in the business a long time and learned that anything is possible. Now tell me why you gave her condoms."

I pulled on my tee shirt. "Because, like you said, she'll do it again. Did she also mention that I told her not to get herself in a situation where she'd have to use them?"

"She did." Henry looked at me. "What I said earlier, about her liking you. It's true. It will break her heart if we need to find her a new placement."

"Mine, too."

Henry nodded. "You can take her home now. I'll schedule an appointment at the clinic for next week."

I tucked my shirt into my shorts, stepped toward the door, stopped. "I'm going out of town next week. Should I cancel? Shit."

"Hmmm. No need. How long you going to be gone?"

"A couple of days."

"Interesting. Might be a good time for Sam to get to know Ginger. For better or worse." He ushered me to the door.

I stopped in the doorway. "Bob Goldstein left Ginger standing in our driveway with no one home. She had to break in through the kitchen window. You might give him a call to remind him that's not a good idea."

His brow furrowed. "Nice guy."

"Yeah." I went to retrieve my daughter.

❧ ❧ ❧

Ginger insisted on making supper. I tried to help with the salad, but she shooed me out onto the porch. By the time Sam arrived home she'd set the table and dinner was ready. Nothing fancy, homemade mac and cheese and a big bowl of salad. A nice peace offering all the same.

I've participated on both sides of some particularly ugly displays of adult neediness and manipulation, but with a kid, it's different. Maybe she liked us. Maybe she liked the benefits package. But she'd come close to scotching the deal and she knew it.

Sam certainly said thank you. He's a polite guy. But I could tell, and I think Ginger could too, that it was going to take more than dinner and a run to win him back. Broke my heart, but then, I've always been easy. Of course, chocolate brownies for dessert didn't hurt.

TWELVE

※

ll right, I'll admit it. I hate the Fourth of July. I'm as patriotic as the next guy, but all those drunks careening around my lake on water skis, fire crackers scaring the dog and bombs bursting in air all night always put me in a foul mood. There's only one thing worse than sitting on my dock all day on the Fourth glowering at the jet skis, and that's going to an academic picnic.

Thursday morning Sam made potato salad, Ginger made brownies and I made faces, muttered and stomped around the house. Not particularly enlightened behavior, but screw it.

Finally, Sam snapped. "Oh come on. Stop acting like you're about to have all your teeth extracted. It's a damned picnic. Supposed to be fun. You're setting a bad example for Ginger."

She shrugged, continuing to transfer brownies from pan to plastic box. "I don't mind. I'm used to bad examples. But will there be any other kids there?"

Sam stopped filling the cooler and stared into space. After a moment he said, "Probably a few little kids and, of course, the grad students. I don't think there's anyone your age, though. Sorry."

Her shoulders sank and I could see her struggling between the impulse to whine and her resolve to please. Time for me to grow up.

"Did you say this thing's at Kidney Point?" I snatched a brownie from Ginger's spatula. She looked up, startled. I grinned and winked.

Sam opened the refrigerator and began transferring sodas to the cooler. "On the beach, down from the public docks."

"So why don't we take the boat? We can throw some skis in the back in case anyone," I wiggled my eyebrows at Ginger, "wants to ski, or learn to ski."

"Really?" She grinned and turned to Sam. "Can we?"

Sam smiled. "Sure, why not? If driving the ski boat will keep Edward from pouting, I'm all for it."

"I'll finish packing up the brownies for you," I told her. "Go get into a swimsuit. I recommend the one-piece unless you want to risk losing your bottoms in front of the whole university community."

"Eeww." She grimaced and sprinted toward the stairs.

"Well, at least we know she can be modest," Sam muttered.

"Get over it." I scraped the last brownie from the pan and bit in. "You went to the same workshop I did. Kids who get sexualized early act out. It's not her fault. She's the victim here, remember?"

Sam took a deep breath. "You're right, but I didn't expect such a little Lolita."

"Here, you want the rest of this? She makes a good brownie." I held the last bite in front of his lips. He slowly opened his mouth and took it in.

❧ ❧ ❧

It turned out that one of the history grad students used to spend summers as a ski instructor at a boys' camp. He organized an impromptu class on the beach for Ginger, Ruth's ten-year-old son and a PhD candidate from Singapore. I sat on a log bench and watched as one by one they stood from a crouch, leaning back against the tension as he held the rope.

Ruth appeared beside me. She stood with her arms crossed, watching the lesson. Finally she spoke. "Dad says you're doing good things for that girl."

I managed a startled, "Thanks."

She nodded. "Did you know I begged him not to sponsor you?"

"No, but it doesn't surprise me."

She turned to look at me, her large dark eyes narrowed. Tension etched lines around her mouth. "I told him you were a spoiled, rich white guy who went around wrecking people's lives and thinking money could fix it all."

I closed my eyes, took a deep breath and let the punch settle into that old soft spot. I opened my eyes. "I deserve that. But just so you know, I never thought the money fixed anything." I shrugged. "It's a way for me to keep saying I'm sorry."

She nodded. "That's what Zoe says."

We watched the lesson in silence.

Ruth said, "I wanted to let you know that I'm glad you're helping that poor girl. It's good you're cleaning up someone else's mess for a change." She turned and strode back to the food tent. I watched her go.

Paul Johnstone appeared and handed me a diet Coke.

"Thanks. One of yours?" I asked, nodding toward the PhD student squatting in the sand, clutching the ski rope.

"Yeah, started last term. Good kid." Paul twisted the cap off his beer and took a long slug. He smiled apologetically at me. "I don't usually drink this early in the day, but sometimes it seems like a good idea."

I followed his glance. Maggie stood in the center of a group of faculty. She'd pulled her hair back and wore a deep blue body-skimming shift. Bill stood nearby, surrounded by fellow students.

"I don't think that will help." I nodded toward his bottle.

He looked down at it cradled in his right hand. "I suppose you're right. I probably should crawl home—make it an early afternoon."

"You want to ride shotgun in the boat? I'm going to need a spotter."

He tossed back the last of his beer. "I'd like that. Thanks."

The doctoral student proved surprisingly graceful. He got and stayed up on the second try. It took Ginger three, but by the end of her turn she was crossing the wake like a pendulum. After half an hour Ruth's kid gave up, someone found a tube, and we pulled him around on that. After the beginners were through, we let the instructor do an exhibition show, a series of hotshot moves that ended with him somersaulting out of his ski to wild applause from the beach.

By the time I dropped Paul back at the beach, I knew even more about the sordid history of the East India Company. I also knew his wife died of breast cancer in her thirties, his son's a lawyer in Chicago and his daughter lives in town. He's two years older than me, the grandfather of three, and before Bill arrived in town Maggie kept a change of clothes in his bottom drawer.

"That was so awesome. Can I ski back?" Ginger begged.

"It's fine by me, Gingersnap. But first fall and you're back in the boat." I handed her a life-jacket and the skis. Sam tossed me the empty cooler and hoisted himself in.

"That wasn't too awful, was it?" He flopped himself into the spotter's seat.

"It was very educational." I threw Ginger the rope and started the motor. "I'll tell you all about it on the way home."

๙๐ ๙๐ ๙๐

Sunday afternoon dragged on. With Ora upstairs grinding through her Torah portion, Ginger and I alternated between lake and dock. She rotated in her deck chair, browning in some preteen-magazine-dictated secret tanning pattern. I squeezed my chair into an ever-shrinking swath of shade. Daphnia stretched out limply on a shaded spot of grass near the shore. Too hot to talk, we periodically lurched to the edge of the dock and slid in, waking sharply as we plunged through the cool water.

"I think there's ice cream." I swung my legs over to the side so I could stand. "You want to make sundaes?"

Ginger rolled to her side, looked at me for a long sun-dazed moment and grinned.

As I opened the back door, we heard Josh Lev's deep baritone saying, "But that's impossible. We've already sent out the invitations."

I looked at Ginger, who shrugged. I stood aside so she could slip past me and closed the door quietly behind us. We stood together listening to the confrontation in the living room. I didn't catch what Sam said, but Josh boomed out, "Well, you'll have to get her ready."

The kitchen door flew open and Ora almost plowed into me. She stopped, stared at the two of us, sniffed, and ran her sleeve across her nose. I handed her a tissue from a box on the kitchen counter.

"Why don't you take Ora out to the back porch?" I whispered, cracking open the refrigerator and handing Ginger two fizzy fruit drinks. She took the bottles, handed one to Ora and led her out into the backyard. Daphnia trotted behind.

I sat at the kitchen table listening to Sam's reasonable tones punctuated by Josh Lev's sharp outbursts, thinking of Peter Fink from last spring's crop. Sam had argued with his parents, too, begging them to postpone. But, of course, there was no stopping that train wreck once the invitations were out, airplane tickets purchased, party planned. Poor Pete wouldn't look back on the occasion with pride. Probably neither would Ora.

Josh shouted, "I don't care if she has to live here for the next few months. It's already a month later than we'd planned. Her birthday's in September."

Vera Lev spoke. "We could pay you."

I groaned. Just what this family needed, for Sam to take a second job working with someone else's kid. But looking out the window at Ora, weeping beside Ginger in the shade of the big pine, I knew in the end he wouldn't say no. Ora would be rushed to the ceremony, with or without Sam's help. How could he make her do it alone?

The door into the living room opened and Vera Lev appeared. She stopped still when she saw me, blushed, twirled her wedding ring with her right hand, stuttered a few syllables and asked, "Is Ora out here?"

"She's in back with Ginger. Can I get you something?" She was the sort of short, nervous woman that knots up my stomach and makes me want to do something, really anything, to calm her. Clearly Ora inherited her height from her father. I hoped she'd picked up his temperament as well. On second thought, I could hear his forceful pronouncements battering Sam in the other room and I prayed for her sake that Ora'd been switched at birth.

Vera peered out the window at the two girls. She squinched up her face in distaste but began to relax as she took in the view of the boathouse and lake. "This is lovely. Is the boathouse yours as well?"

"My grandfathers built it in the thirties."

"You've kept it up beautifully."

"Thank you. Are you sure I can't get you anything?"

"Oh no, I'm fine." She watched out the window for a moment more. "Ginger, is it? Beautiful girl. Too bad about her history. Still, I'm sure you're doing the best you can for her. I guess you won't have to worry about all that . . ." She fluttered her hand toward the living room.

"Why's that?" I asked, keeping my voice as level as possible.

She gave me a startled look. "Because she isn't Jewish, of course. I mean, she's not, surely you're not, I wouldn't suppose they'd let you, oh my." She sputtered to a stop. "I'll get Ora and we'll go." She opened the back door and called sharply. Ora's head jerked up. She said something to Ginger before springing up and running toward the house. By the time I opened the door to let her in, her mother had already disappeared into the living room.

"Thank you, Mr. Rosenberg," Ora whispered, eyes fastened on my shoes.

"Call me Edward, and you're welcome."

She glanced up at me with a shy smile and disappeared through the living room door. I watched Ginger throw sticks for Daphnia until Sam slipped up beside me.

"You heard?" he asked.

I nodded.

"It makes me crazy. How do they expect her to do in two months what takes everyone else ten? They won't listen to me or Rabbi or anyone else." He shook his head.

"So how often will she be here?"

He looked at me sheepishly. "Sundays, Mondays and Thursdays. I'm sorry. I couldn't refuse."

"I know." We stood silently staring out the window for a long time. "I promised Ginger a sundae. You want one?"

"It will spoil her dinner." Sam walked toward the refrigerator and opened the door.

I shrugged. "What's that old saying? Eat dessert first—life is uncertain."

"Edward, you can't raise a child like that." He pulled a package of hamburger from the refrigerator.

"What, is it 'Ozzie and Harriet' time?" It was supposed to sound like a joke. He straightened, slamming shut the refrigerator door.

"Someone has to be the parent here." He glowered. "Parents set rules, cook meals, check homework. They don't spend all their time going for boat rides or swimming or eating sundaes for dinner." He turned back to the counter and ripped open the package, slapping the meat into patties as he spoke. "I'm tired of being the bad guy because I want a normal home, a normal life, a normal child for God's sake."

"Normal? What the fuck does that mean?" I steadied myself against the table, willing my fists to relax.

"Oh, right. Normal isn't something you'd know anything about." He was slicing tomatoes, the knife flying through the thick red flesh.

"Like you would? If you had the sort of Andy Griffith childhood you pretend to, why haven't you spoken to your parents in what, fifteen years? That's not exactly *normal*."

He threw the knife down and turned around. "That's not fair, Edward, and you know it. So what if my parents can't handle that I'm gay. Before that, everything was great."

"Do you actually hear yourself? Everything was great? You knew who you were by the time you were her age." I pointed to Ginger, still playing with Daphnia. "But you didn't tell your parents until you were a grown man and they fucking sat shiva and made you dead. You call that normal? "

Sam crossed his arms and glared at me. "At least I didn't spend my adolescence with a bottle, a joint or a dick in my mouth."

"Shit." I took a breath. Counted. Took another breath. Counted some more. "I'm going for a drive. Don't wait dinner."

"Wait. Oh, crap. Edward, I'm sorry." Sam's voice broke behind me.

I waved him away and slammed the garage door behind me.

I drove to Neskame and sat in the parking lot until sunset. On the way home, I stopped at a fried fish place and bought a basket of clams and chips. The breading dripped grease and the clams were tough, but I ate every one. By the time I got back, Ginger'd gone to bed. Sam sat in the kitchen, a cup of tea on the table in front of him. He looked up when I entered.

"Oh, Honey, I was out of line. I'd just come from having Josh Lev bite my head off, got mad at you and said horrible stupid things." Tears pooled in his gorgeous dark eyes. "I'm really sorry."

"Me, too." I sat across from him, suddenly very tired. "I've gotta pack. My plane leaves at eight tomorrow morning."

He stood. "I'll help."

"No need. I'll get my prints and toss a few things in my bag. It's only one night."

He was waiting up for me when I got to bed. Of course, we made love. Even so, it was a long time before I fell asleep.

❧ ❧ ❧

The original plan had me landing at JFK by early afternoon, leaving plenty of time to take the train in, check into my hotel, maybe even eat before meeting the editor at five. Instead, a three-hour delay in Detroit left me sprinting to the train and frantically calling Kathy for directions. At the subway station at 23rd, I popped out into thick wet heat. My shoulder ached from the bag and sweat ran down my back. I checked my watch—five minutes, three blocks.

Spotting the bar, I called Kathy again. "I'm here, but I forgot to ask you, what's this guy's name and what does he look like?"

There was a pause, a rustle of papers. "He's new as an editor. I think he used to be an assistant to the publisher. His name is Rob um, let me check. He said you've met before."

"Morgan. Rob Morgan, and yeah, you could say we've met." I hung up as Rob strode toward me.

He cocked his head, smiling with those beautifully capped teeth I bought him. "Edward, you look great. I got us a table in the back room. You'll love this place." He clapped his arm around me and pulled me into the bar. I shivered in the sudden cold. "They recently redid the décor. Look at the detailing around the windows."

"Why am I here?"

"To have a drink, are you drinking again yet? No? Then to have a ginger ale and talk about your book, of course. Come on, here's our table." He pointed to a chair and I sat, dazed. He plunked down next to me, too close. I started to scoot away, but he stopped me with a hand on my arm. "Stay. It gets noisy in here."

The waiter appeared, a big blond gym rat with a Celtic braid tattoo encircling his bicep.

"I'll have a Bombay Sapphire martini, extra olives, and he'll have a, what, a Shirley Temple?"

"Diet coke," I mumbled. Turning to Rob I asked again, "What am I doing here?"

"Edward, you're always so suspicious." He leaned back in his chair, cat-stretching his elegant torso to either side. "I have this new job. The managing editor and I are like that." He rubbed his index and middle fingers together slowly.

"I bet you are." I sat on the edge of my chair and crossed my arms.

He smiled. "You know me so well. Anyway, when your agent mentioned your book, I thought, why not? It seemed the least I could do after all those years together."

The waiter brought our drinks. "No, you thought, I wonder what I can get from good old Edward now."

"Oh, that's so unfair." Rob held my eyes as he swirled his olive skewer around the martini glass, brought it to his mouth, wrapped his lips around an olive and gently sucked it in. "We were good together."

I snorted. "Ten years of you was one of the worst things that ever happened to me."

"I didn't say I was good for you. I said I was good." He slid his hand under the table and onto my thigh. Rob's got this thing for public sex. Hard to take as a steady diet, but it can be captivating. I batted away his hand. He grimaced theatrically. "I can see you don't want to talk about old times. All business, right?"

"What are you proposing?"

His face slithered into a smile. "That together we publish your book. Simple as that."

"Together?"

"You'll give a little something, I'll give a little something, everyone will be happy." He took another sip of his martini and scanned the happy–hour crowd.

"And what, exactly, do I give?"

He turned his huge blue eyes on me and blinked slowly. "I never go anywhere anymore. Remember when we used to fly to London for the weekend? Those were good times, weren't they?"

I took a deep breath and closed my eyes. Those were good times. Mostly. When he didn't leave me waiting alone at the hotel, uncertain when or with whom he'd be back. I opened my eyes. "Rob. I have a good, settled life now. I'm happy." I tried to think of Sam. "My new lover's the real thing." Substantial, like roast beef, potpie, tenderloin.

"Bully for him. Look, baby, I'm not asking for anything serious. No one would have to know." His hand landed back on my thigh. It felt good, familiar and exotic. This time I didn't brush it away. "It'd be fun. Life's so dull on a salary. It wouldn't hurt anything and might spice things up for you and the new boy." He slid his hand along the inside of my thigh to my crotch. His fingers closed around me.

I leaned back and shut my eyes. Maybe he was right. After all, Rob's like a tasty, fluffy dessert. Like meringue, angel's food cake, chocolate mousse with whipped cream. Like sneaking drinks at my older cousin's bar mitzvah, like the hit from that first toke off a Thai stick, like the clean sting in your nose from a line of uncut cocaine.

"No!" My eyes flew open. I grabbed his hand and slammed it on the table, a wash of terror dousing the heat. Other customers stared at us, so I lowered my voice and hissed, "No. I don't know what kind of sick thrill you get from periodically ruining my life, but you're not going to do it again."

He narrowed his eyes. "I thought you wanted to publish that book of yours."

"Evidently not enough." I stood. "You see, that's always been a big difference between us. I don't use sex to get what I want."

He leaned back in his chair, arms crossed. "Well, I've never had your kind of money, so I guess I use what I've got. The only difference between us, Edward, is that you're too afraid to do what you need to succeed. Get real. No one wants to publish a book of pigeon and squirrel pictures. I was willing to do it as a favor. It's not like it'll sell."

"That may be, but whatever you're marketing, Rob, I'm through buying."

When I hit the sidewalk, I started running, dodging other pedestrians, bag slapping against my side with every step. At the first cross-street, I turned the corner and stopped, resting against a wall to catch my breath.

I pressed the speed dial on my phone. Henry answered and I started to cry. "I almost blew it."

When I finished, he said, "Here's what you're going to do. First, you find a meeting. I'm in the car or I'd get on the computer and find you one. But when you hang up you're going to call information and get a phone number, you got that?"

"Yes." I squatted with my back against the wall and wiped sweat from my forehead. I wanted to curl up in a ball right there.

"You go to the first meeting you can and maybe the second. Get yourself together before you call Sam. You are not going to snivel to that good man about being felt up by your ex. He may have been messing up lately, but he doesn't deserve that. You understand?"

"I won't tell Sam."

"No, you will tell Sam, but only after you've gotten yourself together."

I breathed into Henry's growl. "Right."

"Call me when you get to the meeting and it'd better be soon."

"Thanks." I hung up, stood and started walking and dialing.

Half an hour later, I found a seat at the back of a big meeting. A guy my age sat down next to me. "Jim, alcoholic." He held out his hand.

I shook it. "Edward, alcoholic-addict."

"You new here?" he asked. His eyes held such sympathy, I knew I must look like crap.

"I'm in town on business. Had a bad day."

"You've come to the right place." He smiled.

After the meeting, Jim and I went for coffee. I called Kathy and left a message that the deal was off, called the hotel to cancel my reservation, took the train back out to JFK and sweet-talked my way onto a red-eye. Pulled into the driveway about four in the morning. Sam rolled toward me as I slipped into bed.

"I thought you weren't coming home until tomorrow. Is everything okay?"

I wrapped my arms around him, breathing in his spicy Sam smell. "It is now. I'll tell you all about it tomorrow, I promise. Now go back to sleep. I just wanted to be home."

THIRTEEN

꙲

I woke in the near-dark as Sam swung his legs over the side of the bed. Looping my arms around his waist, I kissed the tender spot at the crease of his hip. "Stay," I whispered.

When I next opened my eyes, I had to blink against the bright sunlight blanketing the bed from the east window. I rolled over and paper crinkled by my ear, a note from Sam that read, "Let you sleep. Back for breakfast at eight. Love, S." The bedside clock read 7:43. I managed to get dressed and have the coffee going by the time Sam and Ginger trotted their sweaty little bodies into the kitchen.

Ginger stopped in the entrance. She looked at me, one hip cocked so that her body formed a graceful S in the doorway. "I thought you were in New York."

"I was." I pulled cereal boxes and bowls from the cupboard. "I came back early."

Sam opened the refrigerator and brought out the milk. "So, how'd it go? Did you make a deal for your book?"

"I didn't like the terms." I set spoons on napkins next to our chairs. "The editor wanted too many rights."

"Like what?" Ginger stepped up to the table.

"Oh, technical stuff. But it wouldn't have been a good deal for me." I shrugged. "It isn't meant to be."

Sam pulled out a chair and sat, reaching for a bowl and cereal. "That editor must be an idiot. It's a great book."

"If at first you don't succeed, try, try again, right, Sam?" Ginger smiled, pouring granola into her bowl.

I sat beside her. Sam handed me the frosted flakes. I blinked hard and took a deep breath. Lack of sleep always makes me emotional.

❧ ❧ ❧

Sam went to work. Ginger took Daphnia outside for a game of whatever it is they play together and I called Kathy.

She sounded frustrated. "I thought we had a solid agreement. Then I get your message and Rob calls to tell me the deal's off. What happened?"

I took a deep breath. "I'm sorry you got caught in the middle of that. There was never a real deal. It was all a bad domestic drama. Rob Morgan and I lived together off and on for years."

"Oh." Silence. "I guess that explains it. I've a few more possibilities. In the meantime, I've got a list of photo requests from *Leisure Living*. I'll forward it to you. They want everything for a Thursday press deadline, so look through your files to see if you have anything that might work and email me back today."

"Sure. Again, Kathy, I'm really sorry."

"Not your fault. Any other ex-lovers I should look out for while I'm shopping this thing around?"

"None like Rob."

❧ ❧ ❧

When I dropped Ginger off at the lab, I stopped at Maggie's office. She was peering at the computer screen and glancing periodically at a sheaf of papers in her lap. More stacks of paper cluttered her desk, teetered on the edges of bookcases and lined the edges of her carpet. She looked up as I stood in the doorway.

"Hey, Edward." She laughed self-consciously and checked her blouse. "I hope I look a little more put together now—at least I think my buttons are done."

I smiled. "Maggie, I am in no position to criticize anyone else. Relationships are hard enough without having to defend them."

"That's a relief." She leaned back in her chair. "Between Sam's critical eyebrows and Paul's hangdog shoulders, I've had quite enough of other people's unvoiced opinions."

"Actually, I'm here to ask a favor." I folded my arms, and unfolded them, unsure what they were telling her about my inner thoughts.

Her eyebrows shot up. "Shoot."

"I was wondering if you have time to take Ginger to a movie and maybe dinner tonight, my treat. I could send her over to her social worker's, but that might feel like a big deal and all I really want is to have a little space with Sam."

"And I suppose sending her to a friend's house is out." Maggie shifted the papers in her lap.

"That didn't work out so well last time. Besides, she doesn't really have friends yet, except Daphnia and the rats and I can't ask them to take her out."

Maggie scanned her stacks of papers. "I tell you what. I was going to work late tonight. How about if I ask Ginger to stay, we'll order a pizza and while I work she can do a major cage cleaning. That should take a while. I'll bring her home around nine. Is that enough time?"

I grinned. "I'll make it work. Thanks."

When I poked my head back in the lab, I found Ginger quietly chatting to the rats as she changed each water feeder. "Hey, Gingersnap, I think Maggie wants you to work late. It's okay with me if it's okay with you."

"Sure." She turned and smiled that great, crooked smile. "Do you think we could pick up Ora early on Thursday? She told me she hasn't been swimming all summer. I said maybe sometime she could come swimming before she does her Sam thing."

"Sounds great to me. I'll call her folks this afternoon." I reached for my wallet. "Meanwhile, here's some cash in case you need to buy lunch or dinner."

She stood very still, cocked her head and looked at me thoughtfully. "So this is like a babysitting thing? You're pawning me off with Maggie so you can do something with Sam?"

I smiled. "Sort of. Except you're getting paid and made to clean rat cages."

She nodded. "So are you guys talking about whether to send me back?"

"No, no." I stepped toward her. "I'm making him dinner."

Her eyes widened. "You're making dinner? Did you have a fight?"

I laughed. "I deserve that. But stop worrying. I'll buy a good dessert and save you some. You'll need it after five hundred rat cages."

"If you guys break up, what happens to me?" She flung a hip to the side and folded her arms over her chest.

"We're not breaking up. You're making much more of this than what it is." I squatted on a stool next to the wall so that our heads were level. "Everything is fine."

"I still want to know." She bit her lower lip.

I sighed. "Fair enough. Sam and I are fine and we're not breaking up. But if we did we'd have to arm wrestle for you and I don't know who'd win."

"And Daphnia?"

"Same thing."

She nodded and unfolded her arms. "So what are you making for dinner?"

I smiled. "Don't know. Any suggestions?"

"Something fancy." She picked at a nail. "Google salmon and pick the weirdest thing you see."

❀ ❀ ❀

The weirdest thing I saw when I Googled salmon is that some salmon species grow humps before they spawn, humps for humping as it were, except they don't hump, they drop their sperm in the vicinity of some eggs and move on. I could have done that.

In the end, I emailed Gillian, who sent a recipe for salmon baked in grape leaves with orange slices and marmalade that looked both impressive and easy. I printed it out and left for St. Sebastian's basement. Half an hour later I said, "Hi. My name is Edward, I'm an alcoholic, an addict and a damned fool."

❧ ❧ ❧

Sam got home around six. He entered the kitchen, stopped and stared. "Where's the table and what smells so good?"

"Dinner's almost ready, and I thought we could eat on the porch." I opened the back door. He stepped out and surveyed the table set for two with the grandfathers' china, tall blue candlesticks and the tablecloth we bought in Puerto Vallarta last year.

"It's beautiful." He turned back toward me, eyebrows knit. "Is everything all right? Where's Ginger?"

"She's working late for Maggie, cleaning cages." I stepped back into the kitchen. "The salmon should be done in fifteen minutes. I think the little potatoes were ready a while ago." I opened the refrigerator door and produced the salad and dressing.

Sam stood in the doorway watching me, his mouth slightly open. "You made all this?"

I shrugged. "The salad's a mixed bag of greens, but I did slice the tomato." He continued to stare until I said, "I have to talk with you about New York and I thought a nice dinner might help."

He folded his arms and leaned in the doorway. Cocking his head to one side, he gestured for me to continue.

I took a deep breath. "It was a setup. The editor turned out to be Rob, my ex."

Sam's eyebrows rose. "Your agent set you up with your ex?"

"She didn't know."

"So what happened?"

I stopped mixing the salad and looked at him. "Nothing really, but, well, can I start at the beginning?"

He nodded, his mouth a straight line. I watched closely as it tightened, and eventually relaxed as I told him everything. The oven timer buzzed as I finished. After sliding an envelope of grape leaves and salmon onto each of our plates, I added overdone new potatoes and asparagus that fell apart as I forked it from the pot. We carried our plates to the table in silence. The candles had blown out. I lit them again.

Sam cleared his throat. "You never talk about that relationship. I don't even know how long you were together."

"Depends on how you count." I cut a potato. Crisp on the outside was a good sign, wasn't it? "From our first night to our last was a little over ten years. But there were lots of gaps." I looked across at Sam.

He picked apart the grape leaf envelope, exposing salmon that actually didn't look that bad.

"It was always complicated with Rob. He was there for some of the worst of my using and picked me up when I got out of jail. On the other hand, on the night of the accident, I was driving around, pounding a fifth of Wild Turkey and feeling sorry for myself after he left for yet another pretty guy. I was never sure which was worse, when he took off with them or when he brought them home." I shrugged. "We broke up for good after I'd been sober a few years. Until yesterday, I hadn't seen or heard from him since."

Sam chewed a bite of salmon thoughtfully. "This is really good. How'd you learn to make it?"

"Gillian."

He nodded and took another bite. "So when he handled you last night, outside or inside your pants?"

"Outside."

He smiled. "Good."

I laughed. "That's your definition of faithfulness?"

"No." He squashed a potato with his fork. It collapsed like an overripe puffball mushroom. "That's my definition of stopping in time." He set down his utensils and looked at me. "I'm not sure what more I could ask for. Your sexy ex-lover tried to use a book deal to seduce you, but the thought of losing me sent you weeping through the streets of New York City." He grinned. "And made you rush home to cook me a romantic dinner."

"Sorry about the potatoes."

He shrugged. "We'll save our carbs for dessert."

"I love you, Sam."

"I know." He picked up his fork and poked at his salmon. "Now my turn. On Sunday, I said some awful things."

I started to protest, but he held up his hand. "No, let me finish. I'm sorry. I was really out of bounds. And," he closed his eyes briefly, and opened them to look into mine, "you were right about it being okay to have fun with her. Yesterday Ginger and I spent the afternoon together. We canoed through the channel to Devil's Lake. It was gorgeous. We saw loon chicks. First time in a canoe, but she did her best with the paddle and we had a good time."

I let him talk, unwrapping my own salmon package. The orange slices fell away with the grape leaves. The fish had turned a nice white-pink. I took a bite. It tasted of sweet marmalade, tart orange peel, salty brined grape leaves and rich salmon. Not bad.

Sam stabbed his salad. "It was such a beautiful afternoon. Then almost as soon as we got back, Ora showed up with her family and all that tension. It got me thinking about families and expectations." He stuffed a large bite of lettuce and tomato into his mouth, chewed and continued. "I think my folks had to know. They were always pushing girls on me. I made a pact with Carol Sanders, a nice lesbian from my high school. We 'dated' for years, but I don't think we fooled anybody. When she came out, Carol's mom said something like, 'I wondered when you'd get around to this.'"

He shrugged. "All that lying and pretending, I don't know if it's normal, but it isn't good for anyone. At least with Ginger we don't have to pretend everyone's perfect."

"That's a relief."

He took another bite of salmon and chewed before speaking again. "I don't know where that puts me with all of this." He set down his fork, clasped his hands and looked me in the eye. "Edward, I'm not making any promises. I can't guarantee this is something I can handle, especially if we have to go through something like Qian again." I started to speak, but he held up his hand. "But I will try to remember that it isn't your fault. I think I'm even beginning to get that it isn't hers either. Look, I'm sorry I got us into this mess and I'm sorry I'm the one who can't deal. But I love you. I know you want her to stay, so I'll try to make it work. That's the best I can do. Can you live with it?"

I smiled and reached across the table to stroke his cheek. "You're perfect."

"Hardly." He snorted.

"Perfect for me."

The phone rang. Sam jumped to get it while I cleared our empty plates. Something in the tone of his voice stopped me from fixing dessert. He hung up as I put the last plate in the dishwasher.

"That was Maggie." He looked pale.

My stomach clenched. "Ginger?"

"She's fine, but there's something wrong at the lab. Maggie wants me to come down right away."

I slipped on the flip-flops I'd left by the door. "Your car or mine?"

FOURTEEN

❧

Huge florescent lights blazed around the parking lot and along the deserted campus walkways, part of the chancellor's new safety program, which Sam and his ecologist colleagues nicknamed the light pollution initiative. Light streamed from Maggie's lab on the top floor of the science building. Neither of us spoke as we ran up the steps. Sam hit the door first.

In the lab, Maggie and Ginger stood before the huge bank of rat cages. Ginger held her notebook open and pointed to one of the rats. "See, the first one had black spots on its front left foot."

Maggie watched her, arms crossed. They both looked up as we stepped in.

"What's up?" Sam crossed to Ginger.

She looked up at him. "I've been filling them out like you said." She held out the notebook; her voice sounded high and tight. I stepped up beside Sam and looked at the paper, a form of some sort. A photocopied line drawing of a rat from four angles topped the page. Ginger had filled in the rat's markings along with some notes. "But we didn't make enough sheets. I've had to make extra copies on the photocopier in the office when the new rats came. I ran out of sheets again tonight and asked Maggie to let me in the office to make more copies and she asked why and—"

"What new rats?" Sam peered over her shoulder at the notebook.

"The ones that come on Mondays." Ginger looked from Maggie to Sam.

"I need her out of my lab." Maggie glared at Ginger. "I don't know what kind of game you're playing, but you may have compromised the study. This is serious research. These aren't pets. We don't name them or play with them, we study them." She turned toward Sam. "And I can't believe you've got your kid spying on me. You know my contract with the pharmaceutical company specifies exactly what kind of data I can collect. What gives you the right to mess around in my research?"

"I didn't do anything." Ginger appealed to Sam and me. "I didn't even touch them or pet them once, I swear."

Sam crossed his arms over his chest and looked steadily at Maggie. "I thought Ginger could use some of her free time usefully, get some practice doing science—you know, learn something? What harm could she do by describing your damned rats?"

Maggie straightened her shoulders. "This is a million dollar grant. I can't take chances."

He didn't blink. "It seems like dicey science if a kid writing down a few physical descriptions poses a real threat."

"Go. Get out of here." Maggie gestured to the door.

Ginger's eyes filled. Sam watched Maggie for a few breaths. "I guess we'd better take you home, Honey," he said to Ginger, his voice low.

"But I didn't do anything!" Ginger stamped her foot.

"Get out of my lab," Maggie hissed.

Ginger glared at her. "Fine, whatever."

I put an arm around Ginger, but she shook me off.

She glowered at Maggie. "Fuck you. I didn't touch your stupid rats."

She stomped out of the lab. Sam followed.

I stared at Maggie. "Don't you think that was a little harsh?"

"You don't get it. This," she swept a hand in a gesture that took in the lab, "this is my life. If she fucked up this grant, I might as well pack it in. Who's going to fund someone who lets kids mess around with their experimental animals?"

"You told her not to touch them and she says she didn't. What harm was there in drawing them?"

Maggie gestured toward the door. "Don't bring her back here. Ever."

"Right." I concentrated on controlling my breathing as I strode down the hallway and sprinted the stairs.

Sam and Ginger stood together on the walkway outside, Ginger's arms crossed around her notebook, her left hip flung out to the side, face red and lips a tight line. Sam's hands were buried deep in his pockets. His smile flickered in the halogen light.

He looked up as I burst through the door. "Rise and Shine for pie?"

"Sure. Tuesday's blueberry."

Ginger glared but followed us to the car.

The Rise and Shine is open until ten. Irene's sister, Claire, was surviving her last hour of work when we arrived. Sam guided us to a back booth, ordering on the way. "Three blueberry pies, one plain, two with ice cream, two cups of decaf and—" he paused, looking at Ginger.

"Water." She slid into the booth across from me, clutching her notebook.

Claire nodded and left. Sam sat facing Ginger. "All right now, Honey, tell me what you mean by the new rats."

"I didn't do anything wrong. I swear. I did everything I was supposed to." She flushed and scowled as a tear ran down her cheek.

Sam handed her a napkin. "I believe you. Really. So show me what this is all about."

She wiped her eyes, blew her nose and flipped a page in her notebook. "I made notes like you said. I named them all." She turned to me and explained, "I decided to give them last names so I could use the same first names over and over because I kept forgetting. So there's an Adam Apple, Adam Bancroft, Adam Christopher, get it? I couldn't tell if they were girls or boys so I picked names I like. Adam, Betsy, you know."

I nodded. "Cool system."

She smiled slightly. "But after I named them all and went back to make more notes, some of them were different." She pointed to a page in the notebook. "Like, this is Herbert James. See his feet? The left one was all white, but the right had this dark spot that looks sort of like he stepped in chocolate."

Sam and I leaned to peer at the paper.

"I see that," Sam said.

Ginger turned the page. "Herbert James the second isn't like that. He has black spots on his left toes, see?" She pointed to the form where she had penciled in a mark on the left foot along two toes. Under a category called "Distinguishing Marks," she'd written in careful cursive, "Spots on left toe, dark hairs at the end of tail, likes to sniff fingers."

"Maybe you got them mixed up." I fingered the thick sheaf of papers. "There are a lot of rats here."

Ginger shook her head. "I mark their cage number, see?" She pointed to a line at the top of the data sheet. She flipped between the two pages to show that both carried the number 268 below the penciled-in names, Herbert James #1 and Herbert James #2.

Sam studied the diagrams for a long time. "How many of these are there?"

"You mean new rats?"

He nodded.

Ginger thought for a long time. "I don't know."

He tapped her stack of papers. "When we first made the data sheets, I gave you five extra copies. How many more did you copy on the office machine?"

"Twenty-five the first time and fifty the second. But when I was cleaning the cages this time, I saw lots of new ones that I didn't have sheets for." Ginger shuffled to the front of the notebook. "I keep this one out for photocopying. I was going to make a hundred copies."

Claire brought our pie and coffee. She'd heaped at least two scoops of ice cream on my slice. I grinned at her. She winked back. I spooned off a dollop of ice cream and stirred it into my coffee.

"What does it all mean?" I asked Sam.

"Let's not worry about it anymore tonight." He forked a big bite into his mouth, chewed and swallowed before focusing on Ginger. "Forget about the rats and let's concentrate on running, okay, Ginger? It's late now, so we can take tomorrow morning off. We'll start working on sprints later this week. The race is a couple of weeks away and intervals are a great way to build speed."

❧ ❧ ❧

We got home after ten. Daphnia greeted us with the frenzy of a dog abandoned for hours on a dark night in an uncertain universe. Ginger leaned to pet him and yawned. As Sam walked her upstairs to bed, I heard him say, "Those sheets were well done. I'm proud of you."

Bet that earned him the lopsided grin.

I stayed in the kitchen, watching the moon streak the lake. After a few minutes, he came downstairs and made a short phone call. We walked down to the dock. I sat at the end. Sam crouched beside me, picking at his fingernails.

"So now will you tell me what's going on?" I dangled the tips of my toes in the lake.

"I'm not sure." He shrugged. "Maybe there's a reasonable explanation. Hard to tell yet."

"So what's the story with the data sheets and the notebook?" I sunk my feet into the cool water.

He chuckled. "Sometime in her first week, Ginger wandered into my office saying she was bored. Evidently it doesn't take two hours to water and feed the animals. Also, apparently Maggie doesn't stay in the lab the whole time Ginger's there, which is an interesting piece of gossip on its own. Anyway, we talked a little and I suggested that if she was going to name them, she might as well take notes. I really did think of it as a sort of busywork thing that might have some educational value. So we mocked up that sheet you saw, I ran off a bunch of copies, gave her that big binder and my code number for the departmental copy machine and forgot about it."

He shook his head. "I only gave her the code because I thought she'd have a hard time filling in the forms or she'd change the names or whatever."

"Maggie's angry with both of you."

He rocked back on his heels. "I guess I can see her paranoia about losing her grant. That would be devastating professionally. On the other hand, if Ginger's right and the rats are somehow getting switched, Maggie might be in big trouble." He stared at the water. "It's not my field, so I really don't know how these things work, but if most of the sick animals got replaced by healthy ones that would certainly make a difference in the results, don't you think?"

"So you don't think Ginger messed up?"

He shrugged. "No, I don't think it's Ginger. Can't really think of a reason why she'd fool with the rats. Pet them without permission, maybe, but switch them around between cages and make up new data sheets? It's possible, but I can't see why she'd do it. But I guess we'll know eventually."

"You think we'll find out what's going on?" I splashed my feet in the water.

He smiled. "That's the thing about small towns and universities. Secrets don't stay secret."

❧ ❧ ❧

I woke again at four as Sam slid out of bed. "I thought we were taking the day off."

He patted my belly. "You're taking the day off. I'm going in to work."

"To work?" I sat up on one elbow and blinked. "It's four in the morning, you freak."

He smiled. "I've got something I need to do now. I'll be home for breakfast." He pulled on jeans and a tee shirt and left. I fluffed up my pillow, rolled onto my side, and when I opened my eyes again, light streamed in the window and Sam stood at the end of the bed.

"I brought donuts." He grinned. "Let's all have breakfast on the dock."

After a decadent breakfast of donuts and cheese—don't knock it till you've tried it—Sam drove back to work, leaving Ginger, Daphnia and me free to waste the rest of the day. We lolled some, swam some and eventually I suggested, "There's a marina about twenty minutes from here by boat. It has the best fish and chips in town. Lunch?"

"Can Daphnia come?"

"If you can get him to stay in the boat at the pier."

She grinned. "Of course he'll stay. That's easy."

I looked at Daphnia. He leaped against my leg, panting. "You can come, but you'd better be good."

Ginger ran up the stairs to change. Daphnia trotted behind, his nose almost touching her heels.

When we arrived at the marina, the lunch crowd had thinned and the afternoon heat settled thickly over us. We found a dockside table with an umbrella that shaded two of the chairs. Ginger stationed herself so she could see Daphnia, who curled under the dashboard on the passenger side of the boat. We ordered two fish baskets and lemonade.

"So, how you doing?" I asked as the food arrived.

"I didn't touch her stupid rats." She scowled into her lemonade.

"I believe you."

She stirred her drink.

"So does Sam."

She tapped her straw against the bottom of the glass. "Good. I hate her."

"Maggie?"

She nodded. "What do you think happened to all the other rats?"

"I don't know. What do you think happened?"

"Who knows? But I bet it has something to do with Bill." She chewed thoughtfully on a fry. "He's creepy. I don't like him."

"Why's that?" I bit into my fish sandwich. Tartar sauce squirted all over my hands.

She wrinkled her nose. "I don't know. He's such a poser. Like, even though they're having sex, I don't think he really likes Maggie. Sometimes when she leaves the lab he has this weird look on his face."

"He didn't—" I wiped my fingers with a napkin, unsure how to finish the sentence.

"Nah," she said. "He's not a sex kind of guy."

"What does that mean?" Fries made from sliced potatoes are simply better. I dipped one in ketchup.

She opened her sandwich and began scraping tartar sauce onto her plate. "You know. Some guys are sex guys and some aren't. Bill's not a player, he's a planner. He's into planning and making things happen, which is why it's weird he's making it with Maggie."

It was even weirder to hear this analysis from a kid. "It all looks like a big mess to me."

She nodded and watched the lake. After a while she asked, "Do you think Ora is going to hate my tattoo?"

I poured more ketchup on the fries. "I doubt it, but maybe you shouldn't show her right away."

"You mean hide it?" She looked at me over her sandwich.

"Not exactly." I pulled off a bite of the sandwich and popped it into my mouth. "I'll tell you what I do with the things about me that I'm not sure people I meet will like. I wait until I know them a little better before I share. If they're still weird about it, I know they're not really my friends."

She nodded, chewing her fry.

❧ ❧ ❧

We picked Ora up on Thursday around noon. Ginger and I took her to the Rise and Shine for lunch on the way home. The kid was so shy around me, it took until pie time before she made eye contact. She had me trying so hard to be likable that by the time we got home, I was ready for a nap. Ginger took Ora up to her room to change. Within minutes, they exploded through the kitchen and out the back door. Ginger looked like a gazelle in a bikini. Ora jiggled beside her, carrying an extra year and thirty pounds. Her thick dark braids bounced as she pounded down the hill and across the dock. They splashed into the lake. Daphnia stayed at the edge of the dock and barked.

I transferred images to my laptop and spent the afternoon settled on the porch, previewing, tweaking and cataloguing. Midafternoon I delivered chips, soda and sunscreen to the dock, but otherwise stayed out of their way. By the time Sam came home and changed into his swimsuit, Ora had relaxed enough to join in an impromptu water fight.

"Stay out here and practice on the dock," Ginger said when Sam asked Ora if she was ready to go up.

He cocked an eyebrow at Ora. She blushed and shrugged. "Maybe we'll run through the Torah blessing," he suggested. "Give you some practice with an audience."

He pointed to two deck chairs. Ginger and I sat obligingly. Ora wrapped herself in a towel. Sam slung another over her shoulders like a prayer shawl. He solemnly chanted the calling of her name. She stood beside him, eyes on the dock. A boat drove by and I had to strain to hear.

"Good job." Sam smiled. "Now let's go upstairs and work on your Torah portion."

Ginger and I watched them climb the path to the house.

"So I guess you got along this afternoon?" I stretched out and Daphnia jumped onto my chest and began licking my chin.

Ginger grinned. "It was okay. On Sunday can we teach her to water ski?"

❧ ❧ ❧

I started the grill, Sam made hamburger patties and boiled corn while Ginger created an everything-in-the-kitchen salad with lettuce, carrots, sunflower seeds, peanuts and dill pickles all smothered in ranch dressing. It turned out more creative than edible. We took plates to the dock and dangled our feet in the water while we ate.

"I want to learn the whole portion for my bat mitzvah." Ginger handed half her burger to Daphnia.

Sam stopped mid-bite. "Your bat mitzvah?"

She nodded. "Ora says you're supposed to be thirteen, but she has an aunt who had one as a grownup so it must be okay if you do it later. She wants to wait until she's fourteen so she can learn her whole portion, but her parents are hung up on thirteen. I figure it might take me even longer since Ora says I'd have to convert first." She looked at Sam. "Does it take a long time to convert?"

He set down his burger and blinked at her. "Um, it depends. As an adult you study first, but children, well, it varies. So you want to convert?"

"Sure." She picked up her corn. "You guys are Jewish. It's weird to go to synagogue and not be Jewish."

"Um, right. I guess we should talk with the rabbi." He looked at me. I grinned.

The kid's good. She knows exactly which buttons to push.

❧ ❧ ❧

Vera Lev was almost nice to me at Friday night services, which I took as an omen that Ora'd had a good time. That Ora and Ginger spent the entire *oneg* whispering together at a far table seemed an even better sign.

Bob Goldstein glared at me from across the reception hall. Henry must have scolded him, which was the least the sucker deserved, leaving a kid all alone on the street like that. Sam followed my gaze. Bob looked away.

Sam leaned in to whisper in my ear, "I told him they'd need to find another Hebrew tutor since Brittany was no longer welcome in our homo home."

I looked at him. "You said that?"

He nodded. I high-fived him. Way to go to bat for the family.

I glanced toward Ginger, who was laughing with Ora. Maybe things did always work out for the best.

Rabbi Talia swooped up as Sam and I stood watching the girls. "That seems to be going well." She gestured toward Ginger and Ora.

Sam smiled. "Do you mean the friendship or the bat mitzvah prep?"

"I take it they're progressing at different rates?"

Sam leaned toward her, his voice barely above a whisper. "She's a great kid and she's working hard. Maybe you could get her parents to reconsider October?"

She shook her head. "I've tried. Do the best you can. Evidently, Josh's mother already has her plane ticket. I warned them that Ora's performance will have to be minimalist. They don't like it, but I think they're resigned." She watched the girls for a long moment. "And Ginger?"

When Sam didn't say anything, I answered. "Aside from that one um, event, she's settling in. In fact, she asked about conversion the other day."

"What do you think of that?" She was looking at Sam.

He cleared his throat. "I think that if we adopt her that would be appropriate."

"Uh-huh." She glanced at Ginger and Ora, shook our hands and moved on to the next cluster of congregants.

I watched Sam. He slowly finished his piece of cake. "Ready?"

"I've been ready for a while."

"What?" He cocked his head.

"Nothing. Let's go."

❧ ❧ ❧

By Sunday, when we picked up Ora for an afternoon of pre-Torah-torture water sports, the friendship seemed cemented in that peculiar instant-superglue way with which young girls adhere. They huddled together in the back seat, giggling as they watched each other eat soft-serve ice cream and exploded from the car as soon as it stopped. By the time I made my middle-aged way to the dock, Daphnia sat at the end, barking in harmony with the shrieking girls.

Compared to Ginger, Ora proved less naturally athletic, but strong. It took five tries to get her up skiing, but once on her feet she bent her knees, set her arms and held on with a steely will, lasting a full fifteen minutes and earning my complete admiration. Ginger followed, gracefully popping up and swinging back and forth across the waves.

"You'll look like that soon enough," I told Ora, who sat shivering in a towel beside me as we spun Ginger around the lake.

"I doubt it." She pushed up her glasses and pulled the towel even tighter. She grinned and shouted her encouragement to lithe little Ginger.

❧ ❧ ❧

On Monday I poked my head in Henry's office as I dropped Ginger at her weekly counseling appointment. He waved me in.

"Sit for a minute." He pointed toward a chair. "We need to talk about a few things."

I sat. "You're not going to make me take down my pants again, are you?"

He smiled. "I still have nightmares about your hideous ass. Please, keep it covered."

"Thanks, I guess."

Henry chuckled and reached for coffee cups. "More evidence that Sam's a saint."

"Oh, enough already." But I took the coffee and creamer he offered. "Anything in particular that you wanted to talk about or am I just here to suffer ridicule?"

"Touchy, touchy." He shook his head, dumping a long pour of sugar into his cup. "We need to talk about braces."

"Braces?"

He nodded. "Dentist says Ginger needs them and the state won't pay for orthodontia. Which means it's up to you."

I shrugged. "Sure. We can pay for braces. Why not? Maybe it will make her look a little less sexy for a while. That could be a good thing."

"Maybe so. It's a long-term commitment, you know. Means paying for the next couple of years. It's not something she can stop in the middle if you guys decide to hand her back." He watched me over the rim of his coffee cup.

I leaned back in my chair and crossed my ankles. Henry's coffee tasted as bad as usual, but I sipped it anyway to give myself time to think. "I'm happy to pay for Ginger's orthodontic work, no matter what happens in the next two years."

Eyebrows raised, he asked, "No matter what?"

I sighed. "All I'm saying is that, while I can't guarantee she'll stay, I can agree to foot the bills. It's the least I can do."

He waited.

I fiddled with my coffee cup. "She's doing everything right to get him to come around. It's almost eerie how she's figured out what to say or do that's likely to matter most to him. But who knows what will happen between now and then?"

He nodded. "Anything I should know?"

I looked out his tiny window. A group of house sparrows pecked at a pile of seeds on the sill. "It probably wasn't her fault, but trouble may be coming." I told him all about Maggie's rats.

When I finished he shook his head. "Sometimes I think God uses these kids for target practice. Keep me posted."

I rocked forward to set my empty cup on his desk. "Thanks for calling Bob Goldstein."

He inclined his head. "No problem."

❧ ❧ ❧

We picked up Ora, and Ginger talked me into dropping them at the mall for a couple of hours. I handed her a twenty and my cell. "I'll be back in two hours to pick you up. Call me at home if you need me. Don't talk to strangers. Stay safe."

She rolled her eyes.

This is a mistake, I thought, but it seemed such a normal thing for her to want to do, so I watched them walk in through the big glass doors and drove home to sit by the phone.

An hour later it rang. "Edward? This is Ruth Blake, Henry's daughter?"

"Of course, Ruth, um, what can I do for you?" I sputtered.

"I'm at the north entrance to the mall with your girl and her friend. You need to come pick them up." My stomach flip-flopped.

"What happened? Are they hurt?"

"They're safe enough. Just come get them." She rang off.

I broke several speed limits and arrived at the north entrance within ten minutes. Ruth stood at the curb, each hand affixed to the shoulder of a miserable preteen. She nodded at me as I pulled up and jumped out.

"Here they are. I found them hanging around the side entrance with Terry Lamer's eldest boy, Pete, and his merry band. This one," she shook Ginger's shoulder, "was smoking a cigarette and from the smell of it both took a swig or two out of the flask that boy keeps in his back pocket."

Ginger stared at the ground. "Ginger." I waited until she looked up. "Is what Mrs. Blake says true?" I watched answers fly across her face. Finally she shrugged, nodded, and looked back down.

"Thank you, Ruth. I'll take them from here." As Ruth released the girls, I added, "I can't tell you how grateful—"

She shook her head. "Kids are hard, Edward. That's why we all have to watch out for each other's." The tension across her jaw line softened a bit. "Some take longer to get there than others, but maybe that doesn't always mean they're bad."

I blinked back tears. "Thanks." Looking from Ginger to Ora, I opened the back door and pointed. "In."

I turned to thank Ruth again, only to watch her disappear into the mall.

We drove home in silence with me trying to figure out what to do, and them scared and young in the backseat. In the rear view mirror, I could see Ora crying quietly and Ginger huddled with her knees clasped to her chest. The clock gave me about an hour before Sam was due home for Ora's lesson.

I pulled the car into the garage and shut it off. We sat in silence for a few seconds before I turned on my lecture. Starting with violation of trust, I ran them through smoking, drinking, and hanging out with older boys. By the end, Ora sat sobbing and tears streamed down Ginger's face.

"Are you going to tell my folks?" Ora croaked.

Josh Lev's angry visage swam before my eyes. Of course, I should. What responsible parent wouldn't? "No," I said finally. "Not this time. But if I ever think you've been drinking again, I'll tell them everything and maybe even make some stuff up."

She gasped, gulped back her tears and nodded quickly. "Now go on in and wash your faces. Sam will be home any minute."

Ora flung open the door and slid out.

Ginger bit her lower lip. "Are you going to tell Sam?"

"Of course. Henry, too. I can hardly keep this a secret from him since it was his daughter who caught you."

She shuddered and climbed out. I emerged from the car slowly, feeling about a hundred years old.

When Sam flew in the door, he took one look at the girls' blotchy faces. "What's wrong?"

"I'll tell you later. You ready?" I asked Ora.

She nodded.

"Okay." I looked at Sam. "We'll be on the back porch if you need us."

I placed a hand on Ginger's shoulder, spun her around and pushed her toward the porch. Sam raised his eyebrows inquisitively. I shook my head. "Later. Enjoy your lesson. I'm guessing Ora will be particularly eager to please today."

I grabbed a couple of fruity sodas as we passed through the kitchen, handed one to Ginger, and pointed her toward a chair. Sitting beside her, I opened my bottle and took a long pull before speaking. Ginger sat quietly, holding her unopened drink.

Eventually I asked, "So what the fuck were you doing? Is this about Maggie and the rats? Because if it is, you have to figure out another way to blow off steam."

"I was just . . ." She trailed off. Tears welled. I waited, but she sat staring at her knuckles.

"Gingersnap," I softened my voice. "Don't do this. I know it's hard and we're asking you to make so many changes, but you can't keep using sex to make yourself feel better. For one thing, it doesn't seem to work."

"I was only being friendly. Pete and the guys were being nice. Don't you want me to have any fun?" She hugged her knees.

I leaned back in my chair. "Friendly? You don't really think that's what was going on, do you? Teenage boys feeding booze to young girls are being nice? You're not stupid, Ginger, and you're not naïve and on some level you knew exactly what was going on."

"What's naïve?" Her head rested on her knees.

I watched her watch me while I framed my response. "Naïve means you think the world is a safe place. I'm guessing that's not you."

She scowled. "That's just stupid."

"Maybe, but it's probably a nice way to live."

She shrugged.

I propped my feet on a footstool. "You're right, though. Pete Lamer's group will envelop you like part of the family. You won't have to try to get them to like you. Of course, you'll need to service them appropriately." I paused to watch her blink and take a deep breath. "And you'll be stuck living that life for good. I don't think you want that."

She huddled into a ball, her hair draped over her knees.

I placed my hand lightly on her shoulder. "This is your chance to get out. It's up to you."

"Do you think Sam will send me away?" she whispered.

I took a deep breath thinking, not much gets past this kid. "Not if I can help it. But please. Try to stay out of trouble. For my sake. I've grown fond of you, Gingersnap. It would be lonely here without you."

She sniffed, uncurled and sat up. She gave me a sad, crooked smile and nodded. "I'll try."

"And don't drink. It makes you stupid."

She nodded again.

❦ ❦ ❦

Ora looked presentable by the time the car horn blew and she came back downstairs and waved goodbye. Sam followed her to the car and chatted with Josh for a few minutes. I heated leftovers. Ginger made a salad. The phone rang as we were setting the table. Sam answered.

A few minutes later, he appeared in the kitchen doorway looking pale. "That was Naomi. My mom's had a stroke."

FIFTEEN

✼

It's funny how priorities can change in an instant. One minute you're trying to figure out how to talk about a bit of flirtation, a swig and a puff at the mall, and the next you're at a whole different level of human complexity.

"She thinks I should go out there." Sam stared blankly at his uneaten food. "Says Mom wants to see me. But Dad?" He stopped, breathing back tears. "He doesn't know she's been in contact."

"I don't get it," Ginger said. "Why wouldn't you go visit your mom if she's sick?"

Sam focused on her. "She'd be your foster grandmother, I guess. What a funny thought." He shook his head. "It's complicated. You see, I haven't seen or spoken to my folks in years. I send letters that don't get answered." He shrugged. "My sister sometimes slips me notes from my mom." He passed a hand over his forehead. "God, that sounds sick, doesn't it?" Straightening up, he looked at Ginger. "My father thinks homosexuality is a sin against God. When I came out, he made me dead. Mom's gone along, but sometimes she cheats, through Naomi."

Ginger stared at him. "Made you dead? You mean he pretends you don't exist."

"Essentially."

"Wow." She took a bite of salad and chewed thoughtfully. "So you do fit with Edward and me. Sorry about your parents, but I'm glad you're not as normal as you look."

Sam snorted. "Thanks, I guess. So what was all that fuss about earlier?"

Ginger paled.

I said, "We'll talk about it later. First we need to work on your Rhode Island travel plans."

❧ ❧ ❧

Another couple of phone calls, a quick internet search for flights and it was done. Sam had an open-ended ticket to Providence where Naomi would pick him up and drive him directly to the hospital. While Ginger took in a movie downstairs, I watched Sam fill an overnight bag.

"Do you want me to come with you?" I leaned in the bathroom doorway as he gathered his toothbrush and comb.

"God, no," he breathed, glancing up apologetically. "I'm sorry. Thank you. That was a sweet offer. I'm not even sure I should go, but you'd be more than they could take."

I let him pass into the bedroom. "I could get a hotel and wait for you."

He shook his head. "Stay here with Ginger. I'll be home soon." He stuffed a couple of tee shirts into his bag. "So what happened with Ginger and Ora today?"

I watched him pull socks and underwear from his drawer, wondered briefly if I should lie or minimize or what. But I couldn't do that with Sam. "Ruth caught her flirting with some older boys. There was evidently alcohol and a cigarette involved."

He looked up, eyebrows lifted, then continued packing. "I guess that's progress."

Sometimes it's wonderful when people surprise you. "I thought you'd freak."

He shrugged. "Moving from fucking to flirting seems like the right direction. Ora was quite subdued, so I assume you expressed your displeasure." He zipped the bag, dropped it on the floor and collapsed onto the bed. "Do you realize it's been almost fifteen years since I've seen my folks?"

"How do you feel?"

He shook his head. "Surreal. Scared. Make that terrified. For all I know, Dad won't let me see either of them."

"Maybe." I sat beside him and patted his knee. "But your mom will know you came."

"Right. Do you think there's chocolate fudge ice cream left?"

"If not, I'll drive to the store and get you some. With marshmallows or without?"

"You choose. I'll be watching whatever awful movie Ginger picks."

Much later, after surviving a teen slasher movie and gorging ourselves on ice cream, we sat on the back porch watching the fireflies.

Sam stared out into the night. "I don't want you there, but I know I'll need you. Keep your cell phone charged, all right?"

"Sure. Call as often as you like."

❦ ❦ ❦

On the way home from dropping Sam at the airport, I hit the early-bird meeting at St. Mary's. Not one I usually make, but while Sam flew and Ginger slept, I needed to re-center. Sometimes I forget that I'm one slip away from a new bottom. When times get stressful I need some help remembering how complicated my life could get. This time my reminder came in the form of a kid in his twenties, just out of treatment. His hands shook as he told his story. The rest of us told ours and by the time the meeting ended, I thought maybe everything would all be okay after all. Henry met me for coffee at the Rise and Shine. That helped, too.

Ginger was awake, watching TV when I got home. She sat on the floor, cereal bowl held under her chin, dropping the occasional frosted flake into Daphnia's open mouth.

"Are we out of dog treats?"

She scrunched up her face. "He likes these."

"They're bad for him." I passed into the kitchen, started another pot of coffee and located the dog treats. Ginger met me at the door, took the treats and brought them, along with her frosted flakes and a very attentive dog, into the kitchen. She sat at the kitchen table, Daphnia on his haunches at her feet.

She held up a dog treat. "Want to dance?"

Daphnia leaped onto his hind legs, paws clawing the air and did a lovely pirouette. "Good boy." She gave him the treat. "So Sam's parents don't talk to him and supposedly I have an aunt who does. And I think he said I have cousins?"

I nodded.

"Anyone else I should know about? For example, do you have parents?"

I laughed and poured myself a bowl of cereal. "My family is complicated." She stared at me until I started talking again. "Right, I guess that means your family is complicated, too. Actually, yours is even more complicated. To begin with, I'm almost positive my grandfather was gay."

And I told her about the grandfathers, how they raised Gillian and sheltered me and how my mother never approved of her father-in-law. "My father died years ago. In all sorts of ways, my mother and I made each other miserable for a long time. She's remarried now and living in Florida. We don't talk much. You'll probably have to meet her, but I'm not up to that yet."

"Florida? Can we visit her and go to Disney World?"

I groaned. "Maybe. But you should know, she's not a cuddly sort of grandma. She won't make you cookies or knit mittens. And you won't like her. Nobody does. Except her new husband. At least I think he likes her. Let's wait a while on the visit."

She shrugged. "Do you have pictures?"

I blinked. "Yeah. I've got pictures."

We spent the rest of the morning looking at photos. I told my stories. She asked questions. Eventually it all started to feel very familiar, so I dug out the old, old albums from the attic, full of images of Grandpa Wolf and Grandpa Rosenburg camping, fishing, climbing the pyramids. I told their stories as I remembered them from long rainy afternoons when Gillian and I sat at the same table, trying to picture their lives before us.

My cell phone vibrated. "Sam?"

"My flight gets in at ten tonight. Can you pick me up?" His voice was a thick whisper in my ear.

"Of course." I stepped out onto the porch. Ginger followed. "Did you get to see her?"

"For a few minutes. Naomi lured him to the cafeteria and I snuck in." His breath caught. "She cried. But she didn't want me to stay. Afraid he'd catch her talking to me."

"Oh, darlin'." What else could I say?

Ginger looked a question at me. I mouthed, "He's coming home."

She nodded and left.

"Where are you?" I asked Sam.

"On a bench outside the hospital. I tried—I tried to talk with him in the cafeteria. Edward, he saw me, I know he recognized me. But he looked right through me and walked the other way." He sobbed. "I need to come home."

❦ ❦ ❦

Ginger and I met him with flowers. She'd painted a big sign that read, "Welcome home." and held it above her head at the little chute beside security where passengers funnel out. He saw us, smiled, and burst into tears. We hurried to the car where I handed him the tissue box and Ginger plied him with brownies.

"Do you want to talk about it?" I asked once we'd pointed Ginger toward bed.

He shook his head. "I'm just glad I'm home. But I don't want to be a rejecting father, okay?"

"Okay."

"I mean it. I'm in. No deadlines, no conditions. I am not my father."

I held him very, very close.

❦ ❦ ❦

Later in the week, I talked Ginger into accompanying me to Neskame for one last batch of photos. My book might be dead, but there was still a brochure to finish. Of course, while wetlands in mid-July are beautiful, we had to squirt so much bug spray on each other that the occasional loose leaf stuck to our flesh.

Once on the boardwalk through the marsh, Ginger managed to stay silent for approximately thirty-seven seconds. But "Do you think virginity is a big deal?" isn't the sort of question you're supposed to shush.

"Um, for me it felt like a big deal at the time, but in retrospect, no, I guess not." The sun burned down and a green darner dragonfly whizzed past, its wings buzzing. "Why do you ask?"

"Ora was talking about it. I didn't tell her anything, but I think she knew. Maybe everybody knows." Ginger swiped at a patch of reed canary grass.

I turned around to look at her. "How does that feel?"

She scowled. "You sound like a counselor. How do you think it feels?"

"Sorry." I started walking again. "I bet it feels scary and maybe embarrassing."

She followed. "Kind of. And like I'm gonna throw up when I picture other people talking about me. I wish I could wake up one morning and it would be different. Nobody would know and maybe I'd have grown up here all along and none of that other stuff would have happened."

We'd come to a wide point in the boardwalk. A bench set back from the path afforded a view of the wide expanse of open water that formed the core of the marsh. Laying down my equipment, I sat, and gestured for Ginger to take a seat beside me. Our movements startled a red-winged blackbird.

"You can actually make that happen," I said after a silence.

She gave me that look teenagers throw at particularly dense adults. "Yeah, right."

I shrugged and crossed my legs. "I did. Sure, there are some people like the Goldsteins who still remember what I was like in my using days. But mostly people know me as I am now, which may not be perfect but is sort of respectable." I glanced over at her. "And everything that happened to me was my own fault. Imagine how easy it will be for you to change what they think, since you didn't do anything wrong."

She looked at me as if I was crazy. "Excuse me? Didn't do anything wrong? You don't have a clue."

I held her gaze. "I don't know exactly, but I think I have some idea of what happened and I don't think you had much choice in the matter, did you?"

She looked away.

"Here's the thing." I looked out over the marsh. "When you're a kid, you depend on the people around you. It's not like you could have gone out and found a job to feed yourself, right? You've got nothing to be ashamed of, Gingersnap. I think you're one of the bravest people I've ever met."

While her expression didn't change, tears pooled in her eyes. One escaped down her cheek. I handed her a tissue. She wiped her eyes and blew her nose. We sat again in silence.

The breeze picked up and the buzz of mosquitoes died down. After a long time, she spoke, her voice flat. "Sometimes I liked it."

I nodded. "Of course you did."

Her head whipped around.

"We all need affection. I bet you weren't getting it any other way."

She stared at me.

I shrugged. "I probably shouldn't tell you this, but when I was in high school I used to let myself get picked up by older, mostly married men. In my case, I had a choice and I made the wrong one, but I remember that feeling, like maybe this was what love felt like. Of course, it wasn't, and I felt more lonely after. Maybe it was a little like that for you?"

That's when she really started crying. It was like watching a slow-motion film. At first, her face crumbled and she shook. Then a single sob seemed to rumble through her entire body, followed by another and another until she gasped for breath like a wailing toddler. I wrapped an arm around her. First she held herself rigid but slowly she melted into me and buried her face in my chest.

The thing about crying is that it always ends. I ran out of tissues and shrugged off my tee shirt. I wiped my own eyes on one corner before giving her the whole thing. That, of course, made me a large, succulent target for momma mosquitoes, so we gathered up the gear and sprinted for the car.

"You really are great, Ginger," I told her on the drive home. "And it won't take long for kids around here to figure that out. Having a past makes you more interesting. But it's the present and future that matter most."

She hiccupped. "Hope so."

We drove in silence punctuated by her sniffles. I pulled the car into the garage and turned off the engine. As I was opening the door, she spoke, her voice barely audible. "I think there are pictures."

My stomach did one of those slow, awful rolls. "Where?"

But of course I knew the answer. Where are all the twenty-first-century nightmare pictures stored?

"Online." She sat staring at her folded hands, her hair hiding her expression.

"Do you know where online?"

She shook her head.

"Maybe they're not really there."

She looked at me with disbelieving, reddened eyes. Right.

I gripped the door handle. "Let's go in."

She opened her door and slid out. Daphnia greeted her at the garage door. She patted his head absently and trudged upstairs to her room.

Henry answered on the second ring. I sat on the back porch watching the lake and recounted the events of the afternoon. I finished with, "Finding those pictures might help you find and prosecute whoever did this to her."

He sighed. "That's an impossible task, Edward. Do you have any idea how many child pornography sites are out there? And since it's illegal, there won't be anything to identify either the perps or the kids, which for her is a blessing. I doubt that after your fine makeover, anyone will recognize her from those pictures."

"That's going to be hard for her to believe. I know what it's like to have embarrassing things become public knowledge." A speedboat flew by, sending waves splashing against the shore.

"So do I." His voice rumbled in my ear. "That's kind of the humbling that brought me to sobriety. Sad thing for Ginger and kids like her is that it continues their victimization. So how are you doing with all this?"

"Between Ginger and Sam, I feel surrounded by unresolved childhoods, so all my memories are churned up, too. Nothing like what must have gone on for Ginger, still, it gets you going, like that training session predicted." One thing I love about Henry as a sponsor, he can talk me through anything. We talked and talked until I could feel the breeze on the porch, smell the dry summer pine, and feel myself ease back into the moment, sitting on my porch watching sunlight dance across the waves.

That night Sam and I lay on top of the covers, the ceiling fan twirling feebly through the hot air. I told him everything, even how my chest felt blown open holding her shaking, wounded child body.

He took my hand. "I wonder what really happened."

The next morning, Ginger ran sprints like demons chased her. And maybe they did.

❧ ❧ ❧

By race day Sam looked buff, Ginger fast, and I could lope three miles without stopping. Ginger insisted she wanted to skip the kid's fun run and compete with me in the 5K, by which, of course, she meant she'd stand at the start with me, wave goodbye as she passed the other slow pokes and greet me, looking rested and cheerful, at the finish. Since I always associate outdoor running with humiliation, this made perfect sense to me.

Sam's race began first, so Ginger and I drove with him to cheer him across the starting line. Maybe a hundred people milled around, women in lycra, men wearing loose mesh shorts, their numbers pinned to sleeveless tees. Sam intended to run the 26-plus miles in under four hours. He seems like such a sane man most of the time, but this wasn't one of them. The starting official was a local car salesman who had run every race in the state until his knee blew out, which left him holding the gun and shooting the opening volley as other people jogged past him. The shot cracked through the early morning air and we waved and hollered and watched Sam trot off. When he turned the first corner, Ginger and I walked back to the car, our starting line ten miles and two hours away.

About twice as many people formed a thick press behind the self-same, magically transported starting official.

I passed Tess Conway on my way from the bathroom. I grinned at her. "Getting in shape for patrolling the grade school again next fall?"

"Very funny." She grimaced. "Newspaper this morning said they've caught the bastard. Missed you at the last Nature Conservancy meeting."

I bent to retie my shoes. "I've been busy. Did I miss anything?"

"Joining the planning committee for the winter fundraising dinner." She grinned. "But it's never too late."

I stood and smiled my most charming boyish grin. "I'm way overbooked, Tess. Can I send a check instead?"

She cocked her head. "Sure, it's a fundraiser, right?"

The crowd parted for a group of athletically clad folk in fancy-looking three-wheeled sports wheelchairs. I looked up as Zach grinned and waved. "Hey, Mr. Rosenberg. Have a great race."

"You, too." I waved, too late, and watched as he spun through the press of runners.

Jan and Lois from the Wednesday one-thirty meeting greeted me. "Hey, Edward," Jan said. "Where've you been?"

"Busy. How are you guys?" I watched Zach disappear.

"Not bad." Jan considered me. "You're not coming to meetings. Should we worry about you?"

"No, I'll be back in September when school starts. In the meantime, I'm catching a few here and there. Have you seen my daughter? About this high, skinny, ponytail?" I scanned the crowd.

"I didn't know you had a daughter." Lois fiddled with the safety pin on her number sheet. "I can't get this thing fastened. Can you help?" She turned to Jan.

"Are you running or walking?" Jan refastened Lois' pin.

I grimaced. "Running, sort of."

"Well, you'd better get closer to the front of the pack. This is the walker section. We'd hate to slow you down."

I grinned. "I'm slow enough on my own. Good luck."

"You, too. Hope you find your daughter."

I pressed on. Ginger had wiggled her way toward the front. It took more helloing and excuse me's and sheepish grins, but eventually I stood beside her. I helped her tie the timing chip onto her running shoe and wished her luck. She gave me a wide smile, a thumbs up and turned her full attention to the gun.

"Remember Sam said not to run too fast at the beginning," I reminded her.

She grinned.

The gun spoke and we pressed forward with the accelerating crowd. Ginger took off. I lost sight of her after the first corner. Zach rolled by and grinned at me, thick arms pumping the slanted wheels of his low-slung chair. When had he started racing? My chest ached. Watching him race felt too much like forgiveness. I slowed, letting everyone and their great aunt pass me, and settled into my own pack of limpers. The course led us past the lake, circled Bass Bay, passed the high school, and returned through a wooded neighborhood and across the old railroad trestle back to the park.

I found myself pacing two teenaged girls. They'd sprint ahead and a few minutes later, when they slowed to walk and talk, I'd return the favor. Tortoise and the hare, except I knew from the start that the tortoise didn't stand a chance.

I had to admit it was a great day for an August race. Overnight a front had moved in and thunderclouds rumbled. The wind picked up as we crossed the two-mile marker. And I'd been worried about heat stroke.

With the trestle in sight, I found something resembling a sprint. Felt good about it, too, at least before I got chilled by the wind from the girls whipping past me. Thunder rolled, a lightning bolt cracked across the sky. Ginger yelled, "Go, Papa!" and I hit the timing pad as hard as I could. Thirty-six minutes—not exactly an eight-minute mile, but there I was grinning like a crazy man. What a sap. So what if I didn't have as much time as I used to?

"What took you so long?" She led me to the snack table. "I've been here for ages."

"Oh, yeah? How long?" The cookies looked homemade. I grabbed a cup and filled it with bright orange liquid from a ten-gallon jug.

"Look." She pulled me to the board with posted results. "Ginger McIntyre, 22:47. Second place in my age group."

"Wow. And it looks like you're the fastest girl under eighteen."

I glanced at the wheelchair results. Zach's name topped the list, 20:53. Holy shit.

A tall, thin man wearing a navy-blue jogging suit approached. "Mr. McIntyre?"

"Actually, it's Rosenberg."

His eyebrows pinched together. "Are you related to Ginger?"

"I guess so. I'm her papa." Something flip-flopped in my stomach as the word rolled off my tongue. Ginger smiled up at me.

"Great." He held out his hand. "I'm Gus Winders, the middle school coach. Any chance Ginger's starting at Lacland this fall?"

"I certainly hope so."

We shook. He patted her shoulder. "Cross country tryouts are the first week. I'd love to have you on the team."

She beamed.

The rain held off until eleven. Ginger and I huddled with all the other watchers under the awning over the food table. I weaseled my way into a particularly convenient location near the oatmeal cookies. Sam's goal had been to make it back by eleven-fifty. At half-past, I sprinted through the downpour to the car, found the big umbrella, picked up Ginger at the tent and escorted her to the finish line in time for us to both yell, "Go, Sam!"

Red-faced and soaking wet, his smile couldn't have been wider. The scoreboard flashed 3:46 as his foot hit the timing pad.

I handed Ginger the umbrella. She ran to him, already babbling about her race and the track coach. I stopped by the food table.

"Nice time." I handed him a cup of the Kool-aid stuff and half a banana.

He grinned, still panting. "Sounds like Ginger did great. How about you?"

"Me? I'm ready for a shower and lunch."

"There's another 5K at Gem Falls in October. You can start training next week." He stood on one foot, stretching his other quad.

"Yeah, we'll see. Can we get out of the rain now?"

At home, we showered and changed. Sam put us through a yoga-style stretching routine and would have kept going if I hadn't growled, "Lunch?"

"Burgers and milkshakes at the Rise and Shine?" Putting her hands together in prayer, Ginger begged Sam. "Please?"

"I really can't think of a worse post-race meal," Sam said, conceding.

Plenty of other runners had the same idea and the place was packed. The restaurant had that wet, close summer-rain smell. We found seats at the counter, Ginger between us.

"I'm starved." Without looking at the menu, she ordered a plain burger, fries and a strawberry milkshake.

"Make it two, only chocolate for me." I handed Irene my menu.

Sam followed with a Greek salad and baked potato. I didn't feel too bad since I knew from past experience he'd be hitting the chips later on.

As Irene brought our food, a guy sat down next to me and pointed to the headline in the paper. "What do you think of that?"

The headline shouted, "KIDNAPPER CAUGHT. LINK TO CHILD SEX RING" above a surly-looking photo.

"I think it's a relief." Irene poured my neighbor's coffee. "I've been waking up nights worried about the kid next door."

"About time," someone on the other side growled.

I turned to say something to Sam, but stopped. Ginger sat frozen, holding a fry, staring at the paper.

"What's wrong, Honey?" Sam asked.

She mumbled something and started to shake.

"What?" I leaned closer to hear.

"Daddy," she whispered, before whirling around and sprinting toward the door.

"I'll get her," Sam said. "Pay the bill and meet us at the car."

"What's wrong with her?" Irene asked.

"Doesn't feel well. Must be the excitement of the race." I pulled three twenties out of my wallet and tossed them on the counter. "Sorry about this. Keep the change."

By the time I caught up with them, Ginger sat in a tight ball beneath an aspen, behind the bicycle rack. Sam knelt before her, whispering. She shook her head violently and curled more tightly. Thunder cracked and the rain fell even harder. Sam bent to lift her. She stood and sprinted toward the car.

Following, I fished my cell from my jeans and punched Henry's number. When he answered, I said, "We'll be home in fifteen minutes and I think you'll want to be there."

SIXTEEN

※

Ginger sat on the couch, head down and arms wrapped around her knees, a perfect shivering ball. Not knowing what else to do, I went to the kitchen to make coffee. While it brewed, I stood in the doorway and watched Ginger shake. Daphnia jumped onto the couch and pressed himself against her, licking the rainwater from her bare arms. Sam brought a towel and touched her shoulder. She screamed. He backed away and stood watching her. That's the tableau that greeted Henry and Mrs. Briggs, the counselor from social services.

Henry took in the scene and swept Sam and me out to the kitchen, leaving Mrs. Briggs squatting before Ginger, whispering into the hair cascading over her arms. He softly closed the door and pointed Sam toward a chair. I poured three cups of coffee and put out cream, sugar and spoons.

"So what happened?"

I handed out the coffee and sat next to Sam. "She saw the newspaper story on the captured kidnapper and freaked. She thinks he's the guy she used to live with, her daddy or step-father or whatever."

Sam pulled a tissue from his pocket and blew his nose. "She's been like that for almost half an hour now. She screams every time I try to comfort her." He shuddered.

Henry nodded. "My guess is she's reliving something really bad right now. She wouldn't know you from whoever she's seeing in her mind." He stirred a couple of scoopfuls of sugar into his cup. "When the police picked up the guy they found three kids, girls, stashed in a closet. I've come from the hospital where they're being checked out. Caroline," he nodded toward the living room, "is great. But we're in for a bad time trying to get these kids back to something like normal."

Sam cleared his throat. "So you think Ginger's right about him being her 'daddy'?"

Henry shrugged. "Don't know. But it would fit, wouldn't it? She's got an eye tattoo above her pelvis, right?"

"Shit." I looked at Sam. He paled.

Henry nodded. "So do the others. Evidently it was his way of letting them know he was always watching."

We sat sipping coffee until the counselor appeared in the doorway. "She's calmer, might even sleep." She sat at the table. I got her a cup of coffee.

"What next?" I sat down.

She took a sip. "Good coffee, thanks. I'm afraid I was hard on you the last time we met, Mr. Rosenberg."

"Please, call me Edward."

"I'm Caroline." She took a deep breath. "In answer to your question, it's hard to say. She's withdrawn now. Might come out of it soon or stay there a long time. The most important thing is that you let her talk about it in her own time. I warn you, it's going to be hard to hear."

I nodded and glanced at Sam.

He met my gaze. "We'll do our best."

Caroline stood. "We'd better get back to the hospital, but I wouldn't leave her alone too long. She might not know where she is when she wakes up."

Henry put his arm around me as I walked him to the door. "I'm going to have to tell the detectives investigating this case, you know," he whispered. "It can wait a while, but I won't be able to put it off forever."

I patted his back. "I know. Thanks for coming."

When they'd gone, Sam and I stood together watching Ginger. She lay on the couch, curled around Daphnia, a blanket draped over her. She looked asleep, but who could tell?

"I'll take the first shift," I told Sam. "You'd better get something to eat before you fall over."

He grimaced. "You're right, I'm starving, which feels totally disloyal."

"I know what you mean." I flopped into a chair facing the couch. "Maybe you could make me a sandwich, too? And a change of clothes while you're at it? I'm soaked."

He nodded and pushed open the kitchen door. I sat watching Ginger, listening to Sam in the kitchen and the rain outside. A perfectly peaceful domestic moment, except for the pain that was spilling from the girl curled on couch and filling the room.

I woke to Sam setting a sandwich on the end-table beside me. He'd changed into dry sweats and handed me a pair before sitting in the other armchair and taking up his plate.

"Thanks." I carried the clothes to the bathroom, where I changed and toweled my hair but didn't bother to comb it. Didn't look in the mirror, either.

❧ ❧ ❧

We both stayed close all afternoon. I peed twice, Sam a few more times. We let Daphnia out at least once. Ginger barely moved. The rain stopped, then started, then stopped. Around five, the clouds parted enough to allow through a finger of light.

Ginger sat up. "I'm cold."

Both Sam and I sprang to our feet. I handed her a dry throw from one of the chairs, Sam passed her a small bundle of clothes he'd brought from upstairs. She wrapped up in the blanket and carried the clothes to the bathroom. I heard the bolt slide as she shut the door.

"Are you hungry?" I called through the door.

"Sort of."

"I think there are some peanuts left," I suggested lamely.

She emerged in her jammies and robe and surveyed the living room. I watched her take in the empty plates, fruit rinds, chip bag and candy wrappers. Sam's the kind who eats for two solid days after a marathon and I'm a stress eater. "Are there any chocolate chip cookies?"

Sam dove for the tin, left over from the last time Ginger baked. He opened it. "I'll make some more," he offered as he held out the last four cookie halves.

She shrugged. "It's okay."

We watched her slowly eat.

"You guys are creeping me out," she said. "Can we play cards or something?"

Could we play cards? It turned out we could play several games each of Gin Rummy, Canasta and Go Fish. We all sat around the kitchen table getting used to Ginger's expressionless face and playing hand after hand of whatever she wanted. Sam made spaghetti. We held our plates in our laps and shoveled in a forkful or two between turns. Sunset turned the clouds the color of apricot roses. We switched on the lights and played some more.

Around eleven, I pushed back my chair. "I can't keep this up. It's time for bed."

Ginger froze, eyes wide. "A few more hands, please?"

Sam and I looked at each other. I was about to concede when he said, "I was thinking we could maybe have a campout in the living room. What do you guys think? We've got air mattresses and sleeping bags. We could even light a fire and roast marshmallows. I think there's a package in the pantry."

Ginger's face relaxed a little. "Sweet."

"Okay, then." Sam rubbed his hands together and stood. "Edward, you're in charge of bringing down the camping gear. Ginger and I will search for marshmallows, rearrange furniture and start the fire."

As I passed him on my way to the stairs, I squeezed his shoulder and whispered, "You're amazing."

By the time I found the electric air pump and came back down, Sam and Ginger had moved the couch and chairs to the far end of the living room. A fire crackled in the fireplace and Ginger sat skewering marshmallows on metal kebab sticks, a package of graham crackers and a bag of chocolate chips on the floor beside her.

Later, our hands still sticky from s'mores, we climbed into the sleeping bags I'd laid atop the air mattresses Sam and Ginger had lined up on the floor. Ginger took the middle. I shrugged at Sam and stumbled to the far mattress. The only light glowed from the dying fire. I lay listening to the occasional crackle as it consumed the remaining log.

As I was drifting off, Ginger spoke, her voice low and flat. "He said he'd kill us if we told."

I felt more than heard Sam turn toward her. "You're safe here."

"He burned Angel with a cigarette when she said she wanted to go home. That was after her first party. She cried for a long time. I guess he never burned me because I was already home. That's why he said I could go to school and the rest couldn't. I didn't have anywhere else to go. And I'm older." She must have been petting Daphnia. I could hear the rhythmic scrape of her arm against nylon. "But I still hated the parties."

"What kind of parties?" Sam asked. I held my breath, not wanting to disturb the silence that followed his question.

"Creep parties, that's what we called them," she said after a long pause. "He said the men were his friends but they were different every time. He'd make us do things with them, bad things, while he watched with his video camera. Before he brought the others home, it was just me and only one creep at a time. But after they came, it changed."

"What others?" Sam whispered.

"Angel and Jasmine. First Angel. Jas came right before they left." She lay silent for a moment. "Are they okay?"

"As far as I know." I spoke softly, afraid my voice would crack. "They found three girls. They're safe now. At the hospital."

"Good." She sniffed. "I missed them. When I came home and they were gone." Another long pause. We all breathed together in the darkness. "He said I was dirty. Because of the bugs, crabs. They were crawling all over me down there." She shuddered. "That's why they left me." Suddenly she sat up on one elbow and turned to me. "So now you know."

Her form backlit from the fire, I couldn't see her face. Sitting, I said quietly, "Yes, and I still think you didn't do anything wrong."

Behind her Sam said, "Oh, Ginger, Honey, none of that was your fault."

Then we had to listen to her cry for a very long time. Neither of us touched her. Instead we patted the edge of her bed and clucked and cooed ineffectually. Eventually the sobs subsided. None of us spoke again.

❧ ❧ ❧

I must have slept, because I woke hot and sweaty in a pool of sunlight spilling through the front windows. Daphnia's head snapped up from between Ginger's feet.

"Come on," I whispered. "We'll pee together."

I led him through the kitchen to the sun porch where we each stopped to kiss Sam, who sat sipping coffee. When I opened the back door, Daphnia bolted down the steps. I followed more slowly. Turning my back to the lake, I watered the lilac bush next to the bottom step.

"Funny," Sam said through the screen. "I thought we had indoor plumbing installed some time ago."

"I'm camping." I pulled up my sweats, stretched and stumbled back up the stairs, Daphnia at my heels. Sam greeted me at the top with a coffee cup.

"Thanks." I took a long swallow. "Long night."

He nodded. "We'd better not leave her alone."

"Whither thou goest. Especially if you bring the coffee."

He smiled, handed me a carton of cream and carried his cup and the pot into the living room. We settled into wingbacks pushed together in the corner opposite our sleeping girl. Daphnia walked to Ginger and sniffed around the sleeping bag before trotting back to jump on Sam's lap.

"I'm sorry I've been acting so stupid," Sam whispered, stroking his fur. "Or more to the point, acting like my father."

I sipped my coffee, waiting for him to go on.

"You were right, you know. I've been misremembering. Even before I came out, it wasn't always great."

"Nobody's childhood is perfect." I stretched. Sleeping on the air mattress had left me feeling stiff and groggy.

"I suppose so." He poured himself more coffee. "It's funny. Last night after listening to Ginger, I couldn't sleep. I lay there thinking about what it felt like to be a kid. So powerless. And in my case, nervous all the time, wondering if I'd get the right grades, worrying that I'd said the wrong thing." He grimaced. "It sucked. But you know what?"

"What?"

"It didn't suck anything like that." He nodded at the lump curled deep in the bag.

"Yeah." I crossed my legs. "I really hope not many kids have that kind of nightmare for a childhood."

He nodded. "It's funny. Something about hearing Ginger's story tipped it for me. Suddenly I remembered clearly, for the first time in years, how angry I was as a boy. And at the same time, I thought, get over it already. My garbage doesn't even make a very good secret. Do you get what I'm saying?" Daphnia stretched across Sam's lap, rolling onto his back.

"I think so." I watched Sam scratch the dog's belly. "It's hard to feel sorry for yourself around Ginger. Her story trumps all of ours."

"I think it's more than that." He sipped coffee and stared out the window. "I lay there wondering what the rest of her life will be like and how we could help her heal and it struck me. I'm forty-two. How can I expect her to get past a history that horrific if I can't get over a little parental bigotry?"

The lump stirred. Daphnia went on high alert. As tangled brown hair poked from the top of the bag, he leaped down, sprinting toward the emerging girl. Her face appeared and he pounced, licking her several times in rapid succession. She laughed and held him away.

"Enough, Daph." She patted the space beside her hip. "Here, sit here."

He did.

"How do you do that?" I asked. "He never does what I tell him."

She shrugged. "It used to take treats, but now he just does it."

"Classical conditioning." Sam smiled at Ginger. "Good morning. Did you sleep?"

She stretched and yawned before answering. "Sort of. What time is it?"

Sam looked at his watch. "About ten. Not bad for a Sunday

morning. How do pancakes sound?"

"With chocolate chips?"

ご ご ご

My sense of time went on vacation. Sam made breakfast. I drank coffee. Ginger mostly stared out the window and petted the dog. Eventually we ate pancakes dripping chocolate goo, covered in canned whipped cream—zombie food, guaranteed to smother anger and fear in a thick layer of somnambulism.

Outside, the sky and lake reflected complementary blues, damp cedar planking in the shade of the boathouse the only remnant of the storm. A breeze rippled the water. We stayed inside.

At one-thirty, Ginger looked at the clock. "Ora will be here soon. I should get dressed."

I glanced at Sam. I'd forgotten Ora. I think he had, too. But he simply said, "Me, too. I'll go upstairs with you."

While they were gone, I did what I could to reduce the kitchen mess. I also grabbed a large plastic garbage bag and scoured the living room for detritus. When the doorbell rang, Sam, Ginger, and the living room looked odd and tired but respectable. Thank God her parents stayed in the car and waved.

Ora stepped in and looked around. Her gaze took in the sleeping bags, moved furniture, Sam's weary smile, Daphnia, subdued in my arms, and settled on Ginger's pale face. "Hi."

"Hi," we all said.

"You guys okay? You look a little weird." Ora watched Ginger, whose smile looked forced.

"Life's weird. Come on, let's go upstairs. Sam says I can hang out for your lesson. So I can start getting used to the chants. I mean, if it's okay with you?" Ginger was staring at Ora's hands, but her eyes flickered up long enough to see Ora nod.

"I guess so. I'm not very good, but you can listen if you want."

Ginger grinned and Ora smiled back. They sprinted upstairs.

"That Ora's a sweet kid," I whispered to Sam. "It's the shy ones that break your heart, isn't it?"

"As far as I can tell, they all break your heart." He kissed my cheek and followed the girls upstairs.

I took Daphnia, the phone, a phonebook, and a fresh pot of coffee out to the porch, slumped into the ancient wicker chair and propped my feet on the footstool. Daphnia, of course, curled on my lap. Enough breeze blew through the screens to push the heat around. The woods smelled of drying pine needles and fresh earth. A loon called from the distance, warblers chirped nearby.

First, I called Henry to check in.

"The kids are home with their families," he told me. "The media are all over them. It's gonna be hard on those girls once the details of the case are leaked."

"Does Ginger need to get linked into that?" A muskrat splashed into the water by the boathouse.

He sighed. "You know, he videotaped it all. Guess on top of selling the kids, he was hawking images over the internet. I've only seen some of what's out there, but Ginger had a starring role."

"That's what I figured." I told him about her late-night confession. "Aren't the movies evidence enough? Does she really have to get involved?"

"The police are going to want to talk with her. Beyond that," I could hear him shrug, "I don't know." He paused and drew a deep breath. "These children have all been through hell. Caroline's good, but I confess, our department is way out of its depth with this. There's a real expert in childhood sexual trauma in Chicago. I talked with her about working with all four girls and she's willing to fly out once a week for a while." He paused.

"But it would cost much more than your department can afford," I finished for him. "Of course, Henry, we'd be happy to pick up the bill. I'll call my accountant in the morning and you can work it out with him."

"Thank you. I hated to ask, but didn't know where else to go." Henry sounded uncharacteristically uncomfortable—guess we never talked about money. He told me he'd come by Monday and rang off.

I closed my eyes and focused on the breeze ruffling the hair on my forearms. A thrush trilled, the sound of summer that always sent me back to when I used to spend weeks with the grandfathers chasing frogs, paddling around the lake and healing my young soul.

Next, I called Dan Osborne, our newly elected sheriff and my favorite cop. When I was drinking, he dragged me in a couple of times for disorderly conduct and whatever. Wouldn't cut me any slack, and I always found an AA meeting list in my pocket when I got home. Never went then, of course, but now I think of him as one of my angels. Which is why I contributed so heavily to his campaign.

"Hi, Dan, Edward Rosenberg." I'd had a hunch he'd be working this particular Sunday.

"Edward, just the man I was about to call."

"I bet." Daphnia jumped down, and I stood to let him out.

"We're going to have to talk with her, you know."

I leaned against the door, watching Daphnia sniff around the base of his favorite tree. "Really? I hear you have it all on video. We've got a sex abuse expert coming in from Chicago. Maybe you can get all the information you need through her."

I could hear him shuffling papers. I sat on the steps and looked out over the water. "That would be second-hand evidence, not admissible in court."

"You aren't really going to pull a bunch of traumatized kids into court, are you? There's no way their parents will let them testify."

Ora sang the same line over and over again. Blessed be God who sanctifies us through commandments.

He sighed. "First, I'm not the D.A. so I'm not putting anyone on the stand. Second, the children probably wouldn't be in court. Their testimony would be taped."

"It seems to me like their testimony already has been taped."

"And third, if the D.A. wants someone to testify, Ginger is our best source. She spent the most time with him and she's a ward of the state, which gives us more control. Although if a child is subpoenaed, there's not much the parents can do to stop it."

"No offense, but that'll happen over my dead body, Dan."

"None taken, but you don't have that kind of authority, Edward." He paused. "Look. I understand what you're saying. If it were up to me, none of these kids would have another bad minute in their whole lives. On the other hand, there is nothing I won't do to put this guy away for as long as humanly possible. You have to understand."

"I do." I walked back up the steps and began pacing the porch. "Believe me, if he didn't make it through tonight, I wouldn't shed a tear." I slumped back into my chair. "It's just that I've never seen anyone this scared. If you have to talk with her, can you at least send a woman, out of uniform, and maybe have Ginger's counselor present? No lights or sirens or anything, simply a conversation?"

"I think I can do that," he said quietly.

"And can we keep her name out of the papers? I know it will be hard with the other girls, since they've probably had their pictures on milk cartons. But no one needs to know about Ginger, do they?" I was pleading now.

"Can't promise anything, but I'll do what I can." He paused again. "How about you? Still going to meetings?"

"Yeah, thanks. Don't worry, the last thing I'm going to do to Ginger is to start drinking over this." I leaned forward, resting an elbow on my knee. "Let me know when they're coming. She doesn't need any more surprises."

I hung up and stared out at the lake.

The doorbell rang. Liv Bloomberg and Erma Malamud stood on the doorstep, arms loaded with paper bags.

Liv gestured toward Erma. "You remember Erma's daughter, Julie, who works in dispatch at the police station?"

I nodded, conjuring a vague picture of a stern-faced, dark-haired woman.

Erma whispered. "Julie called. She said that your little girl was one of those attacked by that horrid man."

My face must have registered alarm that this was general knowledge, because Liv put a hand on my arm. "Don't worry. She's not spreading the news and neither are we, but Erma and I thought you might need some supper." She thrust her bag toward me. It was surprisingly heavy. "I had a kugel and some lasagna in the freezer. I attached cards to each so you'll know how to prepare them. There's also a container of cookies, fresh-baked yesterday."

Erma nodded. "I stopped by the store for some basics—fruit, bread, milk, some of that sweet cereal kids like. You shouldn't have to go out, not now when Ginger needs you."

I cleared my throat. "Thank you both. I can't tell you how much this means to me."

Liv made a waving gesture in the air. "It's nothing."

Erma's eyes were sad and kind. "How is she?"

I shrugged.

Liv kissed my cheek. "Call if you need anything."

Erma handed me the other grocery bag. "Give her a hug for us."

And with that, they turned and strode back down the walk. Sam was right, in a small town nothing stayed secret. But that wasn't always a bad thing.

I took the food into the kitchen and followed the scrawled directions for thawing and cooking the lasagna. It looked wonderful.

Afterwards I returned to the porch to watch the lake and think. The singing stopped after about an hour. Sam appeared in the doorway and handed me a soda before dropping into a chair.

"Where are the girls?" I popped the top and waited for the fizz to subside before sipping.

"I left them upstairs. Ginger needs a friend and Ora's dying to be one. Seemed a good time for us to take a break." He rolled his head and his neck vertebrae crackled. I swung my feet off the footstool, pulled it toward me and patted the cushion.

"Here, sit and I'll rub your shoulders."

He smiled tiredly, sliding onto the footstool. I spread my knees and scooted so his back pressed into my chest. It felt like massaging tightropes. I dug in with my thumbs. He groaned and relaxed a bit. As I kneaded his muscles, I relayed my conversations with Henry and Dan.

"Even though it may not make a difference in what happens, we should start the adoption paperwork soon," he muttered as he hung his head forward and I rubbed my thumbs along his spine.

I smiled. "My thoughts exactly."

"What smells so good?"

I grinned. "We had a visitation and we may never need to cook again."

A horn sounded. Footsteps thundered down the stairs. From the living room doorway we watched the girls hug before Ora sprinted out the door, yelling, "Call me," over her shoulder.

≪ ≪ ≪

We were finishing dinner when the phone rang. Ginger froze.

"I'll get it." I looked at Sam. He patted her hand once, very lightly, and asked her to pass the bread basket.

"Hello."

"Edward? This is Paul Johnstone. Is Sam around?"

"Sure, he's right here." I walked the phone to Sam. "Paul Johnstone?"

His eyebrows shot up. He grabbed the phone. "Paul, how are you? I'm afraid I forgot all about it." He stood and walked out of the room.

Ginger and I looked at each other. She shrugged and skewered a lettuce leaf with her fork.

When Sam returned he smiled. "Did you say there are cookies?"

SEVENTEEN

✿

Eight bedrooms in the main house and three more in the boathouse and we continued to sleep like refugees in the living room. Early Monday morning I woke to see Sam quietly slipping through the front door. I'd almost fallen asleep again when I realized he'd said he planned to leave his running shoes in the closet for the next couple of weeks. So where was he going at four in the morning?

I found out soon enough. Next time I opened my eyes, Sam and some guy were tiptoeing through the room, heading for the kitchen, crackling with illicit energy. I sat up. Sam waved as he ushered Paul through. I stumbled as quietly as I could out of the sleeping bag. Daphnia woke, of course, and bounded in front me as I swung through into the brightly lit kitchen.

Sam grinned from the sink as he filled the teakettle. Paul nodded, leaning against the table tiredly.

"Go on out to the porch," Sam whispered. "I'll be there in a minute with coffee."

Paul and I left obediently. He slumped into a wicker armchair. I opened the outer door for Daphnia who, seeing a squirrel, sprinted past me, forgetting even to stop by his favorite pissing tree. The sun sat low on the eastern horizon and early birds chirped way too loudly to be catching any worms. Not my favorite time of day. Except for the light,

195

that wonderful early morning mix of yellow and white tinged with the memory of pink, that tempts everyone to shoot close-ups of dew beads on grass. I took a deep breath. The air smelled sweet. I always forget that, how good the world smells at sunrise.

When I turned back, Paul was dozing in the chair, his skinny ankles crossed. He wore khaki shorts, a dark blue polo shirt, leather sandals, and a baseball cap sporting the university logo. Not bad-looking, aging about as well as any of us. Sam appeared in the doorway with three cups of coffee. I gestured toward Paul. He smiled, set the cups down, took a step toward me and kissed me, hard, long and deep, only breaking when we heard, "Uh, oh."

Paul blinked up at us. "Sorry, I didn't mean to interrupt."

Sam laughed and picked up his cup. "Let's toast to a successful adventure." He lifted his cup. Paul reached for one and I took the other.

"Um, I'm happy to toast whatever," I said, feeling particularly dense. "But I need some cream first. You want anything in your coffee, Paul?"

"Cream would be great." He looked up from his cup.

When I got back, Sam had rearranged chairs so we could sit in a semi-circle open to the lake. I flopped into one of them, raised my cup in a toast and sipped. "I'm sorry. Maybe you could explain what we're celebrating?"

Paul smiled sadly. "I'm not sure we're celebrating. Although it was exhilarating getting away with it."

"You're right." Sam's shoulders deflated. "It isn't really good news, except maybe for Ginger, but it was exciting, wasn't it?"

Paul nodded.

I cleared my throat. "I don't mean to be a pest, but what was exciting?"

"Maybe I should start at the beginning." Sam leaned back, sipping his coffee. "Paul's been helping me collect data on the mysterious disappearance of Maggie's rats."

I looked at Paul.

He nodded. "It feels like betrayal, but Sam assures me it's in her long-term interests."

Sam sat up straight. "It absolutely is. Things are really bad in Maggie's lab, but if we don't get her to see that soon, before she publishes this trash, it will be much worse. As it is, there'll be some tittering within the scientific community about her sexual behavior, but if she publishes faked data?" He slouched in the chair and stretched out his legs. "For scientists, it's sort of like my mother always said about teenaged girls—without our reputations, we're lost."

"Are you going to explain to me what's going on?" I stood to let Daphnia back in. He immediately ran to Sam and leaped into his lap.

He smiled and stroked the dog's back. "Ever since that night, I've been sure that Ginger uncovered major scientific fraud. Paul and I have been working to minimize the damage. If we can convince Maggie in time, we may keep it out of the newspapers." He scratched Daphnia's ears. The breeze picked up and I shivered. "When Ginger showed her the evidence, Maggie wouldn't believe her for a couple of reasons. First, she's a kid, but probably more important—sorry Paul—Maggie thinks she's in love with that slime-ball."

"Bill," I supplied.

Sam nodded. Paul slumped further in his chair and stared at the lake, coffee cooling in his cup.

"So Paul and I have been periodically breaking into Maggie's lab to independently record descriptions of her rats."

"Breaking in?"

Sam shrugged. "All right, not quite breaking in. I got to know the night janitor during all those pre-tenure years, before I met you, when I spent all my time at work. So he let us in the first time. After that I stole the spare key she keeps in the supply closet and made a copy."

"Is she going to thank you for this?" I watched Paul slink even deeper into his chair.

Sam took a deep breath. "Not immediately, but Maggie's a good scientist. She'll come around once we show her the data. Ginger was right. Someone is systematically removing some rats, probably the sick ones, and replacing them with fresh animals. What this means is that Maggie's results are completely bogus. "

"I suppose we need to confront her soon." Paul looked miserable.

"Today, I think." Sam sipped his coffee. "With Ginger's data, we have three independent sets of evidence. It's enough. After breakfast I'm calling her to let her know the three of us and Ginger are coming to the lab."

I glanced at the kitchen doorway. "Do you think Ginger's up for that?"

He shrugged. "Who knows? It might take her mind off things and it could feel good to know we're standing behind her like this. After all, it's her discovery. She deserves the credit."

"Who deserves what credit?" Ginger's voice wafted sleepily through the door before she appeared.

Sam grinned at her. "You do. Paul, you remember our amazing daughter, Ginger. Paul's been helping me prove you were right."

ॐ ॐ ॐ

And so we found ourselves trudging up to the top floor of the science building at about ten in the morning, chilled in the air-conditioned stairwell after walking from the parking lot through the hot August morning. Ginger walked between us, her head down but shoulders on high alert.

Maggie met us at the door to the lab. Her gaze rested on each of us in turn, lingering a long time over Paul, whose sad smile never wavered. After a moment, she stepped back and let us through. Sam pulled three thick notebooks from his satchel and flopped them on a lab bench.

"I think you should look at these."

Her forehead creased. She glanced at Ginger, then Paul. "What are they?"

Paul's eyes never left her face. "More of what Ginger already showed you. Sam and I repeated her experiment and came up with the same results."

"How did you? When?" Maggie stared at Paul. The air crackled. Ginger backed up against me.

He spoke softly. "We broke in at night."

She stiffened. Her jaw clenched. A red blush crept up her neck. "You violated my lab?"

He frowned. "We didn't touch anything, only looked around.

We're not the ones truly violating your lab. Someone is stealing your animals."

Sam, standing by the wall of rat cages, pointed to one about chest-high. "Maggie."

She swung toward him, eyes flashing.

Sam gestured toward the cage. "Look in the top notebook. Find the first entry for number 345."

She gave him a smoldering look, but flipped through pages in the notebook. When she stopped, Sam said, "Tell me about the markings on that rat."

She read, "Black hood extends from snout over pectoral girdle, narrowing at pelvic girdle. White patch surrounding left eye."

"Now look at this rat." He pointed to the cage labeled 345.

"What is this? Some kind of intervention?" But she peered into the cage. From where I stood, all I could see was an ermine brown face. Maggie looked ill.

Sam continued, "Paul and I took data independently. We didn't open the cages and didn't compare until this morning. There are over a hundred anomalies like that one, not including what Ginger recorded earlier."

We watched silently for a very long time as Maggie paced the stack of cages, listening to the rustle of hundreds of rats nosing around their cages. She flipped through pages in the notebooks and examined rats. My feet were numb by the time she sat down.

"Shit. I knew those numbers were too good." She clutched the notebook close to her chest. Paul stood beside her and rested his hand on her shoulder.

"I don't get it," I said. "Who would want to switch your rats?"

She turned toward me, cheeks flushed. "Isn't it obvious? There's a lot of money riding on this drug trial. Enough that the pharmaceutical company provided me with a trained assistant."

Ginger, her face three inches from rat #291, stopped making kissing noises long enough to say, "Bill."

Maggie nodded and covered her eyes with her hand. "Bill." She looked at Sam and shook her head. "Shit."

Paul wrapped his arm around her shoulder.

"What's he doing with your rats? I still don't get why he'd want them." I watched Ginger crab-walk to the next cage, her lips almost touching #292's whiskers.

Sam looked at Maggie before answering. She sat, head in hand. "He doesn't want them. He's simply removing any data points that indicate the adverse effects of the drugs. He's probably disposed of them. At least that's what I'd do."

"Disposed? You mean killed?" Ginger whirled from the cages. "You think they're dead?"

"We don't know that, Honey," Sam said quietly, "but maybe."

She stared at him and turned back to the bank of cages. I was beginning to think maybe we'd made a mistake loading her up with one more misery.

"Why?" I sank onto a lab stool, wiggling my feet to restore the circulation.

Maggie raised her head. "We've been testing a particular drug compound to see if it impacts the DNA of these rats. It's an important step before clinical trials. Our results have been great. We take blood samples every week and so far, no mutagenesis, no change in the DNA, no possible cancer. Only it looks like it's all been staged."

She propped her elbows on her knees and leaned over, massaging her temples. Her hair tented her face. Eventually she straightened. "I've been waking up in the middle of the night trying hard not to think about this ever since Ginger first showed me her data sheets."

Ginger turned to her. "I thought you didn't believe me."

Maggie shook her head. "I tried not to believe you. It looks like I was wrong, and probably mean to you. I'm sorry about that."

Ginger shrugged. "It's okay." But I saw her smile as she turned back to the rats. That was a good sign.

Maggie sighed. "This explains my near-perfect data."

"If it's Bill, how's he doing this?" Paul stroked Maggie's hair as he spoke.

"He must have been coming in nights, running the tests himself and switching out any rats that didn't pass. I wonder how much extra the drug company is paying him for this kind of insurance," she muttered into her hands.

"Wouldn't you notice the extra tests?" Sam asked. "I mean, that would deplete your supplies, wouldn't it?"

She snorted. "We're talking about a major pharmaceutical company. If it's his job to fake the data and he wants more supplies, or more rats for that matter, he has access to plenty of funds."

"But what about the ethics?" Paul interjected. "I mean, surely the company wouldn't want people who take their drug getting cancer. That can't be good business."

She leaned back in her chair and rolled her neck from side to side. "You can justify anything if there's enough money involved. After all, changes in DNA don't always end up causing cancer. Even if they do, it can take a long time to develop and there are so many other things going on in people's environments, it could be hard to blame it on one particular drug. And, of course, rats aren't perfect models of what happens in people."

She half-smiled. "A dicey bet, but if this drug makes it through clinical trials it will earn hundreds of millions a year for the company. And, of course, if it doesn't make it through, the company can always blame some independent researcher, someone out to further her own career by fudging the data sheets. I have a headache. Do any of you have something for it?"

Sam started to speak. Bill stepped through the door. We all stared at him. He took in the tableau. "Odd place for a party. Hey, old man." He sneered at Paul. "Back for another shot? I don't think she's interested, are you, Baby?"

Maggie scowled. "Where are they?"

"Who?"

"The rats. The goddamned rats," she hissed.

He glanced at the bank of cages. "Looks like they're here to me. Hi, kid, I thought you got fired." He glanced in Ginger's direction. Sam put a protective arm around her.

Maggie looked at him. "I'm talking about the rats you stole, not their replacements."

Bill's eyebrows rose. "Now why would I do that?"

"Because you're a stupid, greedy son of a bitch." Paul spoke quietly, his hand resting in the small of Maggie's back.

Maggie cocked her head and looked at Bill. "Did the company ask you to commit fraud or was this your personal idea? A little innovation?"

"I don't know what you're talking about." Bill leaned against the doorpost.

Maggie whispered, "Get out of my lab. You can expect to hear from the academic ethics committee soon."

Bill crossed his arms. He looked from Maggie to Paul and back again. "Do you really think that's wise, Professor Mazzoni, considering how you've taken advantage of me?" He leaned forward with a smirk and stage whispered, "Remember, I have pictures."

Maggie stared at him. "You little shit. That's what our affair has been about? So you could blackmail me?" Bill's smile began to fade as Maggie stood and crossed to the phone. She dialed. Eyes glued to Bill, she spoke into the receiver, "Dean Koons? Maggie Mazzoni here. Not so good. I've discovered that my student, Bill O'Brian, has been falsifying his data. Uh-huh, very seriously. I'd like to meet with you about this at your earliest convenience. Yes, that would be fine. Thank you." She hung up.

Bill's lip curled. "You'll regret this."

"I already do. But did you really think I'd risk my scientific reputation to keep our little fling a secret?" Maggie shook her head. "I'd rather make my living flipping burgers. Now, get out of my lab."

Bill threw a last look at Paul, who gazed back steadily. He turned and left. We listened to his footsteps fade, the sound of the stair door opening, closing, and then silence.

Paul wrapped his arms around Maggie. Ginger, Sam, and I watched while he patted her back and made little shushing noises. Eventually she pulled away, wiping her eyes.

"This is going to be horrid."

Sam nodded. "It is. But you did the right thing."

She looked up at Paul, and over at Sam. "I hate it that you snuck into my lab. But I'll get over it. God knows what would have happened if I'd published those data. To say the least, it would have been embarrassing." She turned to Ginger. "I'm sorry. For what it's worth, I'm grateful. It may not look like it now, but you saved me." She flipped the pages of one of the notebooks. "I need to figure this out before I see the dean tomorrow morning."

"You guys go ahead." Paul stroked Maggie's hair. "I'll stay and help. Or at least make tea and find an aspirin."

☙ ☙ ☙

"I suggest a victory lunch to celebrate the amazing Ginger." Sam opened the door and we fell into the hot air.

Ginger grinned and bowed to an imaginary crowd. "Thank you, thank you." Her smile faded. "But I don't know about going out. Maybe we could have pizza at home?"

Sam nodded, pulling out his cell phone. "Let's see if Ora can join us, what do you say?"

She smiled. "Awesome."

After lunch, Sam and I sipped iced tea on the porch, watching Ginger and Ora splash in the lake. Undecipherable fragments of their conversation drifted to us across the hot and heavy air. I started to doze, and remembered.

"Did you say something about adoption earlier?"

He smiled. "Uh-huh. She's a great kid—a little rough around the edges—but why wouldn't we adopt her?"

"Um, because she might have sex with the lawn boy?"

"We don't have a lawn boy." He propped his feet on the stool.

"Oh, that takes care of it then."

He shook his head. "After what she went through, I don't get why she'd want to have sex with anyone, ever. Be that as it may, I'm not going to hold who she sleeps with against her."

I laughed. "Equal rights for preteens?"

"More like, nobody's perfect." He ran his hand along my arm. "Maybe if we're a stable family for her, she'll settle down."

"Maybe not. What happens then?"

"We get her more help." He entwined his fingers in mine. "And we figure it out together. Isn't that what families are supposed to do?"

I squeezed his hand. "Don't ask me. I have no experience with healthy families. This is all new territory."

"Let's ask her tonight if she wants us to adopt her." He watched the girls swim and brought my hand to his lips.

"Only if you're sure." I watched his beautiful mouth for an answer. "Sam, this is really serious. Once we say something to her, we can't undo it."

He nodded. "I know. And I could regret this discussion. But it's time to either commit or get off the pot."

"I don't think that's how the phrase goes."

But he was already standing. "If you're okay here, I'm going in to work for a couple of hours. I'd like to make sure everything is running smoothly so I can take the next few days off and focus on the family. I'll stop by the store on my way home."

"It's not like we need anything. Liv keeps dropping off casseroles. I think she has the entire synagogue congregation cooking for us now."

He chuckled. "Still, I can stop if there's anything in particular you want."

"Chocolate. It says in the AA big book that during times of stress we should have chocolate. So lots of chocolate and anything sweet."

જ્જ જ્જ જ્જ

It took seconds for her to answer yes. Big house, plenty of money, Daphnia to play with and nobody torturing her, what else was she going to answer? Still, it felt good.

"What's Hebrew for father?" she asked over dinner.

Sam passed her the salad bowl. "Abba."

She used her fork to point first at me and then at Sam. "You're Papa and you're Abba. That way you won't get confused." She forked another mouthful of macaroni and cheese and chewed thoughtfully. "And I'll be Ginger DeCosta Rosenberg."

Sam stopped buttering his bread. "What's wrong with Rosenberg DeCosta?"

She shook her head. "Doesn't sound as good."

I grinned. He muttered, "At least it's alphabetical."

"What difference does that make?" I poured ketchup on my macaroni. Sam and Ginger both wrinkled their noses.

"In a scientific paper, one way to indicate that all the authors contributed equally is to put their names in alphabetical order with an explanatory footnote." He turned to Ginger. "Do you think we could footnote your name?"

"I don't know what you're talking about" She dropped a bread crust to a waiting Daphnia. "But whatever it is, no."

❧ ❧ ❧

The next afternoon after lunch, Sam's dour graduate student arrived for an infusion of his brilliance. Ginger greeted her by name. At least one of us kept track. Sam and Grumpy commandeered the kitchen table. Ginger and Ora changed into suits and ran for the dock, Daphnia racing ahead. I popped a soda and stumbled up to my office. Papers drooped from the tops of piles, some drifting to the floor as I opened the window, hoping to dispel a layer of heat. A set of images gathered dust on the drying rack. Photographer? Who was I kidding. Just another trust-fund baby making an avocation out of a hobby.

I turned on my computer and started straightening piles and slipping Neskame images into a folder to deliver to the association office. Might as well take them while Sam was here.

I had to admit there were a few nice shots.

Email came up. The usual crap: big sale, free shipping, buy one get one free, political contribution requests, a couple of jokes and something from Kathy, probably requests for more pictures of eagles.

Edward, wish you'd answer your damned phone. Are you out shooting somewhere? Have an offer. Good publisher, small advance. Editor's name is Sarah, in her sixties and married forever so I'm hoping you weren't involved. Call me. Kathy.

I stared at the message. Read it three times. Office so hot sweat poured down my back. Read it again. The phone rang.

"Kathy?" I breathed into the receiver.

"Edward?" Henry's voice rumbled in my ear. "Everything all right? You sound strange."

"No, everything's fine, more than fine, just surprising. What's up?"

"I'm making arrangements with Dr. Lewis, the counselor I told you about?"

"Right." Emotional downshift. "What did she say?"

He cleared his throat. "You don't have to agree to this. She's willing to clear her calendar for the next two weeks and work intensively with all four girls, try to get them functional before school starts." His voice dropped almost to a whisper. "The others are in bad shape."

I watched Ginger dive into the water and surface beside Ora. "When can she get here?"

"Wednesday. Edward, are you sure you want to do this? She's asking for a monthly fee that's more than I make in a year."

"Is she that good?"

He exhaled. "She's supposed to be the best."

I watched the two girls splash out to the floating dock. "Do you remember the story of Orpheus, Henry?"

He chuckled. "Not really up on my ancient mythology, but I suspect you'll tell me about it."

"I don't remember much, myself. Only that Orpheus walked into hell to bring back someone he loved. I don't think it ended well, something about looking back, but maybe that was Lot's wife in the Bible. Anyway, what I'm trying to say is that you're supposed to do everything you can to bring the people you love back from hell. Tell her we're delighted she's willing to help."

Before I could call Kathy, the phone rang again. This time a pleasant-sounding woman introduced herself as Detective Kim Schmidt and announced she'd be over to interview Ginger in an hour. She didn't ask if it was convenient. I called Henry. "Should you be here for this?"

He grunted. "I'm on my way."

I allowed myself a few more minutes watching Ginger and Ora bask in the sun before clambering down to tell Sam. By the time Henry arrived, we'd shooed away Grumpy, sequestered Ora with Sam in the Torah torture chamber and hurried Ginger into dry clothes. She sat on her air mattress, pulling a comb through her hair. Henry squatted in front of her.

"Hey, Ginger."

"Hey." She almost smiled at him through a wet tangle. "Are you here about the adoption?"

He blinked.

I patted her head, her hair damp beneath my fingers. "Sorry, Gingersnap, not this time. I forgot to tell you, Henry, we'd like to begin the process as soon as possible."

"That's wonderful news." He smiled up at me. "I'll get the paperwork ready this afternoon." Turning to Ginger he said, "I'm here because a detective is coming to speak with you."

She stopped combing. Her whole body stiffened.

Henry cocked his head. "She wants to ask you questions about before. That's all. You're not in trouble. The police need to know the truth. Everything. It's important. Are you up for that? Should I call Mrs. Briggs or will you feel safe enough without her?"

She peered at me from between long hunks of wet hair. "Will you be here?"

I nodded. "Of course."

She went back to combing. "Okay."

Henry cocked an eyebrow at me. The doorbell rang. Detective Kim Schmidt stood on the doorstep wearing a lightweight summer suit. Over her shoulder, I could see a blue Honda parked by the curb.

I smiled. "Come in."

For the next hour, while above us Ora repeatedly chanted the same Hebrew lines over and over, Ginger described her years in Hades. I had to force myself to stay still as she spoke, soft and flat, about sitting beside her dead mother, waiting for her to wake up. Her stepfather, if that's what he was, took her with him into a nightmare of little rooms and big men and barbaric threats and special treats. Ginger watched her lap while she spoke.

I ping-ponged from shaking rage to sadness so deep it carved a hole through to the beginning of time. She caught me sniffling at one point—I think she was describing one of her earliest rapes. She stared at me. I breathed, trying to school my face, holding her gaze, pulling her into the light but thinking, how can I imagine the world whole after knowing this?

Detective Schmidt left. Henry lingered, watching me as closely as he did Ginger. He left as well. Ginger sat cross-legged on her air mattress, slowly stroking Daphnia's back. Lying on my side on the living room floor, I propped myself on an elbow and watched her. We listened to Ora. I don't remember my Sunday School Hebrew but it sounded like she'd moved onto another verse.

"We could make cookies." I have a limited number of coping mechanisms.

She looked up, her face blank. "You don't have to adopt me if you don't want to."

You know when you're a kid and someone steps off his side of the teeter-totter so you go crashing down, land on your back and can't breathe? It was sort of like that. I think my mouth even fell open. I know I stuttered, "What? You think? Why? Ginger, that's not right."

She stared at me. "You'd better check with Sam."

I blinked at her. "I'll check with Sam."

"Tell him everything." She pulled Daphnia close. "Promise?"

"I promise. Now do you want to make cookies or not? I'm craving oatmeal raisin chocolate chip, but we can make anything you like."

She took a deep breath and let it out slowly. "Oatmeal's okay."

I was pouring in the chocolate chips while she stirred when she said, "Can you pay to get the pictures off the web?"

I stopped pouring. "You mean buy copies?"

"No." She shook her head, eyes on the cookie batter. "Pay so they won't be there anymore."

"Oh, Gingersnap." I took the bowl from her and set it on the table. I knelt in front of her and brushed back a lock of hair. "I'm so sorry. I can't. Nobody can. Not once it's out there."

It physically hurt to see the despair in her eyes. Any other kid I would have hugged close. Instead, I said, "Come upstairs with me. I want to show you something."

It took me seconds to locate the file. I led her to the bathroom and stood behind her. "You see that girl?" I pointed at her in the mirror.

She nodded.

I pulled a photo from my file. "Does she look anything like this?" I held the picture I'd taken two months before.

Her eyes flicked from the photo to her face. The shadow of a smile started in her eyes.

"There may be pictures of this girl on the web." I shook the photo. "But none of this one." I placed my hand on her shoulder. "It's sort of like being in the witness protection program, only better, because you're leaving the fake identity behind."

We both looked at the image of Ginger skunk-haired and tarted up.

"I want to burn them." Ginger said. "All the pictures you took of me from before. I want to make them disappear."

I nodded. "I'll go get them."

She held up her hand, her eyes still fastened on the photo. "Wait until after you tell Sam about everything. If you guys still want to adopt me, we'll burn her."

❧ ❧ ❧

Ora and Sam came down as the first batch emerged from the oven. Probably the smell. Ginger carefully centered a cookie on her favorite flowered china plate and handed it to Sam. Wrapping up a couple more in a paper towel, she gestured to Ora. "Let's take these up to my room until your folks come. Sam and Edward need to talk."

Sam's eyebrows arched as he stood holding the plate and watching them go. He turned to me. "What was that all about?"

Grabbing a cookie, I fell into one of the kitchen chairs. "God, what an afternoon. Sit. I'm supposed to tell you all about Ginger's past in case you want to back out of the adoption deal."

He sat, still holding the plate. "Anything I don't already know?"

I tasted bile and swallowed it down with a bite of the cinnamon-sweet cookie. "Child pornography, prostitution, squalor, death, nothing you didn't guess. But I promised I'd tell you, so I'll start where she did, with her mother's overdose." I told him everything I could remember, watching his skin tone cycle from pink to red to pale green. When I finished, we sat in silence.

A car horn honked and the girls thundered down the steps. We listened as the front door slammed. Then she was there, standing in the doorway looking at Sam.

He opened his arms. "It's okay if you don't want to, but I could use a hug." She paused, and stepped to him and let his arms close around her. I watched her gradually melt against him. He released her, reached for a tissue and blew his nose. "So, Ginger DeCosta-Rosenberg, what do you want for dinner?"

"Can we make a big bonfire? We could roast hot dogs or something." Her voice sounded muffled against his chest.

❧ ❧ ❧

Later that night, I remembered. "Sam?"

"Hmmm?" He mumbled.

"My book—it's going to be published."

His eyes fluttered. "Really?"

"Yeah."

"Cool."

"I know." But by then he was already asleep.

❧ ❧ ❧

The three of us had finished a late breakfast when the doorbell rang. Maggie stood on the stoop, dressed in a beige pants suit, red silk shirt and pearls. Her nose and eyes shone pink against her pale face. Next to her Paul looked warm in a dark blue suit.

"Morning." I waved them in and through to the kitchen. "Coffee?"

Out the window, we could see Ginger and Daphnia playing at the edge of the lake.

Sam straightened from putting the last plate in the dishwasher. "How'd it go?"

She fell into a chair. "I'll have to go before the ethics committee and the personnel counsel, probably before fall term starts." I handed her coffee. She accepted and spooned in two large scoops of sugar. "Dean Koons was gracious, even kind, but clear that fraternization, as he called it, is frowned upon."

Paul sat next to her and accepted coffee.

"What's likely to happen?" I refilled my own cup and started a second pot.

Maggie shrugged. Sam closed the dishwasher and sat across from her. He patted her hand. "You're not the first professor to sleep with a student."

She grimaced. "According to Koons I'm the first woman at the institution to get caught. In the past ten years about a dozen men have gone before the council on sex charges. Three are still here." She twirled her spoon in her coffee. "He said I can expect a certain amount of pressure to polish my resume and move on."

Paul spoke, his eyes on the lake. "I think he overestimates that danger."

I brought out a plate of oatmeal cookies.

Sam asked, "What about Bill? Can you do anything to him?"

"Koons agreed to talk to him, get him to withdraw from school. He'll probably go for it in order to keep things quiet. If it had been a federal grant there might have been a case for fraud, but since it was private money that's not likely. I talked with the grants officer at the company. They're of course claiming Bill acted on his own, very embarrassing, rogue behavior, etc. etc." She shrugged. "And maybe he was acting on his own. Or misinterpreted his corporate charge. Either way, they'd like to keep it quiet."

"It doesn't seem fair that you get all the hassle and he walks away scot-free." I bit into my cookie.

"Fair doesn't have anything to do with it. Sometimes you have to cut your losses and take whatever you can get. I hope I get to keep my job." She sipped her coffee.

Paul draped his arm around her. I passed her the cookies and went to find a tissue.

EIGHTEEN

❧

A nd then, suddenly, everything changed again. Henry'd talked one of the summer people, a sober drunk who comes up for three weeks in July every year, into letting the counselor use his cabin. For the rest of August I drove Ginger over after breakfast and showed up around three in the boat to take the girls skiing and tubing. Angel, a stick-thin, blond ten-year-old, liked to sit in the tube like it was a throne and have me drag her slowly through the water. Jasmine, eleven, dark, tall and athletically built, got up on skis that first afternoon. By the end of two weeks, she could slalom. Turns out Ginger's competitive. She dropped a ski the day she saw Jasmine try. The other girl, tiny, brittle Chandelle, contented herself with riding in the boat, Daphnia tightly clasped to her chest.

Dr. Eileen Lewis sat on the dock and waved. Not the efficient, neatly-suited expert of my imagination, she pulsed maternal good will. The girls clustered around her, showing her rocks, patterns in the wood and their best dives. Back in my twenties I grew pot in my closet. Gold light from the grow lamps glowed around the edges of the doorway. That's how I envisioned her work, making dark places bloom. My knees buckled with gratitude when she agreed to fly up once a week through the school year.

While Ginger and her group blossomed and Sam worked, I rattled around the house and tried to catch a meeting every couple of days. The first morning I cleaned my office, then sat watching an eagle perched in the dead white pine at the end of the point. Through the telephoto, I could see him blink. Got a few shots that ought to work for selling beer or something.

The doorbell rang. It had been doing way too much of that lately. By the time I decided to answer, the ringer was gone. A bright blue and white air parcel package leaned against the doorpost. In the kitchen, I brewed another pot of coffee, read the fine print, found my favorite pen, ate the last oatmeal raisin cookie in celebration, and signed the book contract. I found an envelope and picked up the completed Neskame folder to drop at the foundation on the way. Daphnia and I drove to the post office with the top down, singing along with the oldies station. After all, it really had been a hard day's night.

૭ ૭ ૭

Memorial Day dawned warm and cloudless. I know, because Sam woke me in time to lie in bed watching the pink fade from sky and water.

He sat on the edge of the bed. "Did you order the cake?"

I rolled toward him. "Yes. From Fran. She even let me pay, when I suggested she could donate the money to some worthy cause."

He looked at me over his shoulder, eyebrow raised.

"What? I'm not having some awful white cardboard cake. That's disgusting. Fran promised a giant chocolate cake with marzipan roses." I nestled back down amid the pillows and lay my forehead against his back. "Yummy is more special."

"I'm going down to start breakfast. You want to come?" He slid away from me.

"In a minute."

When you color outside the lines, they tend to blur. Henry warned us that even fast-tracked, the adoption might take another year to finalize. As Ginger said, that seems a long time to wait to be real. That's when we called on the rabbi.

Sam appeared again with coffee. "Up. The caterers will be here at ten. We need to be out of the kitchen by then."

"I love it when you're stern." I propped myself on pillows and accepted the cup.

"Don't be exasperating." He threw me my robe. "I want it to be perfect for her."

"Okay, okay. Is she awake?" I swung my legs over the edge of the bed. Already the day felt hot.

"I hope so. The water's been running in the bathroom for half an hour."

"Rabbi Talia did stress the removal of nail polish and scrubbing behind the ears." I stood and walked toward the bathroom. "I guess that's so no one can call a convert a dirty Jew."

I heard a loud groan before the bedroom door slammed.

"I thought that was a good one," I mumbled into the mirror. No answer.

❧ ❧ ❧

Liv appeared with enough *rugelach* to feed the entire town, along with a lovely Star of David on a delicate chain, which she presented to Ginger as a gift from the Sisterhood.

Fran and Henry arrived as the caterers took over the kitchen. She unveiled a beautiful cream-colored sheet cake decorated with deep red roses connected by lush green vines. "I thought about writing 'family' or something corny like that." She cocked her head, examining her handiwork. "But it's so hard to put those things into words, don't you think?"

"It's perfect." I hugged her. "Thanks so much."

"Wow." Ginger peered at it. "Awesome cake."

"I'm glad you like it, Sweetheart." Fran patted her hand. "You can tell me later if you want the recipe."

Henry took my arm and guided me out onto the porch. "They've decided not to plea bargain. Thought you should know."

I exhaled. "So what next?"

His upper lip curled. "Judge won't give him bail, so he'll stay where he is until trial. His lawyers are pushing for a change of venue, which would be good for the kids—they don't need this in their backyard. The D.A. wants a show trial. Either way, it will be ugly."

I took a deep breath, looking out over the lake. "And the girls?"

"Depends. I think I've convinced the D.A. it's in the children's best interest to keep them out of the trial. She's got a solid case without them. I've seen parts of the tapes." He shuddered. "Hard to defend against. If he's convicted, sentences for this stuff are variable. But a guy in Arkansas got 110 years for making kiddie porn. Add rape, abduction, and the general public mood and who knows?"

"And if he gets off?"

He stared out over the water. "Don't you have relatives in Amsterdam or something?"

I nodded. "Gillian's there. It's a beautiful city."

He patted my shoulder. "We're getting ahead of ourselves."

The door opened and Sam's head appeared. "Rabbi's here."

Fran and Henry settled into wicker porch chairs while Sam, Ginger and I followed Rabbi Talia down to the dock. She wore a long purple and blue dress that swirled around her ankles and billowed across the grass as she walked. Ginger followed, her arms thin and tan against the white of her shift. Sam and I pulled up the rear. He looked elegant in his best summer suit. I looked clean.

So did the boathouse. We'd hired a crew to clean every plank of the deck, scrub the chairs and sweep the bare board walls, excavating at least a couple of summers' worth of dead bugs and cobwebs. I'd stood guard protecting the bats' nest in the ceiling beam, but I did let them scrub away the guano.

We stepped inside, blinking as our eyes adjusted to the dark.

"Where's the boat?" Ginger looked around like maybe I'd hidden it in the rafters.

"Next door. Since no one's currently living there, I thought the boat would be okay for the day."

She turned to the Rabbi. "So what am I supposed to do?"

"We'll do a little ceremony upstairs. Then you and I will come down here for the immersion. You remember the prayers?" Talia squinted into the boat slip. She tested the top rung of the new ladder.

Ginger nodded. "I think so."

"I'll prompt you if you forget." Talia rested a hand on Ginger's bare shoulder. "How are you feeling about all this?"

Ginger looked at Sam and me. "Good. Kind of weird. But it'll make me Jewish like Papa and Abba, right?"

I didn't look at Sam. Didn't have to.

Rabbi Talia smiled. "Right. But what about God?"

Ginger cocked her head. "I don't think God really cares what religion I am, do you? I mean not if God's really God."

"No, I suppose not." Rabbi Talia smiled at the three of us. "You know what, you've got some lucky fathers."

"Amen to that," Sam said softly.

I stood there grinning like an idiot.

જી જી જી

Up at the house, Jasmine, Angel and little Chandelle huddled next to their parents. Ora arrived and took charge, shepherding the three girls upstairs to Ginger's room. "She'll have to do a bat mitzvah now, like me," I heard her explaining.

With Daphnia leaping ahead of her, Ginger trotted after them adding, "Only I'm going to wait a few years 'cause my Abba says that'll be better." I swear she intentionally pitched that last phrase loud enough for a scowling Josh Lev to hear.

Maggie arrived carrying a large square box. Paul followed, a bulging plastic sack slung over his shoulder. As Sam greeted her with a kiss, she thrust the box at him. "I think this is Herbert James the whatever. Although she might want to consider calling her Harriet or Jamie instead."

I took the bag Paul held out. "Stuff for the rat," he mumbled. "Exercise wheel, that sort of thing."

"I hope you don't mind." Maggie shrugged. "I probably should have asked, but they all have to go and she was so fond of them."

Sam pulled the cage from the box. A brown and white rat poked his nose through the mesh, sniffing Sam's proffered fingers. He looked at me. I shrugged. At least she hadn't brought all five hundred. "Ginger," he called up the stairs. "Maggie brought you something."

She scampered down the steps. At the sight of the cage she squealed, "Awesome!" hugged Maggie and ran back up, Herbertina's cage nestled in her arms.

Paul watched her. "I think you should prepare yourself for a house full of pets."

Sam put an arm around Maggie. "How'd it go with the personnel counsel on Friday?"

She breathed deeply. "Don't ask. For now I'm still here and Paul was wonderful."

Paul blushed. "Thank you. I simply told them the truth about what a great asset you are to the institution."

I raised my eyebrows at Sam. He smiled and winked.

Other people arrived and milled around. Half the congregation seemed to be crowded into our living room. Eventually Rabbi Talia called us all together. Words were said, some in English, more in Hebrew. Word glue binding us together as a little family within a larger community, standing together in the living room affirming our new life.

She dipped, we ate, and later, people swam and skied and sat on the dock in small chatty groups. Henry took the other picture I have on my desk, the one where Sam and I stand holding Ginger, glistening wet and swaddled in her robe, her head thrown back, laughing. Right before we tossed her into the lake again.

ACKNOWLEDGMENTS

As always, I am indebted to Laurie Cheeley, my first and best reader.

I would also like to thank all the readers of the first Lacland story, *Releasing Gillian's Wolves*, who encouraged me to continue telling stories with these characters in this place.

Among the many things for which I am grateful to Rabbi Dan Danson, is his thoughtful reading of this story and his sage advice. Dr. Virginia Tinsley-Johnson offered invaluable editorial commentary – I'm indebted to you, oh capitán. Jordan Castillo Price's comments also improved the book immeasurably. The book benefited as well from a substantial editing team, Heidi Thomas and Samantha Bardarik provided content and line editing and Kim Cheeley brought her sharp eyes to the final copy edit. If, after all their efforts, there are still errors, they're absolutely my fault. Pat Bickner of New Leaf has again exceeded my expectations with her beautiful cover and interior designs.

Families, born and found, are at the heart of this story. Everything I know about families I have learned from my own; my parents, who did their best and who have graciously forgiven their own wild child, my brother and his family, my girls and their mother, who so very generously shared her daughters, the delightful family into which I have married, complete with step-children, grandchildren and great-grandchildren, sisters, nieces, a nephew, great-nephews and -nieces, as well as the friends and lovers who created family with me, however fleeting, over the years. And, of course, my wonderful husband, whose love and faith have transformed my life. I have been truly blessed. Thank you all.

While Ginger's experience is extreme, sexual assault of children is all too prevalent. Researchers at the Centre for Child and Family Studies at Leiden University in the Netherlands estimate childhood sexual abuse rates at over ten percent globally. The pain and detrimental life effects of even moderate abuse can go on for a lifetime. This story is a fictional simplification of what could be a young girl's first steps on a long journey from sex abuse victim to survivor.

Releasing Gillian's Wolves
by Tara Woolpy

We frequently see women standing by their Senator/Congressman/Religious figure husbands at press conferences and wonder why they stay as their spouses admit to all sorts of bad behavior. Bats in the Boathouse Press is proud to announce the publication of *Releasing Gillian's Wolves*, the story of just such a political wife, why she stays and what happens when she finally decides to let go.

Thirty years ago Gillian married Jack Sach, now a United States Congressman. Through the years she's remained faithful. He hasn't. Ever. She cooks to soothe herself and others, takes care of her mother-in-law, gardens, sneaks off to the studio to explode with angry paintings and tries to keep Jack's dalliances secret,. As she nears fifty, her friends think she should leave but she lingers, bound by inertia and fear of the effect media coverage of a divorce would have on her family.

Gillian shares a trust fund with Edward, her gay neighbor and best friend. Their grandfathers made a fortune together and left it to the two of them. Over the years, in support of Gillian's marriage, the trust bankrolled Jack's many successful campaigns. Not particularly interested in politics, Gillian survives by ignoring everything outside her kitchen, garden and studio. Edward has his own ragged past filled with bad relationships, drugs and alcohol. Through the course of a summer, Gillian's marriage continues to deteriorate while Edward's life finally starts to improve. He's sober, stable and has found life-changing love with Sam, a Biology professor at the local university. Their happiness shines a stark light on Gillian's loveless marriage. Finally, when Gillian meets Jack's latest conquest, twenty-year-old Ashley, she's forced to confront the rot at the core of her relationship. She travels to Amsterdam, meets Luke, an intriguing Dutch sculptor, and discovers it is never too late for happiness.

Praise for Releasing Gillian's Wolves

Andrew Mason of BookGarden Reviews:

This is a story of life, love and friendship. Gillian's exploits keep you captivated, and the recipes are an added surprise. If you enjoy a good story of personal growth and love, you will enjoy this beautifully written novel.

Martha Cheves of a Book and a Dish

When I first started reading Releasing Gillian's Wolves I had no idea as to what it was going to be about. It turned out to be a beautiful love story with a message that there can be life after love and that we all deserve to be happy. I loved it!

Kristin of Always with a Book

I enjoyed this debut novel by Tara Woolpy. It is a fast-moving book about rediscovering your priorities in life. Gillian has been dealing with Jack's infidelities for years now, but has finally reached her limit. The problem is that Jack is in the political arena and therefore her life, along with her family's, is always in the spotlight. Does she want to be the talk of the town? Deciding to take a break, she decides to take some time for herself, traveling abroad and meeting new people and finding her artistic drive again. With a new romance on the horizon and a few surprises thrown in, the plot moves quickly. The supporting cast of characters are all likable, with the exception of Jack, who is nothing but a sleazeball! I was captivated by the story, especially the love story that Gillian finds on her travels, and absolutely loved the recipes included! I will definitely be trying out the Survive Anything Double-Chocolate Brownies - right up my chocoholic alley!!! I hope to see more from author Tara Woolpy.

Made in the USA
Charleston, SC
12 June 2012